EACH OF
IN THE FAM

A priest with som

a trainer nursing

and a bitter gr

a rich young man with a habit he couldn't afford . . .

a sporting politician who was in over his head . . .

a female jockey with nothing to lose but her sanity . . .

an IRA fanatic who was all too

familiar with violence . . .

a beautiful pianist whose well-trained hands

knew how to handle horses—and men.

One of them had murdered poor Mrs. Caughey.

ONE OF THEM WOULD MURDER
TO TAKE THE PRIZE.

"Mr. Gill knows his Ireland and his police work . . .
his people are very human. And his backgrounds are
authentic. McGarr is an interesting cop; he is suave,
tough when necessary, knows good food, has charm
and blarney. . . . What a pleasure to read a crime
novelist who does not fall back on platitudes and
cliché writing."

—Newgate Callendar,
The New York Times Book Review

Murder Ink.® Mysteries

Scene Of The Crime™ Mysteries

A Murder Ink.® Mystery

McGARR at the DUBLIN HORSE SHOW

Bartholomew Gill

EX LIBRIS

C. C. Forsey

A DELL BOOK

Published by
Dell Publishing Co., Inc.
1 Dag Hammarskjold Plaza
New York, New York 10017

Dell ® TM 681510, Dell Publishing Co., Inc.

ISBN: 0-440-15379-4

Reprinted by arrangement with Charles Scribner's Sons

Printed in the United States of America

First Dell printing—May 1981

CONTENTS

SURFACES, SHEENS,
A CHINA DOLL,
AND A JADE FIGURINE

McGarr eased open a casement window at the back of a house in Ballsbridge, a select area south of Dublin.

The gloaming of a long summer evening had cast a pall, funereal and still, over the neat rows of flowers, the clipped shrubs, and the spiked iron fences that formed an alley in the distance.

Below him he could hear two women talking.

". . . and it's little wonder the police have arrived—her letting the daughter go around all tarted up who knows where with who knows who. And the string of them. A week, ten days—some of them take her out only once." There was a significant pause. "And what she must spend. Just one of those see-through blouses—why, twenty pounds easily. And how old would you say she is?"

"Who?"

"The old one, the mother. Of course, the mother. *If* she's the mother. But the other one too, the daughter. She can't be more than . . . fifteen or sixteen, if she's that."

"She's eighteen."

"Is that a fact?"

"It is, missus. It is."

"How they manage it! And the car over in the garage, the—what is it again?"

"A Daimler, I think."

"A Daimler, no less. Think of it—never touched. Not once to my knowledge."

"I don't think she drives."

"Then why the car? And why the clothes and the deliveries and the way Finlay's is always running upstairs with baskets, *baskets* of groceries. Specialty items all, I can assure you. Nothing but the best." There was quiet for a while. "I ask you where it must come from?"

"I'm sure I wouldn't know."

"Then I'll tell you, missus—from no good, that's where. And how they manage it—her an old . . ." McGarr couldn't catch what was then said and, nudging up the brim of his panama, he stepped closer to the window.

McGarr was a short man. His long face and clear gray eyes made it seem as though nothing could surprise him. In his late forties now, his light red hair was balding and he had taken to wearing hats.

But the woman's voice soon resumed the firm, indignant tone. "And it's not the first time today that the police have arrived, I'm led to believe."

"'Really now, missus?" The second woman was older, but her hair was tinted and permed and her figure not spoiled from childbearing, like that of the first woman, whose children McGarr could hear playing in the house. Pastel colors from a television spilled through sliding glass doors and speckled the flagstones of the patio, muting as the picture changed.

In all—McGarr thought, as he strained to hear what was about to be revealed, doubtless in a low voice—a pleasant and an unusual setting for a murder.

"No, missus—" the younger woman said, "—I've been told a policeman was here in the afternoon as well."

Yet another pause, while the other woman reflected. This was news to McGarr, since the condition of the body suggested that death had occurred during the afternoon, although he couldn't be sure as yet.

"A policeman?"

"I have it on the very best of advice."

"Did you get a look at him?" It was McGarr's question exactly.

"No, no—not me myself, mind you." She glanced up at the windows. "But I've been assured he was a policeman. I mean, who else could it have been, seeing they're here again and all?"

McGarr tried to ease the window shut, but the hinges squeaked and both women looked up.

Another voice came to him as he passed through the darkened kitchen and hall toward the sitting room.

"Through this holy unction, and of His most tender mercy, may the Lord pardon thee whatsoever sins thou hast committed by sight." The priest was down on one knee, dipping his thumb in holy oils and making the form of the cross over each eye of the old woman, who was slumped in the chair.

The daughter had found her there, and, thinking her asleep, had gone into another room to change into evening clothes while her escort had waited below in the car. There had been, she had intimated, some animosity between the young man and the mother, and he had rarely entered the house. Only when she had been leaving and had tried to wake the mother had she realized something was wrong.

Having no phone in the apartment, she had sent her boyfriend for help, and the ambulance attendants had called the police. The woman had been strangled in front of the chair and then eased or allowed to fall back into it. McGarr had examined the nap of the rug. He had found swirls near where her feet had come to rest.

There was nothing missing from the house, or so the daughter thought.

"Through this holy unction, and of His most tender mercy, may the Lord pardon thee whatsoever sins thou has committed by thy footsteps.

"Amen." The priest stood and, crossing himself, moved away.

McGarr bent his head and touched a hand to his brow. He was not a religious man, or at least not formally so, but death demanded some obeisance, and McGarr was willing to go along with what people of all religions deemed mete.

What he now noticed was the chair itself. It was an old Morris copy and out of place in the chic apartment. The arms were worn from years of use, and the ring on her right hand had most probably carved the groove in the arm on that side. As well, the upholstery of the cushions—some garish floral pattern that was now faded—was worn beneath a lace doily. Her head, canted at an odd angle to the side, had moved the lacework off the patch, through which stuffing now tufted.

She had been sixty-five if she was a day, McGarr imagined—a short, plump woman with a button nose and the sort of dark features that he had always thought of as Spanish-Irish. Her cheekbones were wide and devolved to a round chin. Her hair was kinky and lustrous and so dark it was almost black. And like the chair in which she was sitting, the impression she gave—the clean but worn gray dress, the sturdy limbs, the hands which, earlier, McGarr had felt and were calloused—placed her more as a servant in the apartment than as its mistress.

The room was furnished with antiques from many periods and tall, tropical house plants in coppered tubs. A grand piano occupied a space near the windows, its long back sweeping into the room. In the little light that remained and against the black, polished wood, the gold-leafed lettering, BECHSTEIN, seemed almost illuminated from within.

As though he had read McGarr's thoughts, McKeon left off writing in his notebook and ran his hands up the keys. He then hit similar notes in different octaves, again and again, and looked up at McGarr. The piano was in tune.

McGarr moved toward the piano and glanced back at the woman. "Larynx broken?"

"Crushed, I'd say. Whoever did it had a grip, so he did."

"What would you hear, maestro," McKeon added in an undertone so the priest, who was saying a prayer, wouldn't hear. "Brahms. Beethoven, or boogie-

11

woogie? Or how about something—" he followed Mc-
Garr's line of sight to the woman, "—Spanish?" He
had come to the same conclusion as McGarr.

McKeon was McGarr's inside man and usually
handled all the administrative details of their many
investigations. Like McGarr, he was short and stocky,
but he had a thick shock of blond hair that he combed
over to one side. His eyes were small and dark and
mischievous, especially for the past several days that
he'd spent away from his desk at Dublin Castle, filling in for Sinclaire, who was on holiday.

McGarr turned his head and considered the many
photographs that had been placed on a table near
the piano, the frames made of metal and expensive,
the glass polished to mirror sheens. Two dozen or so,
they pictured all the rituals of the family—weddings,
births, christenings, Christmas gatherings, Easter, pic-
nics at the beach, the men near a new car or standing with their horses, the women holding the hands of
their daughters, who were wearing lacy white dresses
and caps on First Communion day.

In one photo a little boy was shown with scapulars
around his neck, white shirt freshly starched, his
palms pressed together, his hair brushed; and then in
a suit in front of the same church, after having been
confirmed; then in a graduation gown, an army uniform, and a tuxedo with a bride on his arm. And
years after and—McGarr guessed—with her gone, he
looked suddenly aged and a bit sad, some toddlers
around him and a baby in his arms.

Yes—McGarr decided, trying but failing to pick out
the dead woman among the older pictures of several
dark, curly-haired girls—she had had roots, in spite of

having lived in the large apartment with only her daughter, whom he could now hear sobbing gently in another room.

And the settings—the many rock walls in the backgrounds; the treeless and hilly landscapes with mountain vistas and a lake beyond—placed the photographs not in Dublin but to the west. Galway, McGarr guessed. Joyce's country, although he couldn't be sure.

Once again he considered her—soft and sturdy and, he supposed, a comforting person to have lived with. She had kept the house spic and span, had made fresh bread, the dough of which had risen over the pans in the kitchen and spilled onto the marble-top table and gone flat. And the way she had kept all the surfaces—not just the window and door panes, the glass on the photographs, the ivory and ebony of the piano, but the parquet floors, the tiles in the kitchen and bath, the banister on the way up—attested to her care. Details.

But they would be ignored now, or a least not attended to with as much or the same kind of care. That was what, to McGarr, had always so marked the finality of death: not the fact of the corpse but that the places and things that a person had—he searched for a term —"energized" were suddenly, peremptorily and irrevocably abandoned. She would not bake the bread, meet the grocer, take the bus, or write the letter. And that the natural course of her life, a facet of the history of the family whom McGarr could see on the table, had been adumbrated at the whim of some intruder was an outrage.

He reached out and picked up a photograph that had attracted him earlier. The man who was pictured in the faded, brown-tone photo was dressed in leathers and was standing next to a motorcycle. He was small and thin and dark, which only made his wide smile, which moved off to one side of his face and wrinkled the skin around his eyes, seem genuine, candid and winning, but he could not be young anymore. Still, McGarr had seen that face and smile, he was sure of it, and in the recent past. And it had had something to do with an investigation. But which one of the many? He didn't know, couldn't remember. It was late and he was tired.

Off the surface of the glass that covered the photo McGarr caught the reflection of Garda Superintendent O'Shaughnessy, standing in the doorway to the dining room, his tall frame looming over the girl who was seated at the table. Hughie Ward, another, younger policeman, was asking her questions, writing in a notebook no different from McKeon's.

Beyond them, down a long expanse of table, sat the boyfriend. He had turned his body away from the others and had his elbows on his knees, staring down at the patterning in the carpet as though he didn't want to be there. McGarr could hardly blame him. He started when McGarr switched on the current, although the crystal chandelier diffused the light, made it soft and colorful, the pendants turning slowly from the movement in the room.

"But can you remember anything extraordinary," Ward was saying, "anybody who ever had words with her or threatened her, or . . . or even would have had, in your estimation, some grievance with her."

14

Ward glanced up, locking his eyes with hers. Both pairs were dark, but hers were swollen and red from crying. She only shook her head and blotted first one eye and then the other, closing each slowly in a way that made her long, dark lashes obvious.

"I haven't a clue. She . . . we have no *enemies*. She was a quiet person. Solitary. She wouldn't harm a soul." Unlike the mother, the daughter was tall and thin and had the sort of delicate facial beauty—a long nose and a slightly protrusive upper lip—that would age well. But her hair too was dark, and she kept it swept back along the sides of her temples and bound in a clasp at her neck. It looked full and very soft and so fine McGarr was moved to reach out and touch it. Tears again were streaming from the corners of her eyes, down cheeks which were creamy and smooth in a way that made McGarr think of a China doll, the sort dressed in a kimono with hands clasped before her and a sculptured, rosebud mouth painted bright.

He felt somebody brush against him, and he turned to find the priest easing himself past O'Shaughnessy and into the room.

"Friend of the family," the man said. "Thought I'd stay a bit. She has nobody now, here in Dublin."

McGarr held out his hand. "Father?"

"John Francis—Menahan, Mr. McGarr." He was short and quite stout and had dark, curly hair. His closely shaven beard made his face seem blue.

McGarr turned back to the daughter.

She was wearing a light blue dress that was summery and open at the neck and made of some gauzy, wispy material, all fluffs and fringes that further added to the overall impression of lightness and . . . grace that she imparted. And the dress—McGarr remembered the conversation earlier between the two women who lived below—almost seemed to be transparent. In the shadows of the table McGarr kept thinking he could see dark areas, rounded and taut, of the aureoles and nipples of her breasts.

McGarr leaned back to the priest. "What's the name again?" he asked in an undertone.

"Mine?"

"No—the young lady's, the family's."

"Caughey. Mairead Kehlen, the daughter. Margaret Kathleen," the priest paused, "the poor mother, God rest her soul."

"That's enough for now," Ward said. "Perhaps you'd like to rest."

Did McGarr see Ward's hand move forward, as though he would reach for hers? He had, he was sure of it, and he noted how much the young inspector resembled Mairead Kehlen Caughey, except that his hair was more like the mother's, curly rather than straight and thick rather than fine. And Ward's skin was sallow, not light.

It was then that McGarr noticed an area, like a collar or shadow, of darkish skin around the girl's long, slender neck, as though recently she had been out in the sun, not all at once but now and again over an extended period of time.

"I have a question, if you don't mind, Inspector," McGarr said, taking a step toward the table. He reached for the photograph in front of her, the one of the man standing by the motorcycle. "Who's this?"

She blinked and had to take it in her hands, to turn it so the glass wouldn't glare.

Their hands touched.

Yes, McGarr realized, he *could* see her breasts. Just. They were long and sloping, suited to her build, and dark, there where his eyes focused.

"My uncle."

"Father's or mother's?"

"Mother's."

"His name?"

"Keegan. James Joseph Keegan."

"He's—"

"He used to be a farmer."

"Where?"

"Leenane."

Galway, McGarr thought. Right in the heart of Joyce's country. He'd been right. He wondered what he farmed out there. Unless his holdings were vast, a farmer would have a hard time making a go of it around Leenane. Sheep or—McGarr remembered the other photographs on the table—horses. "And your father?"

"He's dead." More tears. Her hand moved toward her eyes again, and the bodice of her dress opened to expose a long, buff ridge of what seemed to McGarr the softest skin.

"Long dead?"

Ward squirmed in the chair and forced his eyes down to the page of his notebook.

She only nodded.

"I've got all that stuff, Chief," said Ward.

"Do you play the piano?" McGarr glanced at her nails, which clear lacquer made luminous. They

17

weren't too long for that, but he'd seen no scratch marks on the old woman's throat either.

"Yes."

"Well?"

She began to cry.

The priest touched McGarr's arm. "If I could speak to you in the hall for a moment."

"No need, no need. But your man can."

"Who?"

"Sonny," O'Shaughnessy said to the young man who was to have been the Caughey girl's escort for the night.

When he looked up, the tall Garda superintendent only flicked his hand, motioning him to step into the hall. It was a classic police gesture that communicated at once a kind of boredom—that marshaling people here and there was a routine that long ago had lost any interest to him—and a threat. He would tolerate no balking, no back talk.

O'Shaughnessy was a tall man, well over six-and-a-half feet, and with age his long Western Irish face—high forehead and expanse of jaw—had only seemed to appear more stern. He kept his beard closely shaved, and his skin was pink and clear. Like McGarr's gray eyes, his were light, but of a blue tint that was only slightly less severe, and in police work his demeanor had its uses.

He waited for the young man, who paused in front of the girl. She did not look up. He followed McGarr out of the room, and O'Shaughnessy resumed his vigil at the door.

* * *

McGarr led the young man out of the apartment, down the stairway and into the street, where they met four men from the Technical Bureau who would fingerprint and photograph the apartment. Seeing McGarr, they touched the brims of their hats and hustled past.

Night had fallen, and in all houses but one drapes and curtains made the lights seem yellow and warm and outlined the hedges which, bushy and green now in midsummer, had been clipped into turrets or domes or gently rising crests at the borders of each front yard. Along with leaded-glass front doors that glowed like windows in a church, the little sculptural touch to the shrubs made each house, though similar in structure and style, distinct.

McGarr was—he scanned the neighborhood; the roofs of the stately Victorian row houses that were silhouetted against a mauve sky—in his element. All of it, not just the physical appearance of the street but what went on behind those doors and windows too, was of a piece to McGarr.

Even the slight sweetness of the night air—the special mix of Dublin hydrocarbons from the power plant out in the bay, the other turf that was burnt behind the grates of fireplaces in the neighborhood (more perhaps as a ritual, one that tied the urbanites to a dimly remembered past in the country, than out of any real need), from the roasting kilns of the Guinness brewery where barley malt was being blackened for stout, from the hundreds of bakeries and confectioneries that supplied a nation of tea drinkers with their sweets, from the many streams—the

Liffey, the Dodder, the Grand and Royal canals, the Tolka, and the Bay itself—and even from the #2-diesel fuel that the government still permitted lorries to use—was unmistakable to him.

And sweeter and more particular still were the odors of the neighborhood: the sundry flowers and roses that Dubliners—again the country touch, another manifestation of a people who were profoundly agrarian—prided themselves on, cooking smells of rashers, roast pork, sausages, a mutton chop perhaps, potatoes and vegetables for sure with hot, sweet butter, tea and toast. Perhaps it was only his imagination that led McGarr to believe that he could pick out all those different things, or his years of having lived in the setting, but he knew they were there and why and the knowledge made him feel comfortable, at home.

And what was it that had been different about the Caughey apartment above? Certainly the old woman had been a careful householder, prideful of her possessions, her table, her—. McGarr didn't know, but there had been something . . . awry. Of that he was sure. He had felt it.

In the distance he could hear the sing-song claxon of the surgeon's van approaching, and when it turned up the street, the lights in the sitting rooms of nearby homes began to go out and doors were opened a crack and heads appeared between curtains.

"Which is your car, ah—" McGarr offered the young man his hand.

"Sean Murray, sir."

"From?"

"Herbert Park."

An even better address and not far, McGarr thought, and he took in the young man's tan suit that had been cut in a Continental style, with a tight waist and a deep vent, the shoulders padded square. His hair was long and shaped in some modern fashion, and from the back, as McGarr followed him toward the car, Murray looked almost girlish. Shoes with tall heels made him sway.

"Do you want to see the tax book?"

"What for?"

The car was a lemon-yellow convertible, an MG.

"I thought maybe—"

"Do you work?" McGarr offered him a cigarette but he refused.

Murray would have been handsome, McGarr noted, but for a bend in his nose, which was broad. His chin was round and his mouth thin and somewhat pursed, and he was freckled. His eyes were blue. His upper lip seemed to jump for his nose in a nervous gesture, before he said, "No, sir, I'm at university, at present."

McGarr wrinkled his forehead, questioning.

"Trinity. Senior sophister."

"Plans?"

"The law, sir."

Murray, Murray—McGarr thought—Michael Edward Murray, a T.D. (Teachta Dala, a member of the Dial, the Irish Parliament) and a businessman of note. A glad-hander with . . . aspirations, like his son. "Been keeping company with Mairead long?"

"About a year."

"Plans?"

"Well—" he looked away and touched one palm into the other, "—I don't know about that." He glanced back at McGarr. "I've got a long way to go yet."

"But you see a lot of her."

Murray tried to read McGarr's expression.

The clouds were parting and the corner of an amber moon appeared.

The van had stopped, and the attendants removed a litter from the dimly lighted interior.

Murray only nodded.

"Any rivals besides her mother?"

Murray shifted his weight and looked down at his shoes. "Should I be represented by counsel?"

"Not unless you think you're going to be charged. A girl like Mairead—" McGarr let his voice trail off. "I mean—" out of the corner of his eyes he could see the two women conferring over the hedges again, this time in their front yards, "—she's a looker, wouldn't you say?"

McGarr saw the young man's jaw firm. "You mean, the *others?*"

McGarr nodded.

Murray was visibly relieved. "Like I said, the mother didn't care for me, so when we went out with the gang I'd have one or another of my friends pick her up, but she dated nobody but me, Mister McGarr, and that's a fact."

McGarr again took in Murray and the lemon-yellow convertible and wondered what the girl thought about that. She had the beauty and dressed herself in a way that was sure to attract all sorts of men and certainly those who were as handsome and ostensibly better off than the senior student who was only now aspiring to become a solicitor. "What time did you get here?"

"Half nine, about. Maybe a few minutes after."

"You didn't go up?"

"No, sir. Not until Mairead—"

"What were you doing this afternoon?"

"I was with Mairead."

"Doing what?"

Yet again the shoes. "A bit of shopping."

"Expensive girl."

Murray looked up.

"Expensive clothes, expensive . . ." McGarr's eyes moved up the façade of the building and he saw her at the window, standing with her back against the dim light from the dining room. Yes, he thought, noting the shape of her hair and shoulders, the way her dress tucked in at the waist and her hands were folded in front of her—a china doll. She had the sort of delicate and fragile beauty that seemed to plead for somebody strong, some sort of domination, a person who could and would bend her to his will. ". . . tastes. What did you buy her?"

"Me?"

McGarr nodded.

"Nothing. She wouldn't let me. She's—well, I guess her . . . mother had a bit of money someplace."

"She didn't talk about it?"

"Who? Oh, no. Not at all, though I didn't ask. Of course," he added.

A would-be gentleman, McGarr added to Murray's aspirations.

She was still at the window.

The street was a cul de sac, and the van driver

had trouble turning it with parked cars lining both sides.

"Tell me—what are your thoughts, your . . . impressions about all of this?"

Murray shook his head. "I'm flabbergasted, shocked. I really didn't know much about the mother, and Mairead is—" he too glanced up at the window, "—a little . . . vague, and we just tried to keep off the subject, you know?"

McGarr knew Murray had felt, perhaps unconsciously, that his girl would become too much for him. She was a striking-looking young woman. She had money and was used to all the things he wouldn't be able to supply her with for some time to come, and he hadn't wanted to add to his disadvantages. McGarr wondered if she was talented too. "The piano?"

"Mairead's. She got it last year."

"Only just learning?"

Murray shook his head. "She's going to study in London in the fall. She's gifted."

McGarr thought he detected a new tone, dour or glum.

"A real talent, they say."

McGarr thanked Murray and asked him to report to the Castle the next morning to make a statement. "All routine in cases like this, Mister Murray. But I'm sure you realize that."

The two women watched McGarr approaching them. Obviously they thought he would turn away and enter the house, but when he reached for the small, wrought-iron gate that opened onto the front lawn, one of them turned as though she would flee and the other looked trapped.

"Please don't leave. I just want to ask you a few questions.

"Missus—?"

"Brady."

"And Missus—?"

"Herron."

"I'm Peter McGarr, Garda Soichana." He touched the brim of his panama. "I understand, Missus Brady, you have some information about a policeman visiting the Caughey apartment sometime this afternoon?"

She had rested one hand against her cheek and with the other held an elbow. It was a defensive posture. She turned her head to the other woman, who said, "I didn't say a thing, honest, Mary."

"Can you tell me the time?"

She turned back to McGarr. Her face was long and gaunt, her build cowish with bony shoulders under a cardigan, wide hips, thin legs, and house slippers made of some shaggy pink material. "I don't know."

"You don't know."

"No," she shook her head. "I don't."

"And this source. Is he or she available?"

She blinked.

"Well?"

She shook her head. "No."

"Surely you don't mean to tell me that all this report amounts to is . . ." He considered both of them

closely: two hausfraus, one Catholic, the other Pro-
testant, but as alike as two peas in a pod, except for
the numbers of their children. He didn't want to be
hard on them. After all, what else did they have but
the telly and gossip, and at least the latter was par-
ticipatory and more immediate. Both of their hub-
bies were probably down in some pub, bashing them
back with the boys, but he had his job too. ". . . idle
gossip?"

Her head jerked back, but she had more mettle to
her than McGarr had imagined. Her eyes narrowed,
and through her bottom teeth she said, "I can assure
you it's not." She stepped around him and, taking
long strides, walked out the front yard and into the
house, leaving gate and door wide open.

"Pleasant evening," McGarr said to the other woman, taking a Woodbine from his pocket. "May I offer
you a cigarette?"

She only shook her head and regarded him closely.

Mrs. Brady reappeared with a child in her arms.

It was hard to tell if the youngster was a boy or a
girl, and McGarr considered briefly letting her carry
the bundle back to bed, but it was better to put the
questions now while the memory was still fresh.

"Your name?" He reached out to stroke the child's
cheek, and only grudgingly did the mother allow him
to complete the gesture.

"Antony," she said. Her jaw was set.

"And how old is Tony tonight?"

"Four and a half." Her tone was bold, challenging,
but again McGarr thought it best to placate her. The
source of her rumor could in no way be considered

evidence, but at other times McGarr had received valuable information from children.

"And Tony—did you see a policeman this after'?"

She looked down at the child. "Go ahead, Tony. Don't be afraid of the—" she paused, "—gentleman."

It was a nice touch, and the other woman smiled.

The child nodded. His nose was wet.

"Did you ever see him before?"

The child shook his head.

"What did he look like?"

The child only stared at him.

"Did he have on a blue suit with silver buttons and a cap?"

Again the child shook his head.

"Who did he look like then? Did he look like your father?"

Yet again the child shook his head, but he also raised his arm and pointed at McGarr.

"He looked like me?"

"Yes," he said, lisping. "He was a detective."

"Was he now?" McGarr enjoyed children, especially when they surprised him. "And how could you tell?"

"Because he had a hat on."

"Like mine?"

The child only shrugged.

"Was it yellow, like this, and made of straw?"

"No. It was black." He yawned.

"Could it have been the postman?"

"No," said the mother. "He had come and gone at four. I spoke to him myself."

McGarr didn't doubt she had. "You're sure it was black?"

"Of course he's sure," his mother said.

It was late. McGarr tipped his hat. "Ladies. Tony. You've been most helpful." He did not add that he'd be calling on them in the morning.

Driving back to the Castle to file a preliminary report, McGarr was attracted by all the cars parked in front of Jury's, a modern hotel here in Ballsbridge, and it occurred to him suddenly and precipitously that he had not had a drink all day long.

But McGarr did not stop. The hotel was some executive's idea of the type of setting foreigners would appreciate when they came to Dublin, not realizing that those same people had probably suffered through places more interestingly sterile and had not journeyed to Ireland for a poor imitation of what they had back home. The ersatz bric-a-brac and plastic barstools had the look, the feel, even the smell of chintzy modernity and corporate profits. Then why the crowds? The Royal Dublin Society horse show was only three days off and exhibitioners were arriving.

But something had again reminded him of the man in the picture—small and sallow, dressed in the leathers, standing by the motorcycle, smiling. What was it about him? Where had he seen him before? He still didn't know.

McGarr drove into the city, the streets of which on this summer Friday night were nearly empty, the blat of the Cooper's engine echoing off the hot brick of lightless, Georgian row houses, the glass of shops and businesses, government buildings, and at last Hogan's on South Great George Street, where he was something of a regular. The Castle was only around the corner and up the street.

McGarr imagined that at one time the solid mahogany, the brass and cut-glass and mirrors with frosted patterns had seemed new and artificial, but there was a difference here—that Hogan himself had not thought of profits first. He and his family were proud people, and they had established a premises that would convey that pride for generations, if not longer.

Family—what was it about the man in the picture, Mairead Caughey's uncle? On her mother's side.

Hogan's was also crowded—boutonnieres, tails and morning pants, and tall gray hats that the women were now wearing askew on top of their hair; and flowing pastel dresses, sleeveless, made of the new synthetic materials that clung like finer, smoother skin, and that special smile—. A wedding.

Yes, he decided and not for the first time, his people were tribal, clannish, and the old rituals (marriages, births, christenings, funerals, and wakes) were the ones that mattered.

He thought of the elderly, portly woman slumped in the chair and the bruises on her throat. He thought of the daughter playing the piano in the long front room. Her long, sloping breasts. And the man again, the one in the picture.

The barman caught his eye and rapped his knuckles on the wet wood. McGarr nodded and a large whisky was placed in front of him. It was Hogan's own blend, and it had been aged in sherry casks, down in the dark cellar. Pride again, McGarr thought. And details—that was it—the details mattered. Attention, nothing slapdash.

He raised the glass to his lips and became immediately aware of the slightly sweet flavor of the charred sherry cask, more a perfume on the back of the tongue than a flavor that altered the mellow, amber fluid. And McGarr drank it slowly, standing there amid the hubbub yet apart from the others, the whisky and his thoughts and the customs of the pub providing him refuge. It was not his celebration, and other details—his own—were awaiting him. He finished the drink and walked to the Castle, leaving the car where it was.

At home in Rathmines, Noreen, his wife, had been waiting up for him. She had taken a nap, after having closed her shop on Dawson Street, and was now altering the dress she planned to wear to the Hunt Ball, the premier social event of the Horse Show. It was satin, and in the mirror she could see that the tuck she had taken in the back smoothed the slight wrinkling she had noted earlier.

She was small and trim with curly copper hair and eyes no different from the bottle green of the dress; and standing there in the mirror she looked to McGarr like a jade figurine—her beauty finer and more delicate even than that of the young Caughey girl out in Ballsbridge. It had something to do with the contrast of colors or her proportions, which McGarr thought perfect, or the way that she carried herself without any spare movements. Graceful and fluid and—.

"How does it look?" she asked him, turning only

her shoulders so the line of her back and hips and chest was obvious.

McGarr knew the look and what she really meant—the slight wrinkling of the brow, the special light in those green eyes.

"Try on the shoes," he said, "and that new perfume, the one that smells like—." McGarr couldn't place words on the odor, which was just another detail that was eluding him. "And the jewelry. I like my women redolent of . . . mimosa." That was it. "And sparkling."

"One would think you were interested in a fashion show." Like her smile, the phrase was special to them. "Aren't you taking a lot for granted?"

He watched the green satin flex as she bent for the shoes, the sheen of the flat area at the small of her back, between her hips, catching the light from the lamp on the dresser and flashing, the material whispering as she moved toward him.

"Not after all these preparations."

The satin slid between his thighs, and in his palms she felt both slick and dry, smooth and—he turned her around and drew his lips over the freckled skin that was exposed as he pulled down the zipper—talced and scented and fresh.

Later, McGarr turned his head and looked out the open window, across the backyards at the trees in the distance.

A street lamp and a soft breeze was making them sway together and apart, the leafy patterns breaking and merging and ever changing, almost as though the bed or the house was some sort of bark—an ocean liner, a vessel—that was riding vast, slow swells. Or a horse, say, in slow motion. Those long, graceful strides.

McGarr closed his eyes. He had placed the man, the one in the photo. His details were in place.

Pride. And sleep.

2

A ROLE AND A LENGTH OF TAPE, BE YOURSELF, TEA WITH LEMON, BAIT

Ward awoke in one motion, sitting up and tossing the covers off his legs. A burst of sun through the skylight overhead was nearly blinding him, making the large central area of the loft on the Liffey quay bright and fiery, the corners bluish.

Ward didn't care for that light. It was too harsh, clinical, and made the old warehouse floors, the ancient brick that he and some friends had recently painted, the oily oaken beams overhead, seem old and dirty and nakedly . . . industrial, there was no other word for it.

He preferred the place at night, when the fog on the bay pushed up the river and wrapped the masts of the ships docked on the wall in a heavy gray gauze. Then from the cocktail area near the windows he would watch the patches drift before other lamps, farther down the river toward the sea, catching at their glows and seeming to carry the light away.

But now Ward felt that he was late. Why? Ah, yes— he pushed himself off the bed—the girl. Mairead Kehlen Caughey. She'd be arriving at the Castle to make a formal statement, and with McKeon standing in for Sinclaire, he might have a chance to take it himself.

He took two eggs out of the fridge and broke them into the glass jar of the blender, added some vitamin pills, some corn flakes, and filled it up with orange juice. He switched the blender on low and let it spin while he showered, shaved, and dressed in his best summer suit.

It was Italian, bought while he was on holiday in Ravenna, like the black, glove-leather loafers that he kept polished only to a dull sheen, and the off-white shirt with the wing collar. Ward didn't bother with a tie, only tossed the coat over his shoulders the way the Ravennati did, and paused in front of the mirror.

The recent sunny weather had only further darkened his skin, and he did look—definitely, he decided —Latin, with black, curly hair that he had only tossed dry with his fingers, dark eyes, and rather prominent spaces between his white, even teeth. He undid yet another button. Somebody—McKeon or O'Shaughnessy or even McGarr—would notice, but he didn't care. He imagined Mairead Kehlen Caughey would be a prize well worth the abuse, if only he could find some way to separate his official duties from—.

But he needed something else to complete the image. What was it? A cigarette like a prop, in his left hand. He would talk with it, swirling it around demonstratively. A . . . Gauloise. Sure. Ward didn't smoke, but he thought he'd give it a try. If nothing else, the girl was chic, and that Murray fellow she was keeping company with, well—.

He took three large strides into the kitchen area of

the loft and switched off the blender. He tossed the cover at the sink. It bounced off and hit the floor. Ward didn't notice. He was almost thirty now and a confirmed bachelor.

But forcing the dreadful liquid down his throat, he tried to think of something else—the metallic rasp of a cog sliding over the teeth of a ship's winch; the raucous, greedy cries of gulls; the fart and sigh of a lorry releasing the pressure in its air brakes outside the window—, and he only saw too late the thick, golden dribble that was hanging from the bottom of the glass.

It landed it a streaky tear on the lapel of his priceless, light-gray suit.

"Ah—bloody hell!" he shouted to the oily, industrial beams overhead.

McGarr had been up for several hours, making phone calls and other arrangements. Now he was sitting in a small, darkened theater, sipping tepid tea from a Styrofoam cup.

"Janie Mack," the man next to him was saying, "what a lummox I am. Can't even toss water in a pot. I dunno, Peter, I'm not long for the job." He shook his head and stared dolefully down into the mud-colored liquid that some sort of film, translucent and scaly, was riding. "I can see them giving me the sack any day now."

Flynn was director of sports programming at Radio Telefís Eireann, the Irish national broadcasting network, and McGarr knew him to be good at his job. And he'd heard the lament before, had pondered and spoken it himself. It was a plaint that most of his countrymen indulged themselves in from time to time, a recurrent, metronomal drone—as from a bagpipe or a *bodhran*—of the self-critical Celt, the lower register of an otherwise happy people.

McGarr glanced over at Flynn, a thin man with a craggy face and thick, graying hair no comb could rule. He was wearing a turtleneck jersey with a pendant and chain around his neck, some sort of icon —Celtic or Russian or Greek; it didn't really matter —that placed him immediately in "the arts." It was necessary equipage, McGarr supposed, at R. T. E.

He reached inside his jacket, which was tan and made of the lightest cord, and extracted his flask. "Have a touch, Dermot. You're a right man and you know it. I shouldn't have ripped you away from your missus so early is all. In a half hour you'll be on top of the world."

Flynn eyed the flask as though it contained hemlock, but he let McGarr top up the cup.

The lights went down, and a pattern flickered on the screen in front of them.

"Listen, Peter—why're you at this again? Is it important? What's in it for me?"

"Tea and toddy."

"Ah, don't give me that. What've you got? I need to make a splash."

"Take up swimming. At least it's in sports."

The picture came on of a brilliant summer day and an expanse of the greenest turf that was filled with tall, powerful horses and men and women dressed in riding gear.

"Voice?" Flynn asked McGarr.

McGarr shook his head. He had heard it before

and he wanted to concentrate on the video, what was happening on the screen.

"Kill that voice!" Flynn roared into the darkness.

On falling asleep the night before McGarr had realized that during the judging of heavyweight hunters at the Horse Show last year, a horse ridden by a certain Sir Roger Bechel-Gore had suddenly reared and thrown the man. He had fallen heavily through a sturdy fence and onto his shoulders and neck, which had been broken. The ensuing paralysis of his legs was said to be permanent, and he had complained to the police. He had once been one of the country's premier horsemen; as a young man he had been selected to the national team for almost a decade; since then he had bred and raised some of the most heralded hunters and jumpers in the world. He claimed to have heard a series of short, sharp whistles at the moment that the horse had shied.

"Then you think there was a conspiracy, a plot against you?" McGarr had asked.

"Is, *is* a conspiracy, man. The bastards'll get me yet."

McGarr had only pitied the poor man, lying virtually helpless in a hospital bed, contained by a body cast and perhaps further confined by his own fears, until the chief inspector had looked into the matter.

Bechel-Gore, it had turned out, had had many rivals and even some downright enemies. He had refused to offer his jumpers to the Irish National Team at set prices and instead had offered them up at public sales. German, French, Italian, and English money had dominated those auctions, and Bechel-Gore's Irish horses had become the top performers of other national teams that consistently beat the Irish.

But Bechel-Gore's other business dealings had been similarly ruthless. In particular, he had gulled one M. E. Murray, T. D., who after great commercial success—doubtless aided by his political involvement—had plunged into the prestigious bloodstock business several years earlier. Murray had, however, overcome his initial blunders and had been, at the time of the accident, the most serious rival of Bechel-Gore, whom some considered the last avatar of the old, horsey, Anglo-Irish Ascendency. But that was not why McGarr had arranged the early morning showing of the sports film.

In it Bechel-Gore was standing near a chestnut mare no different in color from his mustache. He had on a derby and a gray tweed coat and was rather heavy, all chest and shoulders. When McGarr had interviewed him he'd already been doing upper-body exercises and his grip had been like iron.

It was a stunning scene and sounded something deep in McGarr, as it did, he well knew, in his countrymen. Horses were a passion, and wherever two or more ran together on a track or over a fence interest was aroused. For some, like Bechel-Gore and Murray, horses were business, but for others they were a pastime, a hobby, or a chance to make a killing with a tenner on the nose. Still, apart from gambling, Irishmen liked to look at horses, to contemplate and caress them, to imagine what they might do if and when. Horses were things of the spirit. McGarr thought of the Houyhnhnms and how Swift's satirical proof that horses were nobler than men had had some basis in fact.

Or maybe it was a darker and more recent facet of the racial memory, the indelible and hated print of the British boot on their necks, when in the eighteenth and for some of the nineteenth century—recent history, that—an Irishman had no legal right to own a horse valued at more than five pounds. Perhaps it was that which made the Irish yearn for horses. Good horses. Big, powerful, intimidating horses that could dominate an island that was one of the finest natural pasturages in the world.

And McGarr well knew that the horse had been the symbol of the landed gentry, the vehicle by which they had conquered Ireland and had kept her in thrall, and fox-hunting—the seigneurial right of charging a small army of mounted men through anybody's planted fields or gardens or backyards, driving everything at bay before them in pursuit of an animal almost as cunning as a native Hibernian—had been more than a simple sport.

But watching the contained energy of the large hunters cantering past, McGarr left profoundly and irrationally a lack. He did not own a horse, did not know how to ride one properly and probably never would.

And it was at the Dublin Horse Show—he managed to find Bechel-Gore, standing with his hands on his hips in what appeared to be a swirl of horses and riders, watching them canter by: bays, roans, sorrels, skewbalds, and a pure white horse such as McGarr had never seen—that the old Ireland of the forty-thousand-acre estates with long avenues of beeches winding down to the "great house"; of tenant farmers and enclosures and conscriptions; of "Yes, your honor. No, your honor. You're right, your honor"; of hunt balls, house parties, and little or no *noblesse oblige* lingered on, a vestige of a despicable and opprobrious caste system.

But it was a credit to the tolerance of the broad mass of the Irish people, or yet another instance of their sheer love of horses, that they had allowed the Show to continue. But in most ways it was only a pantomime of the past, and, scanning the crowd and the riders, McGarr could find few with the long faces and old tweeds and the haughty, disdainful expressions that had marked the Ascendency under siege, although there were those who were trying to effect the image. Once more McGarr's mind turned to M. E. Murray, T. D.

And McGarr concluded, as he watched the riders line up their some twenty-seven horses, waiting for the several judges to inspect the awesome beasts at close quarters, that if, say, he could believe in the proposition that certain peoples did certain things very well—the Germans' technology, the Italians' design, the Americans' know-how, the French things cultural—then the Irish did horses in that way. Very well, extremely well, perhaps as well as the English.

But the tape had progressed, and now Bechel-Gore moved toward a liver-colored mare, a magnificent specimen indeed and larger than the other horses near her. He examined her closely—neck, shoulders, forearms, knees, pasterns, and coronets. And then he proceeded to the rear—haunches, croup, thigh, buttock, stifle, gaskin, hock, and cannon. Suddenly the horse turned her head and seemed to give him a familiar nudge before the rider pulled her around. It could be that Bechel-Gore smiled, although it was hard to tell because of his mustache.

McGarr had gone through it all before with the man, when the allegations had been made. The mare, Kestral, had been bred and trained on Bechel-Gore's farm in Galway and later sold to a neighbor, Miss Josephine Cooke, who had been unable to attend the Show. She had been certain the horse, which had hunted with the Partry Mountain Hounds and was usually extremely well-mannered, though lively, would come away from the Show with some sort of prize. Thus she had sent her nephew to Dublin with Kestral and several other horses. When interviewed, Miss Cooke had been confused and dejected—that Kestral, her favorite, could have gone so wrong, so suddenly and without warning. She had put the mare up for sale.

McGarr now watched Bechel-Gore mount the horse and move down along the white fence, behind which the crowd was contained, taking easy, graceful strides, man and beast as one and both seeming to be involved in the gallop, both knowing and wanting it.

The posts clipped by regularly, evenly, and only less so the bushy lindens.

"Could we have it in slow motion from here, Dermot?"

"Slow!" he bawled, and the steady, rhythmical jouncing of horse and rider became soft and fluid, like a dance or a martial, muscular ballet.

The crowd on the fence was motley, a patchwork

blur of colors and shapes, even parasols, like plumes, overhead.

Then Kestral's head turned suddenly to the left and she seemed to stop, or she threw out her fore-legs, and Bechel-Gore was caught by surprise. His hands weren't collected or he lost his hold, and he went forward roughly, his face coming down on her mane.

The derby flew off and the horse vaulted up, twist-ing like a bronco, in a way that disengaged the right boot from the stirrup, and it was plain that Bechel-Gore would lose his seat.

But again and again she vaulted, each time stag-gering back, closer and closer to the fence where many in the crowd stood transfixed, horror-struck, until a small, thin man in a cloth cap began pushing and shoving them back. But he also turned his head every so often to watch. McGarr couldn't tell. The resolution wasn't so good.

"There," McGarr said to Flynn, think of what Mc-Anulty at the Technical Bureau might do with the tape. Perhaps he could get a blowup, see if the small man's lips were pursed, or his mouth—. Or maybe he could isolate the whistle on the sound track. But would that help? He didn't know. "Right there."

"Hell, the fun hasn't even started yet. The bas-tard's still in the saddle." Flynn's eyes were small and hard; Bechel-Gore had few friends in the Irish Re-public.

But the rider was now off the horse, almost—his left foot and boot caught in the stirrup—and when the horse reared up again, Bechel-Gore kicked out and disengaged himself from it, but Kestral was at the apogee of her twisting leap and Bechel-Gore seemed to fall out of the linden tree, back over and down through the heavy white fence that snapped under him.

He landed on his neck. Even then his legs came down heavy and lifeless and limp.

The horse reared up once again, reeled, tripped over the fallen fence, and toppled toward the crowd.

"There too," said McGarr.

The small man had twisted around to look down at Kestral, then, turning quickly, had snatched at and caught the bridle, pulled her to her feet and out into the ring.

Other riders, judges, and stewards appeared on the screen and the man moved away.

But there he was again when the camera was turned to Bechel-Gore. He was beyond him in the crowd, leading a donkey toward the Angelsea entrance. It was an ancient animal with wicker panniers and red-and-white check ribbons tied through the braids in its mane. Its gait was stiff and arthritic.

"And there too. Especially there."

"Don't want much, do you?" Flynn raised an arm and the lights went on. The tape was over.

"How 'bout yourself?" McGarr went to reach for his flask once more, but Flynn stayed him.

"How many times does this make it?"

"Make what?"

"That you've seen this thing."

"I don't know. A couple. Three."

Flynn closed his eyes and shook his head. "Six."

"Well." McGarr stood up. "I don't think you'd deny that it's a work of art."

"I'd be the last. The last. But I smell a rat."

"You mean you've got smell on that thing along with voice? Next thing I know you'll be telling me it's got touch and I can go to the 'feelies' anytime I choose. You'll make matrimony passé."

Flynn only looked down into his cup and shook his head. "Now you really do owe me one.

"You know, the last man to watch this thing had to pay for it."

McGarr only stared at him, his gray eyes clear and unblinking.

"Bechel-Gore paid us to make a copy of the tape."

"When?"

"A couple of months ago."

"He say why?"

"Something about wanting to correct his style in the saddle. Caught me by surprise—didn't think a character like him would have a sense of humor."

Already McGarr was out in the hall of the modern building, moving quickly toward the door. "Shall I wait for the tape or do you want to send it to me?"

"Wait, wait. Jesus! I'll get it for you myself."

Moments later, McGarr was pushing through the glass doors that opened on the parking lot, Flynn right behind him.

A gust of wind, hot and wet, struck them. On the eastern horizon a bank of clouds, a storm front, had passed in front of the sun and shone like hot, burnished silver. The light in the parking lot was yellow and filmy. In a way, McGarr wished it would rain.

"So you believe all his nonsense about the horse being spooked?"

"I always did."

"Point is—can you prove it?"

McGarr only canted his head. The whole thing—having again seen Keegan's face in the photo at the apartment of his murdered sister—could be a mere coincidence, but he didn't think so.

"Still—it hasn't stopped him much."

"Who?"

"Bechel-Gore."

McGarr placed the canister on the passenger seat of the Cooper and straightened up. The rear of the small car was filled with hatboxes. "How do you mean?"

"He's got a horse in the internationals this year."

"For Ireland?"

Flynn nodded.

"Isn't that a switch?"

"It could be, but then again the horse is Kestral."

McGarr turned to Flynn. "Is he cracked?"

"Maybe, but surely his rider is."

Once more McFarr only stared at Flynn.

"His wife, Grainne." He tapped his forehead. "She's beautiful, there's no denying that, but a sad case."

McGarr blinked. "But can she ride the horse?"

"So it would seem. She's been winning with the mare right along. Came away with the whole bit at the Royal Windsor—puissance *and* the time trials. Don't you read the papers, Inspector, or—" he eyed him, "—watch the news on TV?

"Will you keep me in the picture?"

"About what?"

"You're onto something here, I can tell."

"How?" McGarr turned the switch and the small, powerful engine of the Cooper sprang to life.

"You tell me what you're doing here the morning after a murder, messing about with a case that's at least a year old."

McGarr sighed and slid the shift into first. "You should have been a detective, Dermot."

"I hope you'll remember that when I get the sack."

McGarr waved and let out the clutch.

Ward didn't see McGarr pull the Cooper around the lemon-yellow convertible that was stopped at the guardhouse, waiting for a parking pass to be issued. He was concentrating on the car and the girl in the front seat.

There was another car behind the MG, a long black limousine with an official plate, a Mercedes.

"T. D.?" O'Shaughnessy asked. He was farther back in the shadows of the entry door, leaning against the cool wall.

The light in the courtyard, the first of two that the buildings of Dublin Castle formed, was hazy and blue, and Ward had to squint.

He nodded. "Cigarette?"

O'Shaughnessy only looked down at the package of Disc Bleus. "When d'you take that up?"

Ward shrugged. Nicely, he thought, the fat white cigarette dangling from the corner of his mouth, the jacket over his shoulders.

"And that suit." O'Shaughnessy glanced up and away, over the slate roofs of the buildings.

"What about the suit?"

O'Shaughnessy, whether in uniform or civilian clothes, was always nattily attired, but as in everything else his taste was conservative. He only shook his head.

"Well?" Ward demanded, taking in the other man's light-gray homburg and two-button suit made of—was it linen?—the darker gray tie and the black, woven-leather shoes.

The limousine pulled up to the entry. The chauffeur got out to open the rear door.

"Murray," said O'Shaughnessy, squaring his shoulders and clasping his hands behind his back.

"No, no—what *about* the suit, Liam? I'm interested."

Out of the corner of his eye Ward saw the Caughey girl getting out of the little car, and he turned his attention to her: thin legs, white and birdlike, a black-gloved hand on the yellow enamel, then a flounced hat, black as well. She was taller than Murray but taller than Ward too, and her gait was rangy and . . . was it athletic? Yes. She used her shoulders, twisting them a bit forward with each step. And her face was masked, it seemed, in the first movement of a smile, as though she had practiced the expression in a mirror and decided it was best and would get her through the day. But she hadn't been able to conceal the crying. Her eyes were ringed and she looked tired.

"Well—since you asked—it isn't fit for a pimp, much less for a policeman. And if you've got hair on your chest . . ." O'Shaughnessy was staring down at the Mercedes, the door of which was open. Inside a fat, older man with a florid complexion and a bulbous nose was speaking into a telephone, haranguing whoever it was on the other end. His hair was a mass of silver waves that flowed to curls at the back of his head. He was wearing a pin-striped suit. ". . . that's your business," O'Shaughnessy continued, "and should be kept to yourself."

"Well, I'll be . . ." Ward exhaled a puff of blue smoke.

McGarr had appeared in the entryway.

". . . flogged. Where the hell have you been all your life, Liam—Galway?" O'Shaughnessy was in fact from Galway. "Times have changed."

"They have?"

McGarr stood there, regarding them, a thin package under his arm.

Ward didn't see O'Shaughnessy wink to McGarr as the tall man turned to him. "You mean—dirt is in. You've got egg on your lapel, Inspector."

When Ward glanced down, O'Shaughnessy snatched the cigarette from his mouth and crushed it out on the stone floor. He then placed his massive hands on Ward's shoulders and turned him around, pulling the jacket off. "Now stick your arms in this and keep your mouth shut. Be yourself. She'll like you a lot more for it."

He turned Ward back around and reached for the lowest open button on the shirt, which he fastened. He then put his hand inside the jacket and pulled out the packet of cigarettes. "Smoking is a dirty habit. Once you start it you can't stop, and there's no satisfying the devil in your throat. Ask him." He meant McGarr, to whom he handed the smokes.

"But you smoke yourself."

"And I wish I didn't." O'Shaughnessy stepped past him, out into the sunlight of the entry.

"Jesus, I should've joined the army," he said to Mc-Garr, who was laughing. "Or the priesthood."

"Are you a solicitor or a politician this morning?" O'Shaughnessy asked Murray from the doorway.

McGarr, who had begun to climb the first flight of stairs to his offices on the second floor, turned and saw Murray slide his bulk out of the limousine. Suddenly Murray's face was suffused with his most practiced smile. "A solicitor and a friend . . . Liam, isn't it?"

"It is, it is that, sir. Representing?" O'Shaughnessy took the portly man's hand in his own and steered him to the side, as the girl and the younger Murray entered the building.

"My son. I thought I'd just come along for the ride." He began to chuckle. "Miss Caughey doesn't believe she requires counsel," he said in an undertone. "Poor girl."

O'Shaughnessy tipped his hat to her. "Then you won't mind waiting down here, I trust."

Ward opened a door and O'Shaughnessy ushered father and son into a room.

"You—" Murray Sr. glanced at the long, battered table and the several hard-back chairs, "—you won't be long?"

The tall Garda superintendent shook his head. "We'll try to hurry. For you, sir. But it could be a while." He closed the door.

McGarr smiled and continued up the second flight of stairs, from the landing to the offices.

He heard Ward saying, "Do you smoke? You may smoke if you like. Tea, coffee. I'd like to offer you something stronger but it's prohibited, of course."

"Tea. I'd love a cup of tea. With lemon."

McGarr shook his head. They'd have to send somebody out for a lemon.

"Of course. We'll get somebody right on it."

"I was hoping you'd be here," she said in a strange nearly disembodied voice, her words measured, her tone soft and musical. "Yesterday you were so kind and understanding. I thank you, Inspector. . . . It's curious but I can't remember your last name. Isn't that strange? Hugh is your first, is that not so? My father's name, but that's not why I remembered it."

McGarr leaned over the rail. He saw Ward turn his face to hers and peer into those large black eyes.

"Ward. Hughie Ward. My people are from the West, like yours."

O'Shaughnessy had looked away. At the crack in the wall that followed the stairs to the landing.

McGarr did not sit at the desk in his cubicle, only placed the boxed canister of video tape to the right and then skimmed the sheaf of memos that Ban Gharda Bresnahan, McKeon's new assistant, had placed there for him.

Only three sets of prints had been found in the house: the victim's, the daughter's, and some others around the piano that belonged to a male. The victim's larynx had indeed been damaged. Neither theft nor forcible entry had been noted, although both front and back doors had always been kept locked and the old woman had been a cautious sort. And finally no Garda official, uniformed or otherwise, could be placed at the scene of the crime or even in the immediate neighborhood at about a quarter past four, the estimated time of the murder.

McGarr turned and stepped to the window, which he opened. Somewhere down in Dame Street a jack-hammer was blatting away at concrete, and he could see men up in the girders of a new office building, slapping red-hot rivets into sockets and flattening them home with pneumatic tamps. Higher still, through the orange structure of the tall building, McGarr could see a patch of azure sky, covered only by a thin veil of cirrus clouds. Muggy summer weather with neither sun nor rain, just a damp, hot, nettling flux, but—he glanced up once again—a hope, a promise of relief.

What did he know about the Caughey murder? Little, as yet. But the murderer had been known to the victim, that much was plain. She had either let him in or he'd had a key. And the murderer had been strong—no, no; that was wrong: the murderer had had strong hands. McGarr remembered the rug he had examined and the swirls in the nap where her feet had come to rest. And her odd, slumped position in the chair—no attempt had been made to arrange her in it—made it plain that the killer had strangled her right in front of the old Morris chair and had then eased her down into the cushions.

And then there was the business of the report of a policeman having stopped by, just at the time of the murder. Tony Brady, the little boy. That would have to be checked into.

What else? The victim's brother, James Joseph

Keegan, had been present at the scene of the crippling of Sir Roger Bechel-Gore. Keegan, so his niece had said, was from Leenane, the very area of barren but beautiful hills in which Bechel-Gore had chosen to raise his horses, having bought large holdings there in . . . McGarr couldn't remember; it was just something else he'd have to find out.

And what did all that mean? Nothing really. It could all be mere coincidence, but he didn't think so, having just viewed the TV tape for the sixth time. Bechel-Gore was not the sort of man who was mistaken about anything. He was bluff, peremptory, but accurate. He wondered if he was vindictive and revengeful too, and why he had paid to have R. T. E. make him a copy of the tape.

McGarr needed to know more—about the victim especially, but also about Keegan. Maybe he could kill two—no, not kill—*solve* two cases at once. Maybe the crippling and the death were related.

He reached up and closed the wide old window. It shrieked in its track and the pane rattled as it hit the sill. Suddenly the office was very quiet.

He opened the cubicle door and said, "Bernie—when you've got a moment." And while McKeon was finishing up whatever he was doing, McGarr moved through the worn wooden desks of the outer office to the cabinet where he found the Bechel-Gore file. Back at his desk he opened the thick manila folder.

"Chief?" McKeon asked.

Without glancing up, McGarr said, "Two things, Bernie." He reached out and touched the package he'd picked up at R. T. E. "Take this package over to McAnulty in Kilmainham. It's a video tape and

I'm interested in any and all closeup shots ⟨of⟩ the sallow, older man in the cloth cap. He keeps the crowd back as Bechel-Gore begins to fall." McGarr heard McKeon move and he raised his eyes.

The sergeant's smile at the prospect of being given an outside assignment diminished somewhat. "We on that again?"

"I don't see why not. He's a citizen, like anyone else."

McKeon eased his hands into his pants pockets and looked away.

"And I want every available closeup, I don't care if they've got to do dozens. I want to see everything of the man *and* his donkey. And see if they can do something with the resolution. Sharp shots, get me? And while you're out there I want you to take a good look at the man yourself. Understood?

"Then I want you to tell McAnulty that there's a whistle on the sound track of the tape. It's short and sharp, probably a high pitch. It's there and don't let him put you off. I want to hear it." McAnulty was a painstaking professional when he wanted to be, but there was no percentage in the matter, no publicity, no recognition, and the man was jealous of his prerogatives.

"Now, two—" McGarr motioned to the door and McKeon turned to close it.

McGarr noted the accordion folds behind the knees of the sergeant's pants, the collar of his shirt which was a bit rumpled, and the greenish tie, some dark plaid design, that he wore summer and winter. McKeon wasn't slovenly, by any means, only unconcerned with the niceties of dress. Life was too short and those details too inessential to warrant more than a token obeisance—yes, he had a suit, a tie, and a shirt. And yes, he wore them to work. And considering the ease of manner of the short, plump man, the way he could insinuate himself into any conversation or group of people, McGarr judged he was perfect for the task he was about to set him.

"—Ballsbridge, the Horse Show. I want you to go out to the R. D. S. offices. You know where they are—just to the left of the main entrance off the Merrion Road.

"You're a—" McGarr pushed himself back in the chair and clasped his hands behind his head, "—donkey hobbyist. Or, you'd like to be."

McKeon smiled and sat on the edge of the desk.

"I'm serious, now. Anything and everything about the beasts gives you a rise."

"Jack ass me how I knew," McKeon mumbled in a rush, "I'd get to play 'Don Key O. D.' for my debut."

McGarr only closed his eyes. "You've come into a bit of money and you're now wanting another animal. You're wondering if you can purchase a catalogue. They'll have them there, that's certain, but I want you to see if they've got old issues for, say, five years back. If not, they'll have them in their library, which is just across the hall. See if you can get in there. Copy the lists of donkey exhibitors for those years. If you have to become a member, do it—we'll reimburse you out of petty cash.

"And you want to know where the donkeys are stabled and can you amble over there and chat up the owners. Would they mind that? Repeat that you're a buyer. They won't mind a bit. And who's a good

man to talk to? The resident expert, ass it were."
McGarr opened one eye to see if McKeon had caught
it.

He had.

"Now—who we're looking for is a certain older
fellow, name J. J. Keegan. He's the one on the video
tape you'll be seeing. Pounds to pence he won't be
using his real name. Small, dark, sallow skin. Cloth
cap, dark suit, about sixty-five, maybe seventy. Galway.
Leenane. Could be—" it occurred to McGarr, "—a
native Irish speaker. Got the picture?"

"Well—it's not very sharp."

McGarr knew what McKeon meant: Keegan fit the
description of thousands of older Irishmen and he
wondered just how much the grainy picture on the
R. T. E. transmission could help them. "Let's see
what McAnulty can come up with.

"Anyhow, today just let whatever donkey exhibitors
that have arrived get used to seeing you around and
bring back the catalogues.

"If you do run onto him, make conversation but
don't force things. I imagine we've got some time, but
keep an eye on him."

"That's all?" McKeon stood.

"I guess so."

"Can I ask—?"

"The Bechel-Gore thing, and maybe something else
too."

McKeon only lowered his eyes and turned to the
door.

Once again McGarr was reminded of the Anglo-
Irishman's reputation.

After studying the contents of the manila folder

for a while, McGarr wrote out a list of questions that he asked Greaves to take to O'Shaughnessy. They were for M. E. Murray and probably pointless, but McGarr wanted every avenue covered.

He checked his watch. Just 10:15.

He left for Ballsbridge.

3

ARTISTRY, CAUTION,
A FALSEHOOD HUNG,
MOTHER AND DAUGHTER—
ANONYMITY UNDONE

Ward had directed Mairead Kehlen Caughey into the dayroom, where the furniture was somewhat more comfortable than in the other rooms of the Detective Bureau. He had positioned two chairs fairly close to the windows, which he had opened.

"Bit of a breeze here," he said, noting how she eased herself into the chair, the wide skirt of her black dress rustling, the straight line of her back just meeting the old oak.

No wasted movement there. Feminine, to be sure, but the slightly distracted manner—which probably had more to do with her recent loss—made her seem as though only by a conscious act of will was she maintaining contact with the persons and things around her. And she seemed to be listening or watching for or trying to feel any change so she might correct the imbalance.

Ward tried not to bend too close to her when he said, "I'll see about some tea."

"Oh, please don't put yourself to any bother." Her head—the soft flow of her black hair—quivered slightly, but it was plain she could feel him there near her ear and she moved back, closer to him.

A flirt, he wondered? He didn't think so. "No trouble." He straightened up and made for the door. "None at all."

Already O'Shaughnessy had carried a chair to the farthest corner of the room. His hat still on, he had a newspaper in front of his face. He'd stay like that, seemingly disinterested in the entire proceeding. It was their way, once one of them had established a rapport with an interviewee.

A Ban Gharda was sitting at a table in back of the two chairs, a stenographic typewriter in front of her.

When Ward returned, the girl was staring out the window, over the slate rooftops of the Bank of Ireland and Trinity College down at the end of Dame Street, and she didn't turn to him when he sat.

Ward only crossed his legs and clasped his hands over his knee. He followed her gaze to the clear patch of sky that was the lightest blue.

The clouds had begun to break now, almost in two, parting one half from the other so that sunlight slanted through the gap in pinkish shafts that struck north of the city, making the promontory of Howth Head and the golf links on North Bull Island seem very green indeed.

After a while he said, "It must be hard."

She tilted her head slightly, as if listening for something else. "Have you ever lost a . . . parent, Hugh?" Again the measured words, the slightly absent tone.

"Both of them."

"I'm so sorry. It must have been difficult for you."

"At first."

"How old were you?"

"Fifteen."

"How did they die?"

"Smash up."

"Brothers and sisters?"

"All older."

"Who raised you?"

"One of my brothers, although I really didn't need much raising."

She turned to him. "But—fifteen?"

She had a little spot, like a mole but smaller, up from the right corner of her mouth, on her upper lip, which was a bit protrusive. It seemed to tremble.

Ward's eyes followed the line of her long, straight nose to her black and now tear-filled eyes. Under the wide brim of the hat her face was shadowed and again he was taken by the quality of her skin. It was very white but not translucent, like that of so many other fair-skinned people, and it contrasted sharply with the mellow tan on the skin of her neck.

Ward remembered the questions, the ones he'd found in McGarr's preliminary report, but they could wait until he had established the proper mood.

O'Shaughnessy turned a page of the newspaper and shifted his body away from them.

The stenographer's hands were poised on the keys of the machine, and she stared straight ahead at the wall, as though in her own world.

"I knew what I wanted to do," Ward went on. "I had to carry on. I figured my parents would have wanted it that way . . . would have wanted me to be as good as I could at what I had chosen."

She looked away from him, and her nostrils—thin and of that same clear, white texture—flared and her head quivered. "Being a policeman." The voice had little relation to the emotion that was expressed on her face.

"That's right. In the way that your mother would have wanted you to go on with being a pianist. I understand that you're going to study in London in the fall."

"Perhaps." She opened a small black purse and removed a handkerchief.

Ward wondered how long she had had the dress. It seemed new in style, made of some lustrous material he couldn't place, and it was not the usual sort of black evening dress that the women of his acquaintance had in their wardrobes. He couldn't guess the occasion on which she might wear such a thing, except for a funeral or while in mourning, and certainly she couldn't have bought it so early on Saturday morning. And the way she was built—tall and thin but full—he guessed her clothes had to be fitted to her. Even her feet, which were long, were remarkably thin in black patent-leather pumps.

"It wasn't your idea, I gather—to study in London."

She shook her head and blotted the far corner of each eye. "It was Mammy's."

"Why? Aren't the piano teachers in Dublin—"

She shook her head. "London or Paris or New York."

"You're that advanced."

She closed her eyes.

"Who was your teacher here?"

"Oh—I've had many. Father Menahan is my teacher presently."

"The priest . . . last night?"

She nodded slightly.

"Is he a good teacher?"

"The best I've had. He's very good in theory. He was a fine pianist and a composer and taught in university, before it was decided that he should do some parish work.

"In a way he was my first teacher and my . . . only real teacher. The others were . . . interim, when we were away."

Ward didn't understand. "You mean, you've been to university?"

"No, no—I don't think I'll ever go to university. I'm not . . . bookish." She looked up again, into the clouds. "I'm an artist, or at least I will be soon."

She turned to Ward. "Father John, you see, is from home. He was teaching at the university there when I was a child."

"Galway?"

She blinked.

"And you came here to Dublin and Ballsbridge when the father was transferred here?"

"In a way." Still she did not take her eyes from his. "We'd been abroad for a time."

Ward cocked his head.

"In Rome and then London."

"Studying?"

"Yes, I guess so." She hesitated. "You're—very kind, do you know that?"

"Scholarship? Grants? Rome and London are expensive places."

"No, nothing like that. I've won some prizes, but Mother—" she looked away and sighed, "—said she didn't care for other people's money, that there were always strings attached, that we had enough of our own. Father John was good enough, and then he never charged."

"Until now."

Her brow knitted, the lines longitudinal and soft as though she was unused to frowning.

"I mean, until now when it was decided that you should go to London."

She held out her hands and looked down at them—long tapered fingers ending in neatly shoped nails and clear lacquer. "Yes, Mammy—I mean, Mother—didn't think I was growing any longer, that I needed new direction, needed to learn some of the more difficult modern music. She was right, of course, but—"

"The Royal Conservatory?"

"Yes."

"You sat for the prize?"

She nodded.

"And won?"

She nodded again and averted her head.

"That carries a stipend, doesn't it?"

"Yes."

"Did your mother plan to go with you?"

"Certainly."

"How did you feel about that?"

She turned back to Ward. "Mammy was all I had. And she I. Of course I wanted her with me."

"There's nobody else? Back in Leenane?"

"It's not Leenane exactly. Oh—I suppose there's Uncle Joseph somewhere. But we haven't . . . hadn't heard from him in years. He liked to . . . drink, you see. Especially after he lost the farm."

Ward only waited. "Debts," she explained. "And the others—we lost touch. There weren't many anyhow. Some in the States, Australia. I once stayed at a cousin's house when I played in Montreal." A short pause. "Would there be tea now?"

"It's coming. Any moment now."

Ward then put his hands together, fingertips to fingertips. He turned to her. "Please realize, Mairead —may I call you that?" It was a gesture and a question that he had learned from McGarr.

"Of course. Certainly."

"—that this is an official inquiry. The next few questions are necessary, as hard as they may be. I'm only doing my job. Did your mother work?"

"No."

"How did she support you?"

The girl looked down at her small, shiny purse. "I don't exactly know, but I suppose I must find out. She never spoke of it, even when I was being . . . extravagant."

"But yours is a lovely flat—the piano, the automobile. A Daimler, isn't it?"

"I don't know, I think so. But that's Uncle Joseph's, or so Mam—Mother said. And the piano was a present."

"May I ask from whom?"

"Father John."

"He must think highly of your abilities."

"I believe he does."

"Does he play himself?"

"As I said, not much anymore, because of his . . . duties."

Ward paused, collecting his thoughts, not wanting to blurt out the question that had been forming in his mind for the last few moments.

O'Shaughnessy had lowered the newspaper.

The stenographer still was staring off in front of her, at nothing and at the wall, her fingers on the keys.

Down in Dame Street the jackhammer had begun again.

"Did he ever play your piano? The Bechstein."

Her brow wrinkled again, and once more he was struck by the long furrows. But then—she was only eighteen, he reminded himself. Only eighteen.

"Well, when he was giving me a lesson, of course. But I don't understand the purpose. . . ."

"All pro forma. Strictly pro forma. I just want to know if, say, he ever came to practice for himself. Such a marvelous instrument, and his being a pianist himself, as you said. We found his fingerprints on the keys, and it's just a question that must be asked."

She looked down at Ward's hands, as though trying to determine who or what he was or could mean to her. "Yes, he did."

"Often?"

"Not often for a . . . performer, but yes, often enough, I suppose. That's how Mammy came to decide, you see."

Ward only waited.

"Being there all day she had listened to both of us and—" Her voice trailed off.

"She decided you were better than he?"

She turned to Ward. "But it was unfair, really. Mammy wasn't one who could judge."

"But she decided."

"Yes."

"How did the father feel about your going to London?"

"Well, at first he was against it. He's been my teacher for so long. But then Mammy convinced him it was best."

"Did Father John come and go as he pleased?"

She nodded.

"And he had a key to your flat?"

She glanced up at his face. "Are you intimating—?"

"No. Certainly not. Not a thing, Mairead. Please understand me—the question would have to be put sooner or later. Every job has its difficult moments and I'm trying to make this as easy as possible. Can you understand that?"

She turned her head and looked down at her leg, which she had crossed toward Ward. "I understand," she said in a small voice. "Yes—he has a key. He's like one of the family." She turned to Ward. "The only one. Now."

"And not Mister Murray?"

She turned her head to him. "Sean? No—certainly not."

The door to the dayroom opened. It was Greaves with a tea tray on which there was a lemon.

Ward started to stand up, but O'Shaughnessy stayed him, signaling Greaves to place it on the table.

"Now, yesterday—tell me everything that happened."

"But I did last night."

"Just one more time, please—it's all according to procedure."

65

The stenographer's machine made a light clicking sound that was only audible when the street noise ceased for a moment.

"I'd had a hard day Thursday. I'd practiced until ten, then Sean took me out for a bite."

"Where?"

"Neary's."

It was one of the most famous pubs in Dublin. The Gaiety Theatre was directly behind it and at that time of night the old premises was filled with actors and other theater people and—Ward remembered the forceful way she had used the word, as though unsure of herself—artists. And stylish young people too. The downstairs bar, which old wood made dark, was usually crowded with them, especially on a Friday night.

"And so Mammy let me sleep."

" 'Til?"

"Morning. Eleven or so. I had some coffee. She made me brunch, but I couldn't eat a thing. I felt, well—I hadn't really been sleeping because of the heat, but somehow I had managed—and I felt—" one of her hands, the left one, crimped into a tight knot, the knuckles white, "—I felt like . . . Satie, and the piano—" She turned to Ward and her eyes were suddenly different, no longer soft and deep but hard and bright. "I don't imagine that you or anybody can know what it means to me—rich, pure sound, a *big* sound without being big, and—" She drew in a breath and let it out, her chest rising so that Ward's eyes fell on the long, sloping line of her breasts, the gentle curve of the tendons in her neck, shadowed between.

"I played until Sean arrived to go shopping. Poulenc, Honegger, Auric, even Milhaud.

"Seldom one has a day . . ." and then her eyes suddenly glassed and she looked away. "I mean, please understand me. My mother died. She was . . . murdered, I know, but earlier—" Her left hand reached out and clamped on Ward's arm, the nails digging into his skin even through the material of his suit. It was as though she had become transfixed but for seconds only—one or two, several, a few.

"And then you went shopping," Ward said gently.

Quietly O'Shaughnessy rose from his seat and approached the table. He poured two cups of tea. He sliced the lemon and placed a wedge on one of the saucers, then carried the tray and a chair over to them.

There he glanced at Mairead Kehlen Caughey, but she didn't see him. Her black eyes were glazed and she was staring out the window.

He straightened up and returned to his newspaper, but the tall Garda superintendent was puzzled. Perhaps the young woman's . . . vagueness was the result of her mother's death and the manner in which she had died or merely an instance of her "artistic" personality, but O'Shaughnessy didn't think so. He sensed something else there, something that they were missing.

Again Ward was waiting for the proper moment to renew the interview. He stood and walked toward the window, teacup in his hands.

She was an enigma to him too. Countless times over the past several years he had dealt with the survivors of tragedies, but never had he met anybody who had so easily dissociated herself from a loss that was only a day past.

He paused, then turned to her, placing his tea-cup on the sill.

The sun had broken through the clouds momentarily, and the light was hard and white and made her hair seem no longer black but rather some deep brown color, lustrous and slick with a rainbow sheen.

"Your friend, Mister Murray, goes to Trinity, does he not?"

She raised her cup to her lips and drank. "Yes." Then she glanced up at him. "Are you always so official?"

Ward smiled, knowing that his white, even teeth would flash, knowing that she was staring at him. "In official circumstances." He watched her eyes move down his face.

"Do you like piano music?" She still had the tea-cup in front of her, the saucer balanced on the palm of her left hand.

"If you mean, would I like to hear you play, the answer is yes. Anytime, anywhere, but I'd especially like to hear you play your piano. The Bechstein."

She looked around for a place to set the cup and saucer, and Ward took it from her. Their hands touched, and did Ward see her blush? He did, he was sure of it.

"You were saying—you practiced and then Mister Murray picked you up to go shopping. You went to—?"

She stood and moved toward him, staring at his chin or his teeth or his lips. She tilted her head to the side and ran a hand under her hair, fluffing it. "Un Coin de Paris."

"Which is in—?"

"Duke Lane. Number two, I think."

"Were you there long?"

"I don't know. Perhaps."

"Did Mister Murray accompany you into the shop?"

"I—I think so. Yes. I shop to . . . relax. I try not to think about my work and things." She turned her back to the window and leaned against the sill, the slick black material of the skirt smoothing around her hips. "No—now that I think of it, I was alone for part of the time.

"Ah, yes—" she glanced up at Ward and again her eyes dropped down his face, "—Sean had to take the car around to a garage, a repair shop. He said it had something to do with the clutch. An adjustment or something.

"When he didn't return I left a message that I'd gone on to the Pia Bang Boutique."

"What time was that?"

"I have no idea."

"How long were you at the boutique?"

She only bit her lower lip and shook her head.

"That's where?"

"Johnston's Court, it's off—"

"Grafton Street."

"And Mister Murray found you there?"

"Well—" she looked away, "—not actually.

"Is all this being recorded?" Only then, it seemed, had she seen the stenographer. She looked from her to O'Shaughnessy, who was pacing in front of an open window, hands in his pockets, his expression grave.

Ward took her by the arm, again surprised by her body. The muscle was long and thin but hard. He led her back to the chairs. "It's strictly by the book. Procedure.

"You were saying—?"

"Oh, well—I know this man who studies in the National Library. He's a friend. I stopped up to see him, but he wasn't there, and walking down Molesworth Street, Sean pulled up."

"Time?"

"Does this mean so much to you?"

Ward smiled again and looked down at his hands. "No, not time itself, but details. As in a—" he thought for a moment, "—a musical composition or . . . I should imagine . . . playing a piece on the piano, it's the details that matter. Anybody with a little talent can slog through it, but—"

She was smiling again. "Do you have to work all the time?"

"It's not work, really."

"You enjoy it that much?"

"Never more than now."

"You're very un-Irish."

"How so?"

"You're not afraid of me."

And she herself, Ward concluded, was too; he wondered if she had thought about her mother even once in the last several minutes. "But I am. I'm afraid of your—" he lowered his voice, "—talent and your beauty. You have a bit of a tan on your neck. Have you been out in the sun?"

She flushed. "I don't think I've ever met anybody like you." She glanced down at the small area of skin that was exposed near the collar of the dress. "Yes—I've been horseback riding of late."

"Do you ride well?"

"Well enough, I suppose. I love it. I've been at it for quite a long time."

"Do you have a horse?"

She glanced up at him. "Yes. Several. But mostly I ride the Murray horses."

"The father's?"

She nodded.

"You must be quite an accomplished rider. I understand his horses are none but the best—spirited and expensive. Jumpers, aren't they?"

"Hunters and jumpers, yes."

"Is that where you went with Mister Murray, after he picked you up on Molesworth Street?"

"Are you prescient too, Inspector Ward?"

Ward smiled. "And after that he took you out for 'a little bite.'" Ward had tried but failed to keep his tone neutral.

She only glanced at him, her eyes again soft and deep.

"I wouldn't know myself," he went on, "but riding horses must be taxing. And everybody has to eat, now and then. Even artists." He let his eyes drop down her body; it seemed as though she had no stomach at all. "Let me guess where he took you." Ward frowned in concentration, and resumed. "Mister Murray keeps his horses?"

"In the Agricultural Institute."

Ward raised an eyebrow. It was a state-owned operation, quite close to the R. D. S. Show Ground and the Caughey apartment, and Ward wondered how

Murray had managed to place his horses there even with his political connections.

"Oh—I think he rents the stable. Everything Mr. Murray does is aboveboard. It has to be, because of his position and all."

Could she be that naive, Ward wondered? "So—after Sean and you finished riding he took you—" where would a young man with a wealthy background and a lemon-yellow convertible take a girl like her? he asked himself: dozens of expensive places, "—to Lamb Doyles," he said. It was a wild guess.

She laughed. "Sometimes prescient, but fallible. The Tandoori Rooms."

O'Shaughnessy stood. He had kept the Murrays waiting long enough.

On the way to the door he heard Ward ask, "That's such a lovely dress. Rayon, isn't it?"

"Silk, Mr. Ward."

"I hope you'll understand the intent of this question—I don't want to remind you of the situation—but do you wear it often?"

O'Shaughnessy didn't have to see her smile diminish. "Sometimes. When I'm performing," she said in a small voice.

He eased the door shut.

McGarr hadn't turned down the fashionable and quiet cul de sac on which the Caughey apartment was located, but instead had driven past and swung into the laneway that led to a bank of garages. What was it Ward's report had stated? The fourth garage on the left, facing.

Like the houses they served, the garages were built

of brick that glossy ivy now covered and the doors were wooden, heavy and solid and painted brown. Inside, McGarr knew, it would be hot with the sun beating down on the black asphalt roof, and he doffed his tan suitcoat and draped it over the seat of the Cooper, making sure he had his ring of keys in his right front pocket and his pocket torch in the other.

The padlock was old, but somebody had taken pains to cover the keyhole with a square-cut section of inner tube, and fiddling a pick through the mechanism, McGarr quickly had it open. And oiled too. McGarr wondered if the old woman, the victim, had cut the patch and oiled the lock. The apartment had been well cared for, but that was woman's work.

Having to put his shoulder to the doors, he opened first one side and then the other, and turned, hands on hips, to examine the automobile.

It was some light green color that looked turquoise in the direct sunlight and chartreuse in the shadows, but what struck McGarr was how shiny it all seemed, as though somebody had taken a chamois to it and recently. And it was a lovely thing—four-door, postwar, just; probably a '49 or a '50, he guessed—built when cars were still roomy and had a sturdy look to them, as though the manufacturers had been loath to turn away from tank design.

And perhaps it was that thought which caused McGarr to stop as he advanced on the car. He took out the torch and, keeping well away, moved into the garage, shining the light down at the dirt floor where he noticed a pattern, as though somebody had dragged something over it. Squatting, he peered under the car, and the narrow beam of the light glinted on the yellow plastic handle of a screwdriver, one with a Phillips head. Near it was a small length of electrical wire.

McGarr stood and examined the garage: the dark corners, the insides of two old wooden barrels, and up above where the roof beams met the brick walls of the building. There, over the door, he saw what he was looking for—a rag, part of an old army shirt. With the staff of a flagpole he tapped it down, turning his head away from the dust that fell with it.

The rag was very dusty and looked like it had been used to wipe down the car. He wondered if whoever had cleaned the car had also oiled the lock to make it look as though the old woman had kept the garage and car . . . but why? She herself owned the car, didn't she? McGarr could and would check and right there.

But first he held the rag to his nose and breathed in—dust, lots of it, and something like car polish but something else too. He opened the rag out and sniffed at different parts of it—oil and then something sweet and sawdusty, almost pleasant, like the inside of a cedar chest or lemon oil on old wood. And around the smears a chemical odor—potassium nitrate.

What was wired, he wondered, the door latch, accelerator, or gearshift? Or the choke? He couldn't know, but he bet it wasn't a complex device. The dropped screwdriver and length of wire ruled that out. The rigging had taken place on the spot, using cheap materials that couldn't be traced. And in a hurry too.

Bending to examine the front-door handle, passenger side—a shiny chrome lever that had to be twisted down—McGarr played the torch over the surface and found that it had been wiped clean. The material of the oily shirt had left streaks. Using his handkerchief so he wouldn't cause the Technical Bureau any undue trouble, he glanced up, said a small prayer, and gently prised it down. Locked.

Selecting another device from his key ring, he jimmied the lock and carefully swung the door open. He noted the tax number and then opened the glove compartment.

Outside, beyond the hedgerow and spiked iron fence that bordered the laneway, he could hear the cries of children at play.

The interior of the car was stuffy, and the battery was weak, the map lamp only a dull yellow glow.

The tax book read, "Matthews, Dr. Malachy S., D. V. M., Slane Road, Drogheda, Co. Louth."

McGarr placed the triple fold of brown, official paper back in the glove compartment but did not close the lid. He slid out of the car and left that door open too.

Out at the Cooper he called the Castle and the dispatcher put him through first to the Bomb Squad, then to the Technical Bureau, and finally to Garda Soichana headquarters at Phoenix Park. The neighborhood would have to be evacuated and that required manpower.

Only while waiting for the others to arrive did McGarr realize that caution had become second nature to him, but that worried him. Sure—it had kept him from climbing behind the wooden wheel of the car, even though it had especially attracted him, but McGarr wanted always to be thinking caution, to have it consciously in his mind. What if he had grasped the wheel, had pretended he was taking it out for a spin on a sunny, summer Saturday morning, had depressed the clutch, and stepped on the gas? No more car, no more garage, no more McGarr. It was when things became routine that tragedy struck.

Up the alley he saw several small heads peeking around the edge of a wooden fence. One of the children pushed another out into the alley where he fell in the dust. The others squealed in delight. The child picked himself up and dashed back among them.

Otherwise it was quiet, a lovely green sunlit alley with potted plants in the open windows that McGarr could see from the car. Through the spiked iron fence closest to him he caught a glimpse of a large black dog gamboling with a stick in its mouth, easily eluding a toddler who shambled after it through deep green grass. Arms outstretched, the infant was delighted but turned back every once in a while to make sure Mammy was close by and watching.

The dog's collar was red, a bit brighter than its tongue. It dropped the stick and rolled its neck on it, as it would on a trophy. The child fell on the dog's chest and spilled off into the grass, laughing.

A bomb. Here. And a murder. McGarr wondered what it meant.

O'Shaughnessy had not glanced at either of the Murrays upon entering the room. He had only nodded to the stenographer, who had been busying herself with some paperwork, and then walked to the window where he clasped his hands behind his back and looked out into the courtyard.

He thought of the hot, blue haze and how, on such a day, it would lay over the sea and make the swells heavy and slick, like quicksilver or fine gray oil. Sea gulls, diving for bits of jetsam or chum, would drag their bills through it, cutting wakes, and the rap of the lobster boat's diesel would carry far over the water and sound pleasant and soft, like a sewing machine, to those on shore.

Well—he'd be on holiday himself come the first of September and he needed the rest. He was nearly sixty now and getting tired, especially of people like Murray, who—he turned his steely blue eyes on the fat politician—insisted with every word and gesture that he was special, one of God's elect, when in fact the man's very presence offended the eyes.

In a glance O'Shaughnessy noted the man's red-veined nose, the eyes that were shifty and quick and streaked—again the booze—the way he was sweating and breathing heavily even here in the cool lower room, uncomfortable, impatient and squirming in the chair, his body bulging in the expensive, pin-striped suit. O'Shaughnessy would treat the man fairly, but he did not have to like him. Many years ago he had realized it was perhaps the only prerogative granted a policeman and he guarded it jealously.

"Where's Peter?" Murray demanded. "Isn't he going to do this?"

O'Shaughnessy ignored him. He glanced at the son, then turned back to the window in which, he knew, his large body was framed. "You are?"

"Sean Murray," the young man said. "Sean Thomas Murray."

"Address?"

"Seventeen Herbert Park, Ballsbridge."

"Age?"

"Twenty."

"Occupation?"

"Student."

O'Shaughnessy paused, still thinking of how it would be in the West on a day like this: there'd be sun, of course, but it wouldn't be visible by itself. Instead, it would be spread across the sky, everywhere and nowhere, white and hot, and in toward shore, near the rocks, the sea water would be the lightest green, the ocean swells slow, the Atlantic cold.

A fly was blatting against the pink glare on the window, which he now opened.

There were many questions he could ask—those which would further explore young Murray's relationship to the victim, that would pinpoint the times at which he picked up the Caughey girl, dropped her off at the clothes shop, picked her up again, how long they rode the horses, and when exactly they had returned to the Caughey apartment, what he knew about the comings and goings of people who visited the apartment, the priest in particular—but O'Shaughnessy thought them redundant and inessential.

Only one question would establish young Murray's alibi, and O'Shaughnessy had a feeling about him and his fleshy, sweaty father. O'Shaughnessy had heard so many lies in his time, had interviewed so many con men, frauds, and prevaricators that he could almost smell them—the acrid sweat, the rolling eyes, the quick glance to the left; the, "If you really want to know the truth . . ." "The fact is . . ." "I swear to God. . . ."

or here, "Just coming along for the ride. . . ." and the hearty chuckle and glad-hand.

Horseshit, mister—O'Shaughnessy thought. The bastard had come here to front some sort of falsehood, and nothing bothered O'Shaughnessy more than being lied to and by the likes of a Murray, a man who was, in his opinion, nothing but a leech.

He turned on them. "What is the name of the garage where you had the brakes of your car adjusted?" he asked, knowing well that the girl had said it was the clutch that had been worked on. But he had succeeded in catching them off guard.

The son glanced at the father, who only passed a hand over his upper lip and looked away.

The son then directed his gaze at the stenographer's machine, the back of it. He couldn't even look her in the eye. The lie. It was the one Murray Sr. had come to the Castle to help his son utter. O'Shaughnessy was sure of it.

"It was the clutch. Ballsbridge Motors."

"They're at?"

"One sixty-four Shelbourne Road."

In no way did O'Shaughnessy alter his expression. He kept his eyes on young Murray. Ballsbridge Motors sold Mercedes automobiles, like his father's limousine, and O'Shaughnessy was willing to bet they did not service other types of cars.

"For your automobile, which is a—?"

"An MG."

"You got there when?"

"Half three. Thereabouts."

"Did they take the car right away?"

"Er—no. I had to wait a bit."

"How long?"

He squirmed but did not take his eyes off the machine.

"I don't rightly remember." Perspiration had appeared on young Murray's upper lip.

O'Shaughnessy studied him—the flowing, wavy hair that seemed permed or at least tossled carefully, the common, even tough-looking, face that denied whatever delicacy the hair-do established, the sculptured upper lip but with a bent nose above. But, like father, like son, O'Shaughnessy thought, and he pitied the young man. He had a long, hard road ahead of him. "Four, a quarter to?"

"Could be. I don't know."

Nor I, thought O'Shaughnessy. Nor I. "And what did you do while you were waiting?"

"Nuttin'." Suddenly he had lost the Trinity polish and was just another young Dubliner, a jackeen, O'Shaughnessy concluded ruefully. Like his father.

"I guess I read a magazine."

"Which one?"

"Oh—I dunno. I can't rightly remember. I just turned the pages and thought about something else." He was still concentrating on the machine, staring right at the black metal case, one arm on the table, the other elbow on his knee.

"What was it about?"

A pause. His head and shoulders moved slightly and he reached up to touch the paisley ascot in the neck of his off-white shirt. He was wearing a cream-colored blazer. "Automobiles, cars—" then his eyes flickered up at O'Shaughnessy triumphantly, "Mercedes."

"What about Mercedes?"

His father twisted his body in the seat and the wood creaked. "Is all this really necessary, Liam? I mean, Christ, what has all this got to do with anything?" He checked his wristwatch. "And we've really got to rush. The Horse Show. Sean is managing the arrangements for me."

"Where did you sit? In the showroom or in the garage?"

"The showroom, I guess."

"Where in the showroom?"

The young man hunched his shoulders, his hair fluffing around the shoulders of the blazer. He crossed his legs away from O'Shaughnessy—a dark brown worsted material, the pants; yachting moccasins with buff soles, no socks. "The showroom."

"Where did you sit in the showroom? Are there chairs?"

Now his forehead was beaded with sweat.

The fly had gotten trapped between the panes and blatted angrily.

"In a chair, I guess."

"And where was the chair located? Near the cars or near the window?"

"The window."

"Which window. Street side or alley side?"

Again the shoulders. "I didn't notice."

"Many cars in the showroom?'

"Some."

"Colors?"

"I guess."

"Aren't you interested in cars, son?"

"A bit."

"And you didn't notice the types and colors and styles."

"No."

"Not even a fleeting glance?"

"No."

"Your father here has a Mercedes himself, does he not?"

Young Murray glanced up at O'Shaughnessy. "Three of them."

Was it a challenge? It was. His father was monied and powerful, and he was making sure the lowly Garda detective, whose superintendency was by government appointment, appreciated the fact.

O'Shaughnessy turned and looked at the father. Was it pride on his face? It was, and O'Shaughnessy could only pity the boy more. "Who called you to say your car was ready?"

"The service manager." His voice was definite.

So—it was upon the service manager that the lie was to be hung.

"How much did it cost?"

Yet again the shoulders and his eyes on the machine. "A few pounds."

"Five?"

"I guess."

"Or ten? Was it closer to five or ten?"

"Really, Superintendent," the father objected, placing both palms on the table, "is this quite necessary?"

O'Shaughnessy ignored him. "You must have signed for it, since you can't remember."

The son wanted to glance at his father, but he kept his eyes on the machine. "Yes—I signed."

The father's eyes darted away, down to the side and at the floor.

"You signed the service slip?" O'Shaughnessy moved toward the stenographer.

"Yes."

"And the work was extensive?"

"No, no—just an adjustment." He was irked now. "That's why I took it there and not to the garage I bought it at."

"Which is?"

"Harold's Cross Garage."

O'Shaughnessy held out his large hand, and the stenographer pulled the sheets of paper from the machine.

"Would you sign this statement, Mister Murray?"

The young man eyed the sheets, the four copies of which O'Shaughnessy began collating.

"When it's typed up, of course," the father said, standing. "When it's typed up and readable and we recollect it's what was said, then well and good, we'll sign. But not that stuff, Liam. No sir, not like that."

"Then would you mind waiting? We'll have it typed up right now."

"Oh, no—you've kept us waiting long enough as it is. We have business, big business, Superintendent, and I can't allow you to keep Sean from it."

"Then you won't mind returning at a later day, say, Monday morning. By then we'll have it just as it was spoken, neat and in English. And I'll have additional questions to put, of that I'm sure."

The son looked away.

"Monday morning? You must be joking."

O'Shaughnessy only stared at the father.

The hand moved over the upper lip, the harried eyes flashed. "Please try to understand, Liam. We're not . . . civil servants. We're businessmen and the Horse Show—why we've worked all year for it. It's more than just important to us, it's vital. The auctions, the prizes, the competitions."

Still O'Shaughnessy said nothing.

"I'm afraid I'll have to call Peter on this. And Commissioner Farrell. It's . . . extraordinary. Harassment—that's what it constitutes. Harassment."

O'Shaughnessy only moved to the door, which he opened.

The square of buildings had caught the heat and the courtyard was an oven. The lines of the shiny black Mercedes were blurry and difficult to look at. The chauffeur was standing by an open rear door.

O'Shaughnessy turned to Murray. "No hard feelings, sir. I'm only earning my keep."

Murray's facial features were suddenly transformed. "Why, of course. Of course." He pumped O'Shaughnessy's arm, his son behind him. Sweat seemed to pop from his forehead and upper lip, and his skin was the texture of tallow wax. O'Shaughnessy wondered if he was ill and not just from booze alone. "And I mine—as a counsellor, you understand. Strictly as a counsellor. You can't be too careful. I've learned that." Murray held O'Shaughnessy's gaze. He was long used to lying.

O'Shaughnessy began walking him down to the car. "The Bechel-Gore thing. Do you know we're investigating that again?" It was a question McGarr asked him to put to Murray, one of those on the slip of paper Greaves had handed him earlier.

"A sorry situation," said Murray.

"Tragic. Such a vital man. Do you see much of him?"

"Unfortunately, too much." Murray began chuckling. "The tragedy has only made him more . . . aggressive, channeled his efforts. He's a fierce competitor, Liam, make no mistake about that. Ruthless, utterly ruthless.

"But you know," he turned to O'Shaughnessy, "I don't think my life would be as . . . bracing without him, if you know what I mean."

O'Shaughnessy only nodded and looked out over the shimmering cobblestones toward the lemon-yellow convertible. Ward was standing by it, talking to the girl. The echo of the door closing pinged around the brick and masonry of the courtyard.

"And James Joseph Keegan. Do you see much of him?"

"Who?"

"Keegan. J. J. Jimmy-Joe. Leenane. He's a man with a certain interest in horses."

"Keegan, Keegan." Murray's brow was suddenly furrowed, the bushy eyebrows knitted. And O'Shaughnessy could smell him now—the stale, fruity but astringent odor of an alcoholic.

"Horses, you say?"

"Probably, but more definitely donkeys. Small man —sallow, cloth cap. Sixty-five. Seventy."

"No—can't say that I have. Should I keep an eye out for him?"

"If you would, if you would, sir. Peter and I would appreciate it."

"Until Monday, then?"

Murray bent to ease his heavy body into the back seat of the limousine and he either coughed or cried out in pain. "The old bones. They're not what they used to be."

"I know the feeling, sir," O'Shaughnessy said, but the look on the man's face was one of real torment and he reached for the console attached to the back of the front seat. A lid snapped down to reveal a small bar.

"Can I offer you—?" There was a ruptured vein in the corner of Murray's left eye that was shaped like a corkscrew. It seemed to be skewered right down into his eyeball.

"Not while on duty, thank you."

"Then I'll close the door. The air conditioning, you know."

"Monday."

"Well—" Murray's hand was shaky on the bottle, "—early then. Monday's a busy day. For us."

"As early as you like."

The chauffeur closed the door.

Already the lemon-yellow convertible was out the gate, leaving Ward standing in the glare, but O'Shaughnessy didn't wait for him. He had business of his own, at Ballsbridge Motors. If he hurried he could get to the service manager when he knocked off for lunch.

*　*　*

Again an oiled lock. Under the pressure of McGarr's double pick, the dead bolt of the front door to the Caughey apartment rolled over like a corpse.

Before stepping into the cool lower hall, McGarr glanced down the street toward the corner and caught sight of two uniformed Gardai. Each had taken a different side of the street and were advising householders that the neighborhood was being evacuated. It would make the other job—that of canvassing the residents about the report of a detective having visited the Caughey apartment yesterday afternoon—all the easier, once they got them all together. Nobody could part a curtain on the second floor, peek down, and pretend he wasn't home.

McGarr smelled wax, years of it, and carpet-cleaning fluid of the sort that was put on with a brush from a bucket of water and then scrubbed—hard, laborious work. And the staircase was long—seventeen steps, two of which creaked audibly and wanted nails. No man here, they said to McGarr; he wondered if they could be heard in the apartment below. Another thing to check.

Wallpaper of Grecian urns, highly embellished and of a gold color on a beige background, new and expensive.

A second door at the top of the stairs, a large pane of plate glass, lace curtains, below which he could see the gleam of another polished floor—the hallway leading to the interior rooms of the large apartment and the kitchen beyond.

The door was made of oak with tapered panels and little crenellations on the trim around the window. He bent and sniffed the lock—more of the same oil.

She had been careful, painstaking, and McGarr concluded she herself had oiled the padlock on the garage. Whoever had booby-trapped the car would not have taken such care with the oil can only to have left behind the screwdriver and the length of wire. And there were fingerprints on the handle and shaft of the tool as well. Careless. Not at all like the old woman.

New pins of shiny brass in the hinges, McGarr noted, as he closed the door. The Caugheys had had it added to the premises when they moved in, and, now that he came to think of it, the door had the look of a country item, the sort of ostentaciously elegant touch that some farmers with a bit of money to burn would lavish on the front doors of their cottages. The doors seemed ludicrous, of course, but one look and you could tell they cost a pretty penny, that nothing was too good for that family, humble as they were. McGarr rapped the glass—plate, all right. And nice joining work. It closed with a solid, reassuring clump.

He turned to the desk, a drop-top antique that stood near the piano where the light from the tall bay windows flooded the plants, the parquet floor, the Oriental rug. The latter was burgundy with dark green-and-gold patterns—of a knight on a charger, castles and fortifications, a battle scene with lances locked and reserves in tight rows behind—and it had been well used, the rug, but not worn. Quality stuff and tasteful too, even if graphic. He wondered if the old woman had selected everything. His eyes strayed to the tattered Morris chair where they had found her.

He unlocked the desk and everything was neat inside. He found mainly bills from expensive women's clothiers, two recently arrived and outstanding; rent receipts (sixty-five pounds, all inclusive); a piano tuner's charges—but no letters from relatives or friends, not even a postcard. McGarr turned and considered the framed and glassed photo portraits on the table near the piano. Why hadn't she received anything from any of them? Could they all be dead or forgotten? Certainly, in spite of all the . . . pretentions, the dead woman had been very Irish.

He went through the drawers, looking for stationery, the sort in pastel colors with or without Margaret Kathleen Caugheys name (her daughter, her namesake, although in Irish) engraved or printed on top, the sort that was sent out as a personal note, a friendly, chatty letter. None. Not a single sheet of paper. Just business envelopes that were prestamped and had been bought at the post office, a pad of cheap, lined paper, a little Herme's Rocket typewriter that was fitted neatly into the corner and had French punctuation keys and had been bought at a certain shop in Paris. Pencils—a mechanical model in fourteen-carat gold. Pens—again only one, a Parker that was modern in design and looked like it belonged in the pocket of an airline pilot.

But where were all the details of years of living, of having to communicate with this one and that, of having to mail envelopes and packets, of needing staples and clips or labels or—. Even the ribbon in the typewriter was new.

He closed the desk and thought of the phrase he'd used in his preliminary report of the night before,

". . . the apartment must be examined in greater detail to more fully assemble a picture of the victim, her involvements, her family, her circle of acquaintances and friends."

And she had them, McGarr was sure. Why else the pictures?

He lifted the seat of the piano bench. Nothing but sheet music and difficult stuff, pages of complexities of sharps and flats and rapid transitions. He closed the lid.

What now? Basic signs of life, things that were impossible to conceal—food, clothing, toiletries.

McGarr stepped back across the carpet, past the mantel and the eight-day clock with the porcelain face and the golden ballerina who was pirouetting first one way and then the other, past the Morris chair toward the hallway and the kitchen beyond.

Out in the alley he could hear the men from the bomb squad and the Technical Bureau conferring. Van doors were being slammed; Gardai—now at least several squads of them—were blocking off the streets and laneways with sawhorses. People were complaining, dogs barking at the intruders in the dark-blue uniforms.

But here in the Caughey apartment all seemed in place, tranquil, and—was it cool; yes—McGarr could hear the dull drone of a cooling unit in an air conditioner and, pausing in the shadowed hallway, he listened for the location of the sound.

Opening the door to a bedroom, a bank of cold air fell on him, smelling of sweet, spicy perfume. The windows of the room were curtained and draped and, unlike the rest of the house the room was cluttered. The bed was unmade. Already the effects of the mother's death were being felt, but he'd save this room for later. At the moment McGarr was concerned with the victim.

The fridge was still well stocked. McGarr imagined that the girl probably hadn't been able to think of eating since the mother's death.

Chesses—but not the crumbly orange Irish cheddar or the processed Galtee varieties, but brie and camembert and port du salut and some unusual brown sort from Norway made of goat's milk and tasting of the udder. Cottage cheese. A tall chocolate layer cake with chocolate icing. Yogurt. Skimmed milk. Where, he wondered, had they found that here in Ireland? "Specially Prepared For Finlay's Select Customers." They were that all right. With distaste, McGarr slid the bottle back into the fridge. It was bluish and frothy, like soapy dishwater. McGarr preferred his milk with a thick collar of cream around the top . . . when he drank milk.

A bottle of Médoc from Pauillac, nothing expensive, but it had a full, burnt-ruby color when McGarr poured some into a wine glass and the characteristic tartness that he greatly admired. It was a shame that it was chilled and corked and he left it on the kitchen table the cork by its side—for future reference.

Now then—he raised the glass to his lips; it was full-bodied but smooth, and its bouquet, while slight, was pleasant—what had the mother eaten? She was plump. Certainly she hadn't lived on air, and all the fresh fruit and vegetables he could see under the glass in the hydrator seemed more like the daughter's fare.

He stopped and looked into the shelves of the large refrigerator, really too big for two people, and saw several covered pots: simmered calves' hearts with slices of onion, some bacon, and a bay leaf for flavor; a stew—he dipped his finger into it and tasted—beef and without any wine or condiments, just a plain dish with carrots, onion, potatoes, and stock. Some ham slices wrapped in waxed paper. McGarr slid several into his mouth, decided the daughter would only end up throwing the rest away, and so finished them off, tossing the paper in the garbage bin which he sorted through.

Nothing unusual there either.

The cupboard shelves in the large well-lit pantry also held two types of things: specialty items like smoked baby clams, tins of salmons, boxes of wild rice, Italian cookies from Perugia, Droste's chocolate, bottles of *aqua minerale,* an espresso maker; and then cans of tomatoes, peas, beans, corn. Daughter and mother. What a difference.

And in the bedrooms too.

The daughter's: posters of her concert performances framed and under glass; and pictures of horses, her in the saddle; others with roses in her arms, standing on brilliantly lit stages, orchestras behind her, bowing in one so that the bodice of her dress hung loose and much of her breasts were visible.

Even as a youngster McGarr concluded, she had been . fetching and whether out in green rocky fields with her hair braided and pinned to the back of her head or in a white dress with some older mustachioed man holding her hand in—was it Rome? yes, St. Peter's, the Vatican; she had to squint because of the sunlight—she looked worldly and knowledgeable. Not a child. No, never really a child. But still . . . childlike.

And all the rouges, emolients, unguents, powders, eye-shadow sticks, lipsticks, fingernail polishes, powders, vials of perfume and such that lined the top of her dressing table; and the black flimsy things—garters, negligees, a kind of chemise and housecoat of embroidered silk that McGarr had only seen once in a movie, and that portraying the life and passions of a courtesan—in the drawers of her chifforobe, her deep closet, and her armoire all bespoke a certain sophistication.

McGarr found letters in French and Italian, one in Spanish, another in German which somebody had translated onto another sheet. It was about one of her performances—all technical and impersonal and erudite.

But still, the look and feel and smell of the bedroom was not girlish by any means. Had McGarr not known of the mother's death, he would have bet two people had spent a strenuous, sleepless night in the rumpled bed, the sheets of which were silver satin.

The mother's: a picture of Jesus and His Sacred Heart over the mantel, His hand raised gracefully, His face long and gaunt with a thin, shapely beard; a white robe with a red collar to match the color of the heart. And those haunting eyes.

McGarr turned away from the portrait, having seen it thousands of times before, having been frightened and shocked by it even from his first remembrance—God showing His heart. It was . . . macabre, savage, part of the terror that had been his first impression of the religion he called his own but had not practiced for many years.

The mother's closet: black, dark gray, brown, and navy blue dresses, all nearly ankle length. Strong, serviceable shoes in only two or three styles. Heavy winter coats of good quality, but again plain. Only one summer dress made of some thin, lilac-colored material with a green leaf pattern—willows—running through it.

Hats: little woven bonnets or pillbox caps representing years of changing styles were on the top shelf with a few broad-brimmed summer types; and she had been soft on purses too. McGarr fished through every one, and what struck him was the absolute care that had been taken to purge each one of every scrap of—was it evidence? yes, in a way—that the items had had an owner who had an identity. Not a bobby pin or a toothpick or a hanky was left. He wondered if the liners had been pulled out and smacked clean of lint. No, there was lint, but evidence was the key word.

Keeping it in mind, McGarr carefully checked the rest of the bedroom, the dining room, the back entry, kitchen cabinets, pots, lid drawers, the sideboard and the silver, but he found no . . . evidence that would help him put together a picture of M. K. Caughey, the elder.

Where were their personal documents? Passports, since they had traveled; birth certificates, since they had required those for passports; and financial records like deposit slips, bank or check books, since everything McGarr had seen so far had cost money and it hadn't just appeared whenever the daughter had wanted a flimsy, see-through blouse from some fancy shop. And baptismal records, Sunday offering cards, school reports, other photographs than the ones on the table. In a safe deposit box? Then where was the record of that kept? Had the killer come for that?

McGarr opened the back door and stepped down the stairs to the dustbins in the latticed compound near the side of the house. He dumped the contents of the bins onto the concrete and went through the trash, only to come up with nothing and have to replace it all, bit by bit.

It was well past noon before McGarr trudged back up the stairs and closed the door to preserve the cool, rarefied atmosphere that the air conditioner was now straining to maintain.

He washed his hands at the kitchen sink, then dried them on a towel in the bathroom and noted the contents of the medicine cabinet. It was a good Irish object—aspirin, corn plasters, a mild laxative, and some eyedrops. But clean as a whistle—toothbrushes in a holder except for one that he assumed was the daughter's.

In another cabinet, though, he found a range of soaps and shampoos, bath oils, body oils, cold creams, cleansing creams, hand creams, creams for dry skin, night creams, conditioning creams, cream rinses, and even a talc that looked in McGarr's palm just like fresh cream. All the daughter's. And to think, he said to himself, spilling a handful into the water of the toilet bowl, she drinks skim milk. He wondered if she was allergic to cream, the real stuff.

And prescription drugs. Codeine, ergotamine, dihydroergotamine. Ergotamine tartrate—lots of that. Valium, Librium, phenobarbitol. And reserpine and phenothiazine. In all, quite a wallop. The substances had been purchased at a variety of chemists' shops in Dublin and abroad, but he noticed also that none had been much used, apart from the ergotamine tartrate. In the bottle of Librium that the label said contained thirty-six tablets, thirty-two remained. In others only one or two tablets had been taken.

He replaced everything, opened the sliding glass doors of the shower and noted the massage nozzle on the shower head, wishing he had one himself for those difficult mornings-after that sometimes plagued him. He then examined the toilet bowl and even lifted off the top of the tank to peer into the dark water there. Nothing still.

Scented toilet paper and a bidet, of all things. In Ireland. He shook his head once more.

McGarr then raised the frosted glass window and looked down across the backyards toward the garage. The vans were no longer there but had moved to either end of the laneway, except for one which was bulky and windowless. Only one man was inside the garage. He was working under the hood by the light of several brilliant portable lamps. He wore an asbestos suit and mask and a flak jacket. Gillis, McGarr thought. He didn't work much, but he could have it. And it was taking some time. Whoever had rigged it had had some experience.

He lowered the window and returned to the kitchen and the glass of Médoc. He poured himself a bit more.

96

McGarr needed to think and time was running out. He didn't know how long Ward would keep the girl at the Castle. It was perfectly within the law for him to be in the apartment, but he preferred to form his conclusions alone. And the privacy of the evacuated neighborhood was now near total.

He carried the bottle and glass into the old woman's bedroom and sat in the rocker near the small hearth. It was cool here too, and at least the comfort was not mechanized and . . . precise. That was it. The old woman had been precise in everything—careful, attentive, and reasoned about the details of the house, almost to a fault. Why? He had never seen anything like it. No—again he thought of evidence—proof of her having lived here, Margaret Kathleen Caughey herself, the person who must have had some attachment to the world other than her daughter.

But where was her husband? Which one of the photos on the piano was of him?

Proof. Evidence. Had she been trying to cover up something? What was it the girl had said last night? "They're either dead or we lost track of them." Emigrated. Perhaps, but in a big Irish family from the West somebody eventually returned home, sooner or later, to brag about his success, or to remember what was past and feel sad, or just to feel the soil under his feet again. And those people looked up their relatives. It was upon returning that they felt most—again McGarr thought of the word—tribal.

And what was it that had so bothered him the night before? Something had been out of place. The Morris chair itself, the sole concession to the old woman's comfort in the chic apartment, other than the room in which he was presently sitting. Otherwise everything was neat and clean and—.

McGarr stood. The bread, the dough that had risen up over the pans and spilled. And the corpse, the old woman herself. What was out of place about her? Or . . . missing from her person? Her outstanding characteristic—no, no, no; *not* characteristic, her passion—was neatness, cleanliness, a careful, attentive, reasoned approach to the details of her house *and* herself. The bread. Would she have made bread, a messy chore with sticky dough and flour and oiling or greasing pans, without an apron on? No. But she would have taken it off if the visitor had been somebody other than a delivery boy or the postman.

The postman. He had asked the woman downstairs if the man who had been seen leaving the flat could have been the postman. No. He had come an hour before, perhaps about the time she was kneading the dough. Perhaps.

Had McGarr yet examined an apron? No—he had passed them by. They were hanging on the back of the pantry door.

It was there that he found the evidence, the one piece of proof of who she was that Margaret Kathleen Caughey had not had time to destroy.

A letter, brief and pointed. But it was enough and from Drogheda. From Dr. Malachy T. Matthews, McGarr was willing to bet.

> Sis,
> Get out. He's onto me.
>
> Jimmy-Joe

McGarr searched the entire apartment for a telephone to call the Castle, but he remembered the girl saying there was none.

Studied anonymity and to a purpose, he was convinced of it.

4

STROKES, VOICES,
A SQUELCH AND A LAUGH.
PRIEST, PARISHIONER,
A SOT AND AN ASS

The man who was standing in the middle of the large garage had glanced up at them, then back down at the work on the slope of the small porter's desk in front of him. Too quickly, too disinterested. He was O'Shaughnessy's man.

The Garda superintendent had had his driver pull the Cortina up in front of the doors of the service bay, which was open. Now he got out and approached the man slowly, noting the many automobiles with hoods raised or on lifts, red metal cases of tools on dollies near them, snakes of rubber hoses for pneumatic tools and air guns, and the sweet fresh oil and raw gas smell that he'd always associated with mechanical exactitude, a knowledge that he'd found elusive and therefore respected. And Mercedes, all the cars were Mercedes.

The other workers were sitting in a clatch on some tires, munching sandwiches and drinking tea from thermoses. Silently they watched O'Shaughnessy move toward the desk, the whites of their eyes bright in the begrimed or permanently sallow complexions of mechanics, their once light-blue coveralls now a dirty gray.

O'Shaughnessy waited by the man's side, watching him add up a column of figures on a bill of particulars. There were three copies underneath. He was small but square, and his face looked cropped, his nose beaklike and sharp. "Sir?"

"Your name, please?"

His eyes quavered toward the police car. "And yours?"

"O'Shaughnessy, Liam. Superintendent, Garda Soichana."

"How do I know that?"

O'Shaughnessy had been looking directly at the man, but now his eyes concentrated on him—the quick, nervous squint of the eyes, the way he shifted his weight from foot to foot and tapped the ballpoint pen on the top of the desk. His wedding ring glinted on a grease-smeared finger, and it bore a single and small, clear stone. "I want your name."

"Doyle, Nick. Service Manager, Ballsbridge Motors," he said, affecting O'Shaughnessy's tone and inflection.

O'Shaughnessy picked up the receiver of the telephone on the desk. "How do I get an outside line?"

"Try climbing a pole." The man scratched at the corner of one eye, trying to look coy, his eyes moving toward the men who were watching him.

But a dial tone came on and O'Shaughnessy dialed the Castle.

Ban Gharda Bresnahan answered. "Doyle, Nick," and then cupped a hand over the mouthpiece. "Address?"

The man sighed. "Five Uppercross Road, Dolphin's Barn."

O'Shaughnessy repeated the address. "I'll wait."

He only stared at the man, whose mood was changing perceptibly. A kind of resignation—a firming of the jaw, a slight wrinkling of the brow, which was freckled like his face and neck, the eyes that looked out the open doors at the Garda patrol car and seemed to glaze, having seen trouble before, O'Shaughnessy guessed, having been acquainted with the trance that was necessary to get a man through hours or days or years of contention.

The salient details came back quickly, thanks to the computer. He'd been jailed twice for I. R. A. activities, once in connection with a bombing. As a youth he'd been detained a number of times, charged once with aggravated assault and convicted. He was married, the father of six.

"I want a complete rundown on him. Begin a new file. Have it in the dayroom by five. A stenographer. Greaves and Delaney. And call in another team to spell them. I'll check in on Monday."

O'Shaughnessy replaced the phone in its yoke.

Now it was Doyle's turn to be quiet. He was no longer glancing at the other men. And he mumbled something.

"I didn't hear that."

"I said—" his eyes met O'Shaughnessy's for a moment, "—just because a fellow's done a stroke in the shovel—"

"Two strokes. Two long strokes. Long for a man with a wife and four children and a—" O'Shaughnessy let his eyes survey the large garage, "—a good job.

"I'd like to see the service chit on Sean Murray's MG."

"I don't have it." Not, whose car? Or, what day?

Or, an MG? No—Doyle had a record, and Murray had gone to work on him. Why? And how?

"Where is it?"

"The office."

"Who worked on the car?"

"I did."

"Brakes?" O'Shaughnessy caught Doyle's eyes and held them.

"No—clutch."

"What was wrong with it?"

"An adjustment."

"Difficult job?"

Doyle looked away and his shoulders seemed to say, hard enough.

"Where'd you work on it?"

Doyle paused. He seemed to be pondering something, weighing possibilities. His jaw firmed again and he turned to O'Shaughnessy. "In Phoenix Park, right in front of the Taoseaich's palace."

"Suit yourself." O'Shaughnessy knew it was senseless to question him further, there.

Of the other men, two said they had seen Doyle working on the MG during the midafternoon. The car did not leave the garage until half four or thereabouts. O'Shaughnessy took their names, and went into the dealer's office.

There the young sales manager, O'Reilly by name, went through the service slips of the day before and found the Murray bill. £12, 30p., and paid in full.

"What's the problem? Mister Murray's one of our best customers."

"Did you see the car?"

"No." O'Reilly was tall and slim, with an easy flow

of speech. He spoke with his hands in his pockets, informal, as though making a sale didn't really matter to him.

They were standing by the side of a long, cream-colored car with light brown seats that gave off the rich and mellow reek of tanning fluid and leather dressing. And other odors came to O'Shaughnessy—new tires and new material and all the recently manufactured components that comprised the exquisite machines in the showroom—and formed a mix that was unmistakable and communicated power, quality, luxury, and great expense; and in a way the Garda superintendent felt uncomfortable there. Bright sunlight through the windows made the shiny lacquer gleam, and outside on the street other cars were passing in fiery blurs.

"Did you see the son?"

"No."

"Do you know the son?"

"Yes, I think so. Really, what's this all about? Mister Murray—"

"Did you see him yesterday?"

"Well—no, but—"

"Isn't it unusual for this garage to be servicing an MG?"

"Yes and no. After all, Mister Murray—"

"Had you ever serviced it before?"

"I don't know. I couldn't say. I manage the overall operation, but service—"

"Were you here in the showroom yesterday afternoon?"

"Yes, from time to time."

"Did you see Sean Murray here?"

O'Reilly paused. A hand came out of a pocket. "A sort of short young fellow with long hair and . . . a kind of crook in his nose?"

O'Shaughnessy nodded.

"Yes—I saw him."

"What was he doing?"

"Ah—" now both hands were out of the pockets, "—poking about. Looking at the cars."

"You spoke to him?"

"Ah—" with a finger he stroked his brow, "—not actually."

"Why not?"

"Well—the price of this convertible is sixteen thousand pounds and most fellows his age just don't have that sort of money to chuck about. I can't talk to everybody."

"Do you have a place to sit down?"

"O'Reilly pointed to a window beyond the cars. There were several chairs and a couch of modern design clustered around a glass cocktail table. On it were some magazines.

O'Shaughnessy walked him toward it. "And you saw him sitting here?"

"Yes."

"Reading one of those magazines?"

"Yes. He was, now that you mention it."

The magazines were indeed about automobiles, Mercedes automobiles.

"I don't know the lad myself, personally, but he does bear a certain resemblance to the father. I'm sure it was him."

Another liar, O'Shaughnessy thought, although he could be wrong.

"Much trade yesterday?" O'Shaughnessy asked as the other man went through the stack of yellow service chits.

"Holidays. Get the car serviced before buzzing down to the country. That class of thing. It's always a busy time for the boys in the garage."

"Your service manager, Doyle. Are you aware that he has a prison record?"

O'Reilly straightened up, handing a sheet of flimsy copy paper to the superintendent. "Really now—if we can't forget a man's past, a man who's suffered enough, as I understand it . . ."

"How so?"

O'Reilly's hand went back in his pockets, deep. "I consider that his business."

Two hours' labor, 2:30 to 4:30, at 6 pounds per hour, 30 pence tax.

O'Shaughnessy asked if he might take the afternoon's slips with him.

"I'm sorry, sir," said the woman at the desk, "but as you can see I need them for billing purposes."

"And we'd have to know what all of this is about," O'Reilly added.

"Then you're going to force me to get a court order for them?"

O'Reilly glanced away. He cocked his head to one side. A man in his thirties, his dark hair was just beginning to gray. He had a round face with a long sloping nose and a prominent chin. "Let's say that for the present I'd just like to think the whole thing over."

After phoning Murray, O'Shaughnessy thought. And the call would go through post haste.

* * *

"Have you no children yourself?" the woman asked McGarr.

"None. No—" McGarr reached up and with two knuckles plucked at the child's cheek, "—nippers." He looked fondly at the little boy who was sitting on his knee and bounced him a bit. With his right hand he reached for the teacup on the table, which was covered with an assortment of biscuits, breads, jams, and a box of sweets—bon-bons and creams mostly.

The kitchen was startlingly modern, all porcelain and chrome appliances with stark white walls that the sliding glass doors to the terrace and back garden made brilliant. On a counter a portable television was showing a soap opera beamed in from a commercial British station, and at the beginning of the viewing hour a replica—rather, the model—of the kitchen had appeared in most of the advertisements for home-care products. Now the volume was turned low.

McGarr had gained access to the Brady household by dropping the fact that it had been he who had discovered the bomb in the Caughey car.

"A bomb and not just a scare, was it?" she had asked.

"Aye, a bomb, Missus Brady. And wired to the clutch. Didn't I almost step on it myself." McGarr had then touched his brow.

"Why, you look . . . famished. Parched. Amn't I right, Inspector?"

"Chief Inspector," McGarr corrected, knowing it would matter to her.

The other neighbors who had been led to safety several streets away had only just been returning, and they had stared inquiringly at the Brady doorway and the many hatboxes that McGarr had stacked in it.

"Would you care to see my papers?"

"Ah, no, no—come in, sir. Out of the sun. It's blazing today."

And in the Brady flat, too, McGarr had found the welcome relief of air conditioning. Brady himself was a manager at the Phillips Electrologica data processing firm. "We got a big mark-off on the machine," which she pronounced *mashsheen*, "but I needn't tell you the current is expensive. It's only on days like this—

"But they're Belgians, you know. Phillips. And they make my Tommy work awfully hard. He says we can afford it. Still, it's only on days like this—

"It's about the poor old woman that you've come." She had scurried around the kitchen, readying the table, filling a pot with water, taking this and that from the metal cabinets around the kitchen.

"Tony, you little brigand, put that down."

She was from the country and her mind was quicker than her tongue. She was again wearing the cardigan and the gray woolen dress that he had seen her in the night before, and the pink fluffy booties that looked like two dust mops on her thin legs.

"He's gone most of the time now, my Tom." She had paused and glanced at McGarr, who had bent to shake the child's hand.

"About last night—" he began saying.

"Ah, say no more. The poor, unfortunate, lonely, old woman and that tart of a daughter, no sense to her, out with this one and—" The water had come to a boil.

"Are you a detective, a real detective?" the child had asked.

"He's McGarr, McGarr himself," she put in, "like your father told you. Now, that's a strange name." She directed hot water into the pot, emptied that, added tea, and filled it, dropping the lid into its groove. "From the north?"

"Originally, I should think."

"Have you been married long?"

McGarr wore no rings on his fingers, but it was plain she had found out something about him. "Three and a half glorious years." McGarr waited, handing his Garda Soichana badge, #4, to the little boy, wondering if she'd have the courage to ask him directly.

Finally, when the tea was poured, she put it to him straight, "Catholic?"

McGarr glanced over the edge of the cup and nodded, and he could almost hear her saying to herself, Three and a half years and no children!

"And your wife now," she looked down at the jelly donut, her eyes darkening before she bit into it, "I understand she's . . . younger than you."

McGarr was not surprised. It was a small country and information was undoubtedly the woman's stock-in-trade. "Twenty."

"*Twenty?*" A hand went to her throat as she swallowed the bite of donut.

"Twenty years younger. Nearly. Eighteen is closer to the mark." McGarr again glanced at the child, as though his smile was for him, while she worked on the figures of exactly how old both of them were, when they'd been married, and what had happened or gone wrong to find them now, so many years later, child-less.

"Where's your gun?"

"Down in me sock."

When the child looked down, McGarr clapped a homburg—one of the hats he had in the boxes by the side of his chair—over the little boy's head. "Now do you look like a detective, Tony, or haven't you a clue, there in the dark?"

With both hands the child pulled the hat off his head and looked at it, then reached it up on top of McGarr's head.

"Business woman?"

McGarr looked at her inquiringly. "How's that?"

"I mean," again the contemplation of the pastry, "it's what I've heard. She has a shop in Dawson Street, does she not? Antiques, isn't it?"

"Art."

"Oh—art." It was obvious the word meant little to her and was therefore suspect.

"Now, Tony—do I look like a detective or a gun-man?"

"Foreign things, I take it. She must be abroad a good deal?"

McGarr canted his head to the side, concurring.

"You're not a detective."

"Says who?"

"Says me."

"And says I to you, says I—we're always on the look-out for detectives down at the Castle, and I'm won-dering if you can find me hat, the real one, in all these boxes."

"And you've got your job, here at home."

McGarr nodded.

"And you're right up there with them—the commissioners and all."

"I wouldn't say that."

The child had hopped off McGarr's knee and was now tugging open the boxes, pulling out the hats and casting them aside one by one.

"You needn't be modest, Mister McGarr. My Tommy told me about you when he got home from work. No use complaining about him, says Tom—he runs the show. Only the commissioner is above him, and there's no sense trying to track him down at this time of year. He's probably in—"

"Cork," said McGarr.

"Is that where he holidays?"

"Ballydehob."

"Farrell, his name is, is it not?"

McGarr nodded.

The kitchen floor was now littered with hats, hatboxes, and lids.

He glanced at the clock, a new digital contraption that gave the time in odd-shaped figures, the seconds flashing in an electronic blur, and he eased himself back into the chair. 12:47. He had called the rectory of Father Menahan's church and learned that the priest would be saying a 1:30 offertory mass. If he didn't hurry he'd have to sit through—.

"A swell place, I suppose. Posh. I suppose he's hardly ever at his desk."

McGarr ignored her. He was watching the child turn the hats this way and that, running his fingers over the bands, peering inside at the silk liners.

"And I suppose he wouldn't even listen to the likes of me, just an ordinary citizen."

Not if he could help it, McGarr thought. To his way of thinking Mrs. Brady was a bit . . . unpredictable and spoiled. Perhaps she was the queen in her castle, maybe even something of a figure in the neighborhood, but he was convinced she knew little of how the world—the big world—worked.

"Is it your opinion that this Farrell would have listened to me, Mister McGarr?" Her eyes, seen over the teacup which she had raised to her face, both elbows on the table, had grown small and hard. Her imagination was getting the better of her.

The child grabbed the sleeve of McGarr's jacket and gave it a tug. He was holding a derby off his ears, smiling up at McGarr.

"Now—is that the hat I'm supposed to wear?"

The child nodded.

"Are you sure, Inspector Brady? If you're wrong, you know, it might cost you your job."

The smile fell somewhat, but he nodded again.

"And that's the hat you saw the detective wearing yesterday afternoon, the one who came out of the Caughey apartment upstairs?"

Again the nod.

"Was he going out or coming in?"

"Going out," he said, his voice just barely audible.

"Well—I think I'll call him this minute." She stood; two patches of red had appeared below her cheekbones.

"Who?"

"Why, Farrell, of course."

"About what?"

"Just to see. Inaccessible, is he? Not good enough for the common run of citizen. Sure, me and my Tom, we haven't had a proper holiday in . . . years. Years and years, and here he himself is, big as life, down in Ballydehob with all the swells and foreigners, and the others of you always off in one capital or another, buying who knows what—*art*." The last word sounded like a bark. Her face was contorted with sarcasm.

"How do you know he was going out?" McGarr said to the child. He didn't think she'd grant him much more time.

The child glanced from McGarr to his mother, suddenly shy.

"Well—go ahead, Tony. Speak up, now. Don't let him scare you."

"Because I heard the stairs. Before."

"You mean, the stairs up to the apartment of Missus Caughey? Can you hear them from here?" McGarr glanced at the mother. She was staring at him and her jaw was working, as if she were chewing on something.

"Not here, but . . ." The child ran toward the other end of the kitchen, still holding the derby off his head with one hand. With the other he pulled open a door. ". . . in here. I was playing in here."

McGarr had followed her. "May I, ma'am?"

"Of course. Surely." Her tone was icy.

It was a long, deep closet that functioned as a pantry. The walls were lined with canned goods and household supplies, right under the stairs to the second floor.

"Can you hear people going up?" he asked the mother.

"I wouldn't have the slightest idea."

"Can you, Tony?"

The child glanced at his mother and then turned away.

McGarr squatted down on his haunches. "Tony—something bad happened upstairs yesterday, do you know that?"

He nodded.

"Did you hear any voices yesterday? On the stairs?"

He turned and looked at his mother, letting go of the derby which bounced on the floor. He then ran to her and buried his face in her apron.

McGarr sighed and stood. "Missus Brady—I hope you can appreciate the seriousness of this situation. The . . . tragedy yesterday, and now the bomb. We're not dealing with a house breaker here, or a—"

"You're no better than you were last night, are you?"

No, not much, McGarr thought. "Tony—was it a woman or a man's voice that you heard?"

"Missus Caughey," he said into her skirt.

"Harassment, I'd call it. Harassment of a toddler, a mere baby."

Now McGarr knew why her husband was always working.

"And the other voice, Tony. Was it a man's or a woman's?"

"Come, Tony," she lifted him into her arms, "I'm putting you to bed for your nap, and when I return the man had better have packed his things and left. My husband will hear about this, don't think he won't, and he'll be having a word with you, so he will."

She was flushed and trembling and the child began to cry.

"Man's or woman's, Tony?"

The child only turned his face to McGarr and bawled, as his mother whisked him past and down a hallway.

Inside the rooms of the Philosophical Society all was tranquil. Dust sifted through a shaft of direct sunlight that fell between the bowers of the yew tree outside and onto the old leather of a couch that had been set before a window. Behind a newspaper blue cigarette smoke lazed toward the ceiling. The armchairs were empty, the many other newspapers in the reading frames untouched on the rack.

"Excuse me," said Ward. "Have you seen the porter about?"

"Paddy?" a voice asked from behind the paper. "He's out for a sup."

"The College Inn?"

"Think so."

Ward hesitated. The Irish Press was just around the corner from the bar, which would be filled with reporters and staff lingering over their lunches on this hot summer afternoon. But he closed the door, hurried down the granite steps of the ancient building in Trinity College, and made for the Pierce Street gate. He'd chance it.

The campus and the main buildings of the college —the old library that housed *The Book of Kells*, the chapel, and the examination hall—were thronged with tourists, mostly foreigners. Several tanned blondes walking together and speaking a strange, musical-sounding language turned Ward's head. They had blue eyes, and the hair piled on top of their heads revealed fine blond fluff on thin necks. And they moved languidly, on holiday, unself-conscious of their special ethnic beauty, but Ward hurried on.

At the Coin de Paris and Pia Bang Boutique Ward had found persons who had corroborated all that Mairead Kehleen Caughey had stated earlier, and, stopping at the National Library on Kildare Street, he had determined that the institution was still closed because of building repairs and that the foreman of the crew had in fact seen the girl the day before.

"Who could forget her?" he asked.

Indeed, thought Ward.

"Time?"

"After three, it had to be."

Ward knew he could trust the man's judgment. He looked like the sort who counted his pints. It was only noon and already he'd had a half dozen if he'd had one.

And so Ward had turned his steps toward the old walls and wide green lawns of Trinity. Something that young Murray had said and had been included in McGarr's preliminary report, which Ward had read upon first arriving at the Castle that morning, had been troubling him. Murray had told McGarr that others of his friends had picked the girl up at her house to make it appear as though several young men were keeping her company and not just Murray alone. That in itself wasn't extraordinary, since Ward himself had had to circumvent a suspicious mother or two in his time, but the phrase Murray had used—the "gang"—interested him.

First, Ward couldn't imagine a person like Mairead Caughey, who was so involved in her career as a pianist and her pastime of riding horses, being involved with a "gang," regardless of what the euphemism might mean. And then—Ward had noted long before—other women were not particularly disposed to persons of her . . . perfection. How could most young women, even those here at Trinity, really hope to compete with somebody such as she? And then, if the "gang" was simply Murray's group of friends, Ward was interested in just who they were and what they thought of him, the girl herself, and the death of the mother.

Ward saw a break in the traffic on Pierce Street and sprinted through the white hot, and dusty haze, seen only now in summer, and was suddenly conscious of the familiar drabness of the city, the dirty gray slabs of the police barracks across the way, the bus terminus, the faded brick of the inn in front of him. And the cidery stink of the pub—dark snugs and shadows, the dampness and conversation and smoke—seemed welcome, as though the old wood and brick had subsumed centuries of drear, wet weather that no spate of sun could drive out.

There were tourists in the inn too, which was part of the Mooney chain. Ward knew that they could find themselves admitted to any one of the many bastions of Dublin's peculiar institution, find their sandaled feet in the sawdust, be served and taste the curious, bitter products of a quaint, backward culture, even get a conversation, a laugh, a smile, hear a song, and appreciate the sour dregs of lives which in their terms were misspent, but they'd never get beyond that and really know the people who cozened the dampness, the whisper, the double-meaning, the laugh behind the hand, and what was important and filled the minds of Dubliners.

The day by day of it. Life in a brickyard. Past, present, and future all in a pint. And discrete. Alone. Even in a crowd, be it of tourists or their own. And big families, because they knew they were—and didn't like but couldn't help—being alone. The weave of conversation—an allusion, a familiar, plaintive voice, an old story never the same. History—at once too little and too much—to be spoken only. The peculiar cerebral hardiness in the residents of Ath Cliath. And in his own new way Ward was one of them.

He waited for his eyes to adjust to the darkness, and then walked toward the shadows at an end of the bar where a small man dressed in a blue uniform had leaned his back against the wall and was surveying the crowd.

And it appeared that not only his eyes but also his ears were focused on the others. They protruded from his head like two palms raised. A stub of a cigarette dangled from his mouth. His face was lined and creased but black hair, parted scrupulously at the side, denied the appearance of old age, and as Ward made his way toward the man he was reminded that he knew little about him apart from his being a porter in the student activities building at the college, a friend of McGarr's father, and his having helped them before in other investigations.

Ward stopped beside him and nodded. "Paddy."

"Where's the boss? Out in Ballsbridge?"

Ward pointed at the porter's glass and held up two fingers.

The barman reached for a pint glass.

The porter raised his to his lips and in a long swallow that made his eyes bulge poured his away and set it back down, wiping his upper lip with the side of his index finger in a practiced manner.

"Do you know who she was?" Ward asked him.

"I have a notion." His eyes, which were bleary with drink, glanced out over the tables where the reporters sat, and Ward followed them to see a man at one of the tables turn his chair so he could watch them.

It was Fogarty from the *Times,* and he was McGarr's harshest critic. Ward wondered if he was about to get himself in a jam, coming here. He wondered how much the old porter could be trusted to keep his mouth shut, after he left, and how many pints it would cost him.

"Have you ever heard the daughter play the piano?" He pulled a tenner from his wallet and laid it on the bar between them.

The porter only closed his eyes and opened them.

"Any good?"

He canted his head to the side. "If you like that sort of thing."

"Pretty girl."

The man smiled. "And it's you that'd notice, isn't it now?"

"Lots of friends."

"One or two."

"It's the one I'm interested in."

"Thought as much."

They had kept their voices low, and Fogarty mooched in the chair, wanting but not daring to approach them, doubtless afraid he might queer a newsworthy meeting, knowing later he might get whatever was said from the porter.

"Fine family, the Murrays."

"The best, the very best—if your taste runs to gombeen men." The barman placed the fresh pint in front of the porter, who added, raising it, "May the giving hand never falter."

"And yours Paddy. G'luck." Ward drank in the soft, foamy stout, and set it back down.

"But mind—" the old man went on, "—I've never put a bend on nobody. Nor shopped a feller neither. There's some around here thinks me a mouth almighty, when it suits them, though I hardly say a word." The old man's eyes moved toward Fogarty and flickered away.

"Peter sent me now," Ward said, finding McGarr's first name odd in his mouth. Only O'Shaughnessy called him that, and O'Shaughnessy had age and rank. "He's after wanting an opinion of your man. Nothing definite, no fix, just—"

"What about his friends?"

"What friends?"

"His . . . gang, the ones he goes around with. He's got money and a car and—"

"Ah . . ." The porter turned to face the bar and talked down into his glass.

Ward moved closer,

". . . he's got money and a car all right, but the lot of them are nothing but bowsies and touchers, if you ask me. But mind, now—I've said nothing."

"A studious sort?"

The porter only passed air between his lips and closed his eyes.

"But the law—he's to be a solicitor, I hear."

"And he'll have his days filled with himself, so he will."

Ward only waited.

From the direction of Fogarty's table they heard the rasp of a chair being pulled back, and the porter glanced over his shoulder.

He then spoke quickly. "There's a smell in the rooms they've been in, you know. And them smirking and quipping who knows what and wearing them sunglasses indoors and thinking they was pulling the wool—but mind, not a word."

"Not one."

"And Murray himself thinking because of his gobshite of a father he—but I've said nothing."

"Nothing at all."

Fogarty picked the ten-pound note off the bar. His pate was hairless, his face wizened and tough, his nose bent like the blade of a hatchet. He glanced from the bill to the porter and finally at Ward. "What's this?"

"Paper," said the porter, "and not much better than the stuff you dirty."

"I'd call it a bribe."

The bar crowd near them had quieted, listening to the exchange.

"He would," said the porter to Ward, "but then he's called many a lovely thing by those few ugly words at his command."

Somebody beyond Fogarty began chuckling.

"You're buying information here, Inspector, and I want to know why." The expression on Fogarty's face resembled a snarl.

"Thought I'd do a bit of college, put in a stroke in a legitimate profession—lip work," Ward allowed his eyes to survey the newspaperman's face, "the tripe-writer and all that lot. Paddy here's acquainted with the back door.

"You're a Trinity man yourself, aren't you, Ed?"

"He is like hell," said the porter into his glass. "He's a bully, an ignoramus, and he should take to wearing hats."

Now all around them were very quiet.

"Just look at his speckled, pink pate," the porter went on. "It's got the size, the shape, and the consistency, I'm told, of a baby's shitty arse."

Somebody behind them began a high, falsetto laugh that was contagious and spread around the bar.

"When you're through waving your flag," Ward said to Fogarty, making for the door, "you can pass it back to Paddy. It's his, and I'd hate to prefer a charge against an innocent man."

Livid, Fogarty dropped the bill.

Ward felt good, very good, and he only wished McGarr and the others had been there to hear.

"Flattened him," somebody whispered, as he passed. "Have a drink."

"Hughie—have a drink, for chrissakes. Don't rush off."

"Luvely," said another. "Right on the money."
Several others laughed even harder.

Only the odors of spikenard and myrrh were familiar to McGarr, along with the vestments of the priest—cassock, biretta, breviary in hand—and the ruby glow of the sacristy lamp that he could see through the window of a small door. All else in the modern church, the roof of which was absurdly rectilinear and more an insult than a challenge to older forms, was strange and a disappointment. The abstract shapes of the leaded glass in the windows, pure colors and brilliant, were better suited to a pub, and the pendants hanging near the old altar—*Let us lift our voices to God, God is love, Let His word go forth*—reminded him of revivalism and the tracts that were handed out by proselytizing members of newer faiths.

At the door of the church the priest, Father John Francis Menahan, had shaken his hand. Later a woman in front of him turned and shook it again, saying, "Peace be with you," her smile contrived and forced. He was then tapped on the shoulder and made to offer it to several other worshipers.

Another priest, who had a curly beard and red, wet lips, led the singing of an alleluia that was called, "Alle, Alle," and had a syncopated, folksong beat that made McGarr want to walk out of the church.

Where were the dark interiors of the churches of his youth, the censers, the little tinkling bells, the chants in the Latin language—*Introibo ad altare Dei; Hoc est enim Corpus meum*—, the ceremony in which each worshiper celebrated with his priest and his God a sacrifice which one day would be the fate he himself

would have to face alone—death, the promise of
heaven and redemption, or the pain of damnation
and hell? Where were the choirs and the organs that
could make a deaf man hear? Where were the rich
compositions, the very best of centuries of exquisite
liturgical music that celebrated the glory of God but
also the glory of man who was capable of offering
up such beauty—the high, clear alto joined by other
melodious voices and the organ in intricate, convoluted
patterns that mimicked the complexities of life, only
to break clear and soar, time and again—that trans-
ported the humble supplicant or, at least, had trans-
ported McGarr?

Gone, and only blond ugly pews, plastic tile floors,
a ceremony that emphasized group sharing, and a
big, peasant face—Menahan himself—staring out at
them from over a table, mouthing the platitudes of
the new rite which was downright . . . banal. McGarr
could find no other term.

But he waited until the end of the ceremony, kneeling and standing with the others, genuflecting and
crossing himself when he left the pew.

Again Menahan was at the door of the church.

"Have you come to see me, Chief Inspector?"

Once more McGarr was impressed by the sturdiness
of the man. He was wide, his limbs and hands short
and thick. And with the black, bushy hair that
formed a peak on his brow and fleshy, plain features
he looked more like a country farmer—strong, rugged,
and corporeal—than a priest, although McGarr had
made a few discreet inquiries and knew the impression was deceiving.

Menahan had been reassigned from the National

University at Galway, where he had taught mathematics and philosophy, to this parish on the other coast of the island for having evidenced, in the eyes of his superiors, signs of the first sin—pride—and here in Ballsbridge he was being watched closely.

"It interests me why you're calling about him, Peter," McGarr's source had asked.

"We were thinking of having him speak at a Garda function," McGarr had lied. Who was he to cause the man any undue trouble?

"Ask him. He's a wonderful speaker and a pianist. A real talent. He's . . . a little intellectual, mind, but if he could make a go of it with you fellows, it might take some of the heat off him."

McGarr now said to Menahan, "If I could have a moment of your time, Father."

"The sacristry?"

"I'd prefer to wait outside, if you don't mind. I smoke." That too wasn't the truth exactly. The inside of the church, for all its light, made McGarr feel claustrophobic.

But it was hot outside and bright. McGarr leaned against the trunk of a tall, blue spruce and in its shade watched the others move away from the church in twos and threes, mostly old women.

He glanced across the hot lawn toward the rectory, a stodgy, brick Victorian structure with a glass-enclosed porch painted beige and a long flight of gray wooden stairs. The kitchen window was open and cooking smells came to him. Roast lamb. Menahan would eat well, he decided, although he knew the decision as to what wasn't Menahan's to make. Still, there was money somewhere—the Bechstein in the

Caughey sitting room, a present from Menahan. A *magnificent* present. Why?

For such a large man he stepped nimbly down the stairs, his eyes bright and playful. "Accept nothing as true which you do not clearly recognize to be so; accept nothing more than what is presented to your mind so clearly and distinctly that you can have no occasion to doubt it."

He stopped several steps up from McGarr, so he was speaking down to him. "Divide each problem into as many parts as possible.

"Commence your reflections with objects that are simplest and easiest to understand and rise thence, little by little, to knowledge of the most complex.

"Lastly, make enumerations so complete and reviews so general that you should be certain to have omitted nothing."

McGarr thought back; he had heard all of it before or read it, but it was too long ago and his mind did not run to the niceties of philosophical speculation. "Berkeley?"

Menahan's smile fell somewhat. "No, Inspector—, Descartes, the man who propounded modern, deductive reasoning. But I must admit that I'm surprised you came so close. Then again I hadn't really expected to see you in my church. Are you a religious man?"

McGarr had been watching the priest closely. There was a certain . . . playfulness about him that he found engaging but curious for a man of the cloth. "I am, though not like some."

"Do you come to church often?"

"As little as can be helped, to be frank."

Menahan smiled. He cocked his head and his face seemed almost handsome. But his front teeth had been chipped and a scythe-shaped scar on his chin only emphasized the blueness of his heavy beard. "Then what does religion mean to you?"

McGarr had the same feeling that he'd experienced as a child when being questioned about the catechism —a desire to be exact, but anger too, at the thought that so much could have been made so definite. He dropped his cigarette butt into the needles and placed the sole of his chestnut-colored brogue on it. "It's a system."

Menahan clasped his thick hands in front of him, over the top of his belly. It was a gesture of delight, McGarr guessed. "A system. But aren't all systems . . . impositions, ways of helping you to think of a problem, but false, when all is said and done?"

McGarr again studied the man. He glanced from one of Menahan's bright dark eyes to the other, the sclerae of which were very clear, as seen only in persons who enjoyed great good health and had no bad habits. "No, Father. Religion strives through faith in the unknowable to transcend system itself."

"You were taught that?"

"No, Father."

"That's a pity. It's . . . refreshing and intriguing. How did you come by it?"

"Through . . . observation. And reflection."

"Ah—" the hands opened and closed again, "—the empirical method."

"A system of sorts."

"But can you trust your perceptions?"

"I have no choice."

"But doesn't it disturb you that they could be wrong?"

McGarr cocked his head. "No, not really—a reasonable congruity is all I seek. Were I to know all perfectly, it would take the . . . discovery out of life."

"Then you believe you've been presented imperfect tools for an imperfect world?"

"No—in God and His perfectly imperfect design."

Menahan's laugh was short and sharp but mirthful. "You're an unlikely policeman, I must say."

"And you a priest, Father. I understand you're a pianist, and a teacher too."

Menahan's smile fell somewhat and his eyes strayed toward the rectory. He checked his wristwatch. "Monsignor Kelly is a man who enjoys his dinner, as he calls it, and he's punctual. On the dot. Would you mind walking me that way?"

They stepped out into the sun and ambled slowly toward the large house, which a copse of towering ash trees shaded.

McGarr waited, and finally Menahan said, "You've come about the piano." He kept his eyes on his shoes, which were black and shiny but surprisingly small for a man of his size. "I'd like to get that out of the way before we get close, if you don't mind.

"You'd know why I bought it for her if you ever heard her play. You see—" he looked off, out across the lawn toward the sidewalks where the churchgoers could be seen getting into cars and waiting for the bus, "—most of us, myself included, are really just God's pap. We're rather . . . coarse and talentless, but Mairead is—" his eyes moved up, off into the glare,

"—gifted. Inspired. She has that sure touch, an innate feeling for music. It doesn't matter what it is." He was smiling again. "And not 'soft,' mind you. Not 'romantic.' She's . . . hard in the right way. What she needs now is the right kind of technical instruction."

"In London."

"Yes—I'm only a . . . dilettante, and I must be a priest first, it seems. I have neither the time nor the—" he paused again, "—skill to teach her anymore. When was it? A month? No—maybe six weeks ago she experienced what I can only call a breakthrough. The day or the week or the month before I could teach her something, then the following lesson or the one after, she was too advanced. Way ahead of me. Suddenly I was the student. We'd been working through Shostakovich concerti—difficult, modern pieces. At first she had trouble—then it was almost as though she became Shostakovich. There was nothing I could say or tell her, and she knew it too. She became . . . restless, when I was around.

"I myself had studied in London, so I called one of my friends over there and I arranged for her to sit for the piano prize at the Conservatory. She won, of course."

"How did her mother feel about that?"

They had reached the rectory, and Menahan placed a foot on the first gray stair to the porch.

"She was proud, of course, but she was rather a . . . private person, but a darling, loving woman, God rest her soul." Menahan's eyes suddenly filled, and he struggled to control himself. "It's not as though Mairead would really consult her, I don't think. When was it—

years ago; three or four at least—that Mairead began to—" he glanced down at the length of the long wooden stair, "—act on her own.

"I mean—" he turned his gaze to McGarr again, "—all strictly proper, mind you—having to do with her work, her calling. As I said, she's inspired and I do believe from God." He was now sweating profusely. "But to answer your question, her mother wanted Mairead to stay at home, here in Ireland."

"You visited the Caughey apartment often to give these lessons?"

"Three times a week, at least. But then, you know, it was as though we were family, after all this time."

"What time did you leave the Caughey apartment yesterday afternoon?" It was a guess, but based on Mairead Caughey's and Sean Murray's statements, which McGarr had had read to him earlier, over the phone.

But Menahan didn't even blink. "Three-fifteen."

"What was the victim doing when you left?"

"I don't know. She was busy in the kitchen. I said good-bye from the hall and let myself out."

"Why didn't you tell us this last night?"

"Nobody asked. I didn't think it important. I'm not a policeman, Inspector, I'm a priest. At that point I was thinking only of her soul—may God grant it peace."

What was it—McGarr now asked himself, glancing at the contrite, almost self-satisfied purse to Menahan's mouth—that made most priests seem . . . smug? Was that the word? No—patronizing, that was it. "Keegan, James Joseph. The mother's brother, I take it. You're from that part of the country. Tell me what you know about him."

"Next to nothing, I'm afraid. Only rumor and innuendo and the odd allusion Margaret made about him. He's quite a bit older than I."

"What rumor, what innuendo?"

Menahan glanced up at the porch door of the rectory. "I. R. A. and that class of thing. I guess he was just another romantic, a dreamer. When he came back to take over the farm, it went to hell in no time. He lost it in ten years."

"To Bechel-Gore?"

His eyes shied. "I don't know the particulars of the sale, but I think that's right."

"And your own family's property was contiguous to the Keegans'?"

"Yes."

"And you sold that property to Bechel-Gore as well?"

Menahan turned to McGarr and searched his face. "You're not really asking me, are you, Chief Inspector?"

In fact, McGarr was not, having called the Galway Land Office earlier, he was only trying to assess the priest's answers. "Was that the money you bought the piano with?"

Menahan nodded. "Really now—I must get in there. Monsignor Kelly—"

"Who is Doctor Malachy T. Matthews of Drogheda? He's a vet?"

Menahan's eyes again moved away from McGarr. "That's J. J. Keegan, I believe."

"You believe."

"Yes."

"You have good cause to believe that?"

"Yes."

"Why, may I ask?"

Menahan glanced at his wristwatch and sighed, then looked directly at McGarr. "You may ask, certainly, and could I tell you I would. It's no single fact, no one bit of knowledge. It's just an . . . impression I put together over the years. And the Caugheys' money had to come from someplace. They had none that I knew of before. Mairead mentioned a certain cousin in Drogheda; Margaret would say Doctor Malachy this and that, you know. I also knew Keegan was wanted by you fellows for something or other to do with the 'army,' which is one of the reasons the farm went down. And when I asked after the man, she'd always be evasive and . . . sly. It was her way, you see, but I mean not to libel the dead."

What was the man's tone? It had changed, but McGarr wasn't sure how.

The priest turned and started up the stairs toward the door.

"And who was Caughey? When did he die?"

"I'm not sure he did. A bounder, I hear, but older than I, like Keegan. I know no more than that, I assure you."

"Then who would Mairead have as a friend—a person who studies in the National Library? An older friend, she said."

Menahan tugged open the door and stepped up onto the porch, the glass of which made the light inside pink against the brick of the rectory. "I wouldn't know."

"Pretty girl."

"Not pretty. Beautiful," said Menahan. "A goddess in every way."

"Father!" another voice said, sternly. "You're keeping us waiting with your talk about—what was it that I heard?"

McGarr looked up to see an older man with a boiled face and a shock of white hair. He was standing in the inner door.

"Nothing, Monsignor. Nothing at all."

"And who is that man?"

McGarr turned and walked back the way he had come, toward the church and his car beyond.

"Nobody," he heard Menahan say. "A parishioner, a family matter."

McGarr had a feeling it was.

McKeon had his notebook out. He had placed it on the library table directly in front of him, as he thumbed through the *Official Catalogues* of the Horse Show, not merely five years back, as McGarr had requested, but twenty. In his neat but cramped hand he was noting entrants in the donkey classes (nos. 81 through 88 in most of the manuals), and in particular those from either Leenane, County Galway, or Drogheda, County Louth. He too had put in periodic phone calls to his desk at the Castle, which Ban Gharda Bresnahan was presently occupying.

And McKeon enjoyed the assignment, there in the long room stacked with the leather-bound proceedings of the Society dating back to 1731, the deep shadows which the little lamp with the green translucent shade cast, its circle of light, the quiet there contrasting sharply with the hubbub of the exhibitors out in the Main Hall. There carpenters and trade-show personnel were putting up booths to display their wares—equestrian equipage of every sort, tractors, stoves, prefabricated barns, new-technology silos, craft exhibits, an art show, some Finns who had brought with them a whole factory, it seemed, of stylish furniture.

At one point two men, who were arguing in the stilted accents of the old Ascendency, had entered from the Members' Rooms and pulled down a dusty volume. One of them then proved to the other that an ancestor of his had numbered among the founders of the revered Society that had done so much for the country, more than just the Show itself. Having settled the question, they noticed McKeon writing away in his book. "Sorry, old boy," one of them had said.

Old boy, indeed, McKeon had thought. He was as much an "old boy" as they were pedigreed asses of the sort he was reading about there in the catalogues.

J. J. Keegan had, in fact, been an exhibitor of donkeys from 1959, the year he'd been freed from a British nick, to '69, a year which had been marked by much I. R. A. activity. In '71, Doctor Malachy T. Matthews had begun exhibiting a number of donkeys that corresponded rather closely to those of Keegan, in particular a prize brood mare Keegan had called "Pegeen" and Matthews had called "Meg." McKeon couldn't be sure they were one and the same, but the prizes they gained in the category, brood mare with foal at foot, were always best of show, and he had a feeling they were. Matthews was listed as an exhibitor for the current year, although the Office said he had not as yet registered.

McKeon replaced the volumes and switched off the light. He strolled out through the Main and Industry halls to Ring 2 where the hot, late afternoon sun forced him to doff his jacket.

There gardeners were studiously clipping grass around the fence posts, while others up in ladders worked on the linden trees, rounding their bowls as a foreman shouted up at them from afar—a little here, a little there—to make them equal.

Horses passed McKeon, being led down the path of crushed cinders to the stables, which were located throughout the Show Ground. And people—busy people, expectant or anxious or simply caught up in the excitement of the impending Show—pushed by him, talking among themselves, preoccupied, carefully guiding a caravan or a horse lorry toward the quarters they had been assigned. Many—he well knew—had worked all year toward the next few days, and McKeon found the atmosphere of the place much to his liking.

After—how many years was it, now?—twenty-eight and some months as a policeman of one sort or another, strolling under the vaulted porticos of Pembroke Hall with a horse in nearly every paddock, its half-timbered façade Elizabethan and elegant, jumpers in the exercise ring even now loping over low gates, ridden by grooms or young family members, was the class of assignment that McKeon believed he deserved. The Castle and his desk, while a valuable post in regard to promotion and the like, seemed a bleak prospect to him.

Sure—he had often told himself—Commissioner Farrell would soon retire and McGarr would be given his job; O'Shaughnessy would take over the Detective Bureau for a short time and then he himself would be given the assignment with Ward as his desk man. But McKeon didn't know how much more of it he could take himself. More outings like this, though, and he could hump it. He imagined he might even drag some of his kids along for the first day of the Show, make it look more genuine—the pose and all.

At the animal arrival and departure area McKeon managed to insinuate himself among the clatch of men who had gathered in the registrar's office—smiling to this one, nodding to another, smoking a cigarette with his back against the wall until the man in the R. D. S. blazer moved away from the log book. McKeon then stepped toward it, as though not really interested, but his small, dark eyes had scanned all the pages but one before the registrar returned.

"Can I help you?"

"Just looking to see if a friend has arrived."

"Name?"

"Matthews, Doctor Malachy."

The man cocked his head. "Don't think so. Not yet anyhow. I know him though, I think. Brood mares?"

"After a fashion. Brood-mare donkeys."

The man nearly turned his back on him. "Try the caravan park. We've no stabling room for them this year."

There McKeon found the two entrants that had attracted him in the log book—a car-towed trailer from Maam, near Leenane, and a large animal lorry from Slane, near Drogheda.

The man in the former vehicle was trying to back it into a narrow slot near the Merrion Road wall and a tree that would provide it good shade, and McKeon tossed his jacket over the hood and directed him in, then gave the man a hand with propping up the trailer and leading the animals out.

His name was Goggin, and he had his kids and his missus with him. He offered McKeon a bottle of lager, and under the shade of the tree they talked and had a smoke before McKeon departed.

"Going to be around?" the man had asked.

"Think so. I'm in the market. Retired now. Thought I'd raise a few donkeys."

"Ah—no money in it, I'll tell you that right now."

"I wouldn't be in it for that. We had five of them when I was a lad, and now I'm after wanting a few myself—for my kids."

"Been away?"

McKeon only nodded.

"Stop back. I might be letting one or two go."

One of his little girls had jumped up on the back of a strong young donkey stallion, and he was hopping and bucking, trying to get her off. He sprinted forward fast and then came to a sharp stop, twisting his head, but she held fast to its mane. "You're nothing but a Tinker's ass, hear me, Willy?" she shouted in his ear and whacked his side so he jumped and scampered around the cars, his legs strong and stiff, his lips fluttering over square, yellow teeth as he brayed and complained.

At the lorry, the side of which read, "Homewood Farms, Horses and Donkeys, Slane, County Meath," McKeon found nobody about. It was a large Bedford truck, almost the size of a mover's van, its lettering silver and brilliant against polished maroon lacquer. It had a sleeping cab behind the driver's seat and a grill that was higher than McKeon was tall. Even the six lugs on each wheel had been polished, and an auxiliary engine was working to cool the inside.

There were five doors—two to the driver's compartment, the rear bay flaps, and a small door with a window in it on one side. That a curtain nearly covered. Standing on tiptoes McKeon squinted, trying to see past the glare, and thought he caught a glimpse of a figure reclining or sleeping on a small couchlike berth.

He knocked but got no response. He knocked again, harder, then grasped the handle and found the door locked.

The van was parked near the wall and the door was quite close to it.

McKeon glanced down both sides. There were many people close by and he could hear conversations, shouts, car and van doors being closed, but the lorry had been so positioned that the door was concealed from sight.

McKeon reached in his pocket and, with a few turns with one of the several picks on his key ring, had the door open.

He pulled it back slowly, and the figure on the bed stirred. "Dick?" His voice was muffled against the cushions. "Somebody was banging on the door a while back. Where'd you put the bottle? Christ, I'm dying."

The man turned to McKeon.

His face was pallid and drawn, a large handlebar mustache covering his upper lip. He was wearing white coveralls, like those of the gardeners McKeon had seen earlier, and his eyes were glassy. And he was old, maybe seventy or better.

Before McKeon could speak, a hand was placed on his arm. "Can I help you?" somebody asked close to his ear.

It was a large, older man with a face like that of a professional boxer—the nose flattened off to one side, one eyebrow missing and whitish scar tissue in its place, one ear larger than the other. The grip on McKeon's arm was firm.

"I'm after wanting a peek at your donkeys."

"But the door was locked."

"No, it wasn't. I looked in and saw your man, and—" McKeon glanced down.

The man was holding a whisky bottle, like a club, in the other hand.

"What do they call you?"

"Kennedy."

"From?"

"Leitrim." It was McKeon's mother's name, the town and county where he had been born and raised.

"How's the fishing?"

"Fine."

"What did you catch this summer?"

"Brill. A salmon or two."

The man released his arm. "Why don't you come back tomorrow? We're having a little problem here at the moment." He raised the bottle. He smiled. Several of his front teeth were false and very white compared to the others. He was a massive man, all shoulders and chest.

139

"I'll do that."

The other man had turned his face to the cushions once more.

"Buying or selling?" the large man asked.

"Buying, and that's a certainty."

He twisted the cap off the bottle and discarded it roughly. He reached it out toward McKeon. "No sense in wasting all of it." He gestured with his head toward the man in the lorry. "He won't even taste it."

"After having a drop?" McKeon asked, reaching for the bottle.

The man closed his eyes and shook his head. "The failing, I'm afraid. Desperate. But he's a right bloke when he's off it."

McKeon drank off as much as his throat would permit. "I'll be back."

"I'll count on it."

Do that, McKeon thought.

They arrived at the Matthews's farm outside Drogheda late in the afternoon, and Noreen remarked on the little boy they could see sitting on the stairs leading to the front door, head on his hands. The door beyond him had been broken open. It was swaying on one hinge in the slight breeze off the front lawn, its glass stove in.

The farmhouse was an old, two-story affair that had recently been modernized, the narrow windows enlarged, the stucco touched up and painted a light-blue color little different from the summer sky. The slanting sun made it seem brilliant, and the grass of the front lawn, which grazing animals had cropped, had a bushy summer appearance, as though nothing could keep it back, tufts and sprays burgeoning here and there.

Off one side of the house a kennel had been added, a long, shedlike structure with a corrugated metal roof. From it they could hear the muffled barking of many dogs.

McGarr swung the car around, heading it back down the drive. "Perhaps you'd better wait here. And—"

But she had already reached below the seat for the Walther that he kept in a holster there.

McGarr checked the clip and placed the automatic under his belt. Stepping out, he tugged at the brim of his panama to shade his eyes. A flock of corncrakes, black and raucous, passed overhead, and the sun was hot on his back.

The little boy did not look up at him, only stared at McGarr's bluchers, his eyes again filling with tears. His cheeks were stained from crying. "Pegeen," was all he said.

"Where is she?" McGarr stared down at the tousled head, the sunlight so bright there he could have counted the strands.

The boy stood and they walked through an anteroom to an office, the floor of which was covered with broken glass. Other doors had been smashed open, and McGarr could see an operating table for animals, surgical cabinets, and sinks. Yet another burst door led into the house proper. A radio was playing in the sitting room, one light by a chair left on.

But the boy led him through the house, out to the back where, in a pen, an aged donkey was lying in a pool of blood, wheezing, her old eyes glassy. She shied as McGarr approached her, fearful but complacent too.

She had been pulled or had dragged herself into the shade at the side of the house. There was a horse blanket over her and something that looked like a compress on her head.

The boy stooped and pulled back the blanket to reveal a gunshot wound in her rib cage. "And here," he sniffled, gently lifting the compress away.

The blood there was dark, almost black, but the bullet seemed to have passed through the fleshy part at the back of the neck.

"Who done it, Mister? Not Doctor Matt."

McGarr reached down for his hand. "It happened some time ago and she's still with us. Maybe she's not as bad as she appears. We'll see what we can do, straightaway."

The boy slid his small, limp hand into McGarr's, and they moved back into the house.

"Anybody else about?"

"The dogs."

"When did you last see Doctor Matt?" From the doorway McGarr signaled to Noreen.

"Yesterday."

"What time yesterday?"

Seeing Noreen step from the car, the boy began crying harder, and he walked out onto the stair, toward her.

In the sitting room McGarr found the phone and, grasping the cord of the receiver, lifted it off its cradle. With the end of his fountain pen he dialed the Castle and then, after having consulted the directory, the closest vet.

In the kitchen Noreen washed the boy's face and hands and found him something to eat.

He lived down the road and had a small job with Matthews, cleaning the kennels and feeding the animals.

Upstairs in one of the bedrooms, McGarr found a window open and spent casings from some sort of machine pistol scattered over the carpet in front of it. A burst had caught the roof at the side of the house and had smashed the slates. There was blood too, on the carpet and leading into the hall. In the bathroom there was a towel smeared with blood and the medicine cabinet had been rifled, bottles tossed about, some broken.

Down below in the backyard he found footprints of many men—four or five at least—leading toward the marsh at the end of the property. The Boyne lay beyond, black and tranquil, and in one spot the reeds had been trampled down.

McGarr turned and considered the house and kennel. It was quiet there, with Noreen and the child having now fed the dogs. He remembered the letter he'd found in Margaret Kathleen Caughey's apron. "Sis, Get out. He's onto me. Jimmy-Joe."

Back inside, in the office, McGarr discovered that the desk and files had been ransacked, the contents strewn about the tile floor. On the desk were two manila folders, both empty. The label of one read, "Bechel-Gore," the other, "M. K. Keegan-Caughey." From the bent and rumpled edges he supposed each had been long-standing and substantial.

The medical supplies in the office had been used as well, gauze and bandages and adhesive tape.

"What does it mean?" Noreen asked him after the others had arrived.

McGarr glanced down at the empty folders. He wondered why they had been left behind. "That we know far too little about the Caugheys, the Keegans, and Bechel-Gore, I suspect."

"Does that mean Galway?"

"It does."

She smiled. They had yet to take their holiday and soon the fair, summer weather would be over.

In the car again, she smacked his thigh. "Where shall we eat?"

McGarr hadn't thought about food since the rectory, and he was suddenly ravenous.

But he glanced at her—her ringlets of copper-colored hair, her green eyes which were bright, the slight tan she'd gotten from noontime tennis at the college. She was wearing a turquoise jersey and a white dress. "An outing, is it?"

"Certainly, Chief Inspector. It's the weekend, it's summer, and you'll never see this day again. Where's your joie de vivre, your éclat, your . . ." she gave him a sidelong glance, "youth."

McGarr looked away and slid the gearshift into first.

"We could start with a good, stiff drink."

McGarr blinked.

"I know just the place."

She would, he thought.

"The chef is Italian, the real McCoetaneo. He serves a *fagiano arrosto alla ricca* that's unbeatable, especially considering the birds we have here."

It was a pheasant entree that McGarr particularly enjoyed. Sage leaves and juniper berries were rubbed inside, then it was larded with bacon and browned in oil and butter. Grappa and black olives were added, and, after turning it into a hot oven and basting frequently, hot stock was added to the pan. And then a tablespoon of butter and a few drops of lemon—the final and perfecting touch. It was one of McGarr's favorite dishes.

"They serve a light red wine that the owner says his brother sends him straight from his villa in San Gimignano."

McGarr's stare at her was sidelong and sustained. Perhaps she knew him too well.

ON SHOTS IN THE NIGHT
AND WORRY,
A SPIN, A DEATH, SIN
AND FURY

Matthews could distinctly remember the radio having been on—the late news in Irish—and he had given it half an ear and considered whether he should pour himself another tot of brandy, just enough to color the soda in the glass. And it was only that gesture—looking up from the government report on the alarming upsurge of brucellosis in dairy cattle—that saved him.

He remembered turning his head to the radio and wondering if the sound had come from the cabinet with the dim yellow light, dusty, its top heaped with magazines and other reports long dated.

It was a soft, spongy sound, like a boot being tugged out of wet earth, and it had carried across the garden from the marsh and through the window, which he had opened upon returning from the pub several hours earlier.

And he had even glanced at the clock. Half twelve and late. He had a foaling due sometime in the morning, and the mare had a history of breech presentations.

Then Pegeen had begun braying, her raucous cries spreading out through the darkness and frightening a flock of mallards in the reeds. They rose, flapping and complaining, and with one motion Matthews was on his feet and had his hand on the chain of the lamp.

Outside from the front where his office was he heard a curse and the slam of a car door and other footsteps, many of them running toward the buildings.

The dogs in the kennels were alerted now and began the barking that Matthews had listened to so carefully so many times before; the din they sent up at night whenever somebody passed by on the road, the sound that had always brought him to the window, his hand groping in the darkness for the drawer and the weapon he kept in the desk close by.

But it was too late for that. Something heavy struck the front door and glass showered the tiles in the reception room, striking the wall, the interior door, and skittering under it.

He only just made the landing when the door was kicked open and the beam from the torch, a brilliant funnel of bluish light, flooded the hall.

And then nothing for a moment, as the light flashed up the stairs, down the length of the passageway toward the back door, and then into the now-dark sitting room where the radio was still playing.

From the backyard he heard a shot, and Pegeen's braying stopped suddenly. He then heard her wheeze pitiably. Another shot. The dogs were quieting now, and low voices came to him from the kennels. The murmur of several men.

The light moved into the sitting room, and Matthews eased himself along the wall toward the bedroom and its window that gave onto the roof of the kennels.

How had they quieted the dogs and with what? Mince—it had to be. Could he drop down over them without setting them off again?

Pegeen, he thought. The bastards. He'd had her for twenty-three years, off and on. She had come with him there from Leenane, after the farm had been taken from him and he had needed the new identity. She had been all that he'd had left from the other life, the sole thing that had tied him to his family and his past.

He opened the drawer of the nightstand and slid out the silver automatic, thumbing off the safety and shoving it under his belt.

It had been hot during the day and the window was open, and down in the yard he could see other lights being played around the verges of the marsh.

And a flash in the doorway and feet on the stairs.

He slid his leg out, eased his body under the window, and then tried to lower himself down, but the drop was farther than he had thought and his fingers couldn't hold the sill. One hand slipped, then the other, a fingernail breaking and his fingers scraping down the masonry, catching at last on the hard stone of the house itself.

The flash of light out the window above him was almost tangible, freighted and lethal and blinding, like the blast of a bomb.

But he couldn't hold on and he heard steps approaching and smelled the scorch of a cigar, rank and acrid and strong.

In one motion he let go and grabbed for the weapon.

His heels struck the roof of the kennel, which roared

like a drum, and he jerked the barrel at the window and fired.

The blast snapped back his arm, and he rolled over and skidded, face first, down the sheet-metal roof into the darkness, falling heavily onto a stack of turf.

The dogs were roaring again, and he heard shouts from the sides of the house.

And in the window a gun opened up—something big and quick, like a sten, cutting down into the darkness and through the overhang.

Matthews scrambled to his feet and began running in a low crouch, using the side of the house to shield himself from the fire above.

But lights splashed over the grass of the lawn and caught him halfway to the marsh, and the gun rapped out once more, splattering the ground around him.

The bullet slammed into his lower back and hurled him into the reeds. And then something went wrong with his hand as well. Was he still holding the gun? He wasn't, he didn't think, but it didn't matter, now.

The tide was in and he was up to his neck in water. He pulled in a breath and went under, down to the mucky bottom where he thought he could feel the firm roots of the reeds. He tried to pull himself forward, out into the Boyne, but he couldn't tell if he was moving. His entire back was a burning, searing center of pain, and below that he couldn't feel anything. But he crawled on or thought he did, scratching and tearing at the muddy bottom, trying to keep himself down and moving forward. Until he began to feel himself fading and could no longer find reeds or make his arms move and he had to come up.

Matthews broke into clear water beyond the reeds

where a three-quarter moon made the river seem silver and as tranquil as any placid lake. And he was concealed from the shore. He could hear the dogs and the men, but only now and again did the lights wink at him through gaps in the reeds or pass overhead in shafts that were subsumed by the darkness.

The water was cold there, out where the current flowed, and it seemed to soothe his back like two cooling hands. He tilted back his neck, the better to float. The sky was limpid and bright, stars stacked to eternity, it seemed, and whatever had driven him to flee from the house and into the water seemed to leave him. He no longer cared if he lived or died, and suddenly he was very tired. He seemed to be leaving his body—his arms and legs, even his face and head—and retreating to someplace as distant and small as the stars above him.

He couldn't remember how long he had remained like that, uncaring, inert, simply drifting with the incoming tide, but it had to have been several hours at least, for he remembered only the sky suddenly becoming black and his head and shoulders knocking up against something hard.

The quayside or a pier. And his shoe was on something too. A footing. Slane. He had the right kind of friends there, ones who'd understand that he'd been wronged and what he'd have to do. If only he could recover.

And now, there in the van with the night coming on, he had only his pain for company and his hate, and he cozened and saved every galling throb against the moment when he'd take his revenge. And it would be sweet and he wouldn't care what happened to him after.

The door opened, but he did not turn to it. "How is it now, Jimmy?" the other man asked, bending over him. "Will I call the doctor?"

"Better, Mick," he lied. "Much better. Let's not bother him further. I'm beholden enough." —

Horses—Murray thought, looking up from the computer's printouts that were heaped on the desk in his study—they'd be the ruin of him yet. Not a person or a thing that he'd encountered in the venture had proved rewarding in any . . . well, that wasn't exactly true. He tossed the pencil down on the stack and stood. But maybe about even that he was codding himself. It depended on how he handled it, especially now.

He removed the cigar from his mouth and stepped closer to the window, peering through the gap in the heavy, velveteen drapes, out at the tree-shaded street and the yellow convertible that he'd heard pull up many minutes before.

Maybe he'd wanted too much for Sean, and for himself too. Maybe there really was a born, a genetic aristocracy, people who were just naturally better and finer, and who knew and could handle, buy, sell, and enjoy things like horses and yachts, and who had that certain, sure touch with people that put them in their place.

But no, look at the girl Mairead, the child of a simple country woman, and she had that ease of manner, taste and talent too. She was like those others—content in her abilities and her . . . inabilities as well, not always blundering off after this and that, trying to be something she was not. Like him and like Sean. Not knowing why but simply grasping, wanting what others had and for what? To show them. And what? That they weren't common, when in fact the very effort marked them. Indelibly.

But it didn't help, thinking like that, given their—he glanced at the desk—situation.

And the car door had opened, and Sean had stepped out.

Fool of a father, Murray thought, fool of a son. But it was too late to change that now, and it was one thing to think those thoughts in the quiet of one's study and quite another to act them out. How often had Murray told himself he'd be one way and found himself another and always the same—the man who hankered after success, had all the trappings but none of the appreciation of money and power. And there he'd only succeeded in passing the worst parts of his personality down to his son. And none of the strength that had ... saved him.

Quickly now he moved to the study door and out into the hall. From the front door he called to his son, who had been on the point of walking past the gate.

And he had the sunglasses on again. And the stiff gait, all squared shoulders with his weight on his heels, like a drunk with a jag on who was trying to conceal it. Was that what he'd been doing alone in the car?

Murray felt his gorge rising and his shoulder twitched involuntarily. "Where're you off to?"

"Thought I'd pop down to the pub."

"With the Show and your exams coming up?"

"I don't see you stinting yourself."

Murray heard a door open behind him on the landing and he glanced up.

It was his wife, dressed in a vivid red dressing-gown and looking like a successful tout's moll in a Grade B, British movie. She too tried hard, he reminded himself, but she had even less of an idea of how it was done. Small and squat, her hair dark and curly and as well cared for as a clipped hedge—what could he tell her, what could he say? Should he try to explain, apologize for all he had brought on both of them, for their lifetime of striving? No—it was better to say nothing. Not now. Not with what was facing them.

"Could you step in here now for a moment, son. I'd like to have a word with you. Won't take long, that's a promise."

And that he had to pander to the boy, the pleading note in his voice, the conciliation—it showed him all the more how he had failed, had spoiled himself by giving in so completely to his ambitions, had spoiled the boy by the example.

His wife started down the stairs, her step heavy, beefy, her seeming as out of place under the brilliant Georgian chandelier as she looked on a horse at a hunt. But then, Murray knew he himself appeared no better.

Go to bed! Murray wanted to shout. But this was important and he couldn't afford to lose his temper, to climb into the role he affected in his offices and . . . in the world. "Just a little money matter, Bridie," he said in a soothing tone. "Expenses and the Show."

"Don't go too hard on him now," she said. "It won't be long before he's out on his own." She turned and stepped back to her own study, her ankle still narrow even with her size. A good woman, Murray thought, and deserving of . . . better? No—different.

His son brushed by him, hands in pockets, his hair flopping about his shoulders, the goon's glasses still on his face.

Murray was tempted to slam the door but he held off. And with the study door too.

"Drink?"

"No—why don't you have mine for me. You probably could use it."

But still Murray kept it in.

"They stop round to the garage?" the son asked in Trinity tones, nonchalantly, the final word sounding almost French. "Is that what this is all about?"

"And isn't it enough?" Murray was tempted to fill the brandy snifter but he held off. "You handled yourself rather poorly today."

"And you any better, drunk or whatever it was you were. Anyhow," he sat in a cushioned chair and draped one leg over the arm, "how does it matter?"

"Matter?" Murray asked in a quiet tone, turning to the boy. "Lying under oath doesn't matter? Do you know that they've picked up the garage mechanic who is supposed to have worked on your car? They've got him down in the Castle; they're grilling him right now."

The son only hunched his shoulders and looked away. "I thought you said he was dependable."

"And he is, as much as any man, but don't you underestimate that culchie sonofabitch, O'Shaughnessy. He'd like nothing better than to hook us on this one, with me down there representing you and all." It was getting out of hand now—his temper, his persona.

Murray took a long drink from the snifter. "And don't make any mistake about it. He'll lean on that fellow, and there's only so much—" he glanced at the desk and the computer records on it, "—input I can have in the matter. He'll crack him, he will. And then where will you be?" He moved toward the son.

"But you were representing me, *and all*," he replied, making fun of Murray's thick, Dublin brogue. "I didn't sign, did I? My—" he flicked his wrist, "—memory will suddenly return."

Christ, Murray thought, just what the hell was it he had taken that he didn't appreciate the seriousness of his position? And Murray's own. Something like this, a scandal, and everybody would start looking at him hard. "And what will your memory tell you, I'm after wanting to know?"

The son jerked his head to him. His lower lip, which was protrusive, jumped toward his nose. Through his bottom teeth he said, "Are you *after*, are you *after wanting*—indeed?"

Murray's wrath rose up inside him. He felt the bitter sting in his stomach and chest. Sweat exuded from his forehead and upper lip, and his breathing was suddenly heavy. He glared down at his son, his only child, whose smile was supercilious and foppish, the sunglasses wrapping his eyes, like some guru on the cover of a rock album.

He knew it was wrong—he told himself as his muscles tensed and his torso twisted, cocking his body —that, if anything, understanding was now called for, that he should listen and learn what the problem was and try to help him, but that silly, grinning face taunted him. "Can the truth be any worse than the lie?" he roared.

The smile only spread across the face, crooked and loose, and Murray gave in suddenly, completely to his public self—the blusterer, the pompous bully, the man with money and power who wasn't afraid to use either to get what he wanted.

His hand lashed out and caught the son on the side of the face, more like a hard, crossing punch than a slap, and sent the glasses careering through the pewter mugs that lined the sideboard of the small bar.

Murray stood over his son in a slight crouch, waiting for some small sign that he'd try to retaliate. He was puffing and felt the blood pounding in his ears, the delicious giddiness that venting his anger always brought. But more too—things were slightly grainy, and he didn't hear the door open and couldn't see his wife standing there until the son turned his head and looked up, challenging him, it seemed, with the blood that was trickling from his nose and the corner of his mouth and with those eyes.

They staggered Murray.

At first he didn't know what he was seeing. They looked like the eyes of a fly but massive and popped and an agaty blue color with the merest pinpricks for pupils. And he was smiling—a dreadful, bloody, foolish smile.

Murray roared. It came from deep within him, and he found himself with the son's arms in his hands, having lifted him right out of the chair. "Jesus Mary, and Joseph—what have you done to yourself?"

But the son began flailing with his hands and elbows, catching his father in the face and chest and Murray let him go.

Turning to his wife, he said, "We've got to help him, Bridie. He needs our help."

The son pushed by him and staggered, looking about wildly for the sunglasses, then thrashed out of the study and the house.

Murray began to cry. Tears gushed from his eyes.

The wife didn't know what to do—to go after the son or to comfort her husband.

Murray thought for a moment of calling the police, of turning the boy in, of their getting the best help he could for him, over in England where they knew of such things.

Trinity—goddamn the place and goddamn the whim that had made him want to have his son go there. Ruined him, it did. Corrupted him. Made him into a bloody . . . degenerate.

But then it occurred to Murray, and for the first time, that drugs might not be all of Sean's troubles.

He straightened up. Blearily, through his tears, he could see his wife approaching him, her arms out.

No—he clasped her to him—he remembered the agitation, the despair that had marked Sean when he had come to him saying he needed an excuse, an alibi, for the time during which the Caughey woman had been killed, that it was well known among his friends they had quarreled, that he'd been out ". . . just driving around" yesterday afternoon and in Ballsbridge. "Somebody might have seen the car. Would you know if they'll check?"

Murray had thought of McGarr, and he had known

they'd check, but there were probably dozens of such cars in the country. He knew of another himself. "But where in Ballsbridge were you driving? On that street?" He had nodded. "Why?" "I was just seeing if Mairead would be about, but I didn't stop. Honest." And there had been something in the way he had said that that had told Murray he was lying. But not about murder—that had never crossed his mind. Still, he knew the son well enough and thought it best to come up with something definite that he'd been doing at the time.

It was a mistake, he now knew. Better to have let the chips fall and be done with it. He was their son, but those things he took probably made him into somebody else entirely. Somebody violent and—.

He himself was only after knocking back the son's salary, thinking it would make him more aggressive. What if, by so doing, he had inadvertently driven—.

Jesus! He rocked his wife back and forth—what had they gotten themselves into?

When they parted, she said, "It'll all blow over, you'll . . . And look, you got a splotch of blood on one of your new shirts."

Murray tried to see the stain but couldn't. He turned away. "I think he caught me on the chin—gave me a bit of a scratch."

McGarr awoke first.

Noreen and he had taken lodgings in a small hotel in Leenane, and looking out the low, open window there on the second floor he could see the Eiriff River, nearly dry now with the warm weather, meandering down a stony beach to Killary Harbor. Beyond, steep treeless hills rose toward skies that patches of swift-moving clouds made seem very blue. There was a wind up and chop on the water, and McGarr was tempted to climb back into the toasty bed.

It was only 10:00, early by Irish standards, and, chilled now, he knew Noreen would feel warm and soft and he would sink back into that pleasant, dreamless state between waking and sleeping in which he became conscious of the pleasure the body took in being inert.

But that was cowardice, now that he was awake, and twice already a faint rapping on the door had told him that others knew of his whereabouts. There was no sense in further sequestration.

Dressing, he peered down at his wife—the tousled red locks, the slight freckling of the skin, the thin and straight nose, and the lips that were partially open in sleep. Like that, she always seemed to him so childlike, and yet again he marveled at the abandon with which she slept, on her back or sometimes on a side, but never like McGarr, who slept on his stomach, one pillow under his chest, the other over his head. He wondered what it meant, the difference. Probably nothing.

Downstairs was a bar and a general store, with a dining room off that.

Seeing McGarr on the stairs, the young girl behind the counter blushed and scurried toward the note pad near the telephone. The early-rising locals, dressed for Mass, quieted, making her approach to McGarr all the more painful.

159

Her voice was high and no more than a whisper. "Chief Inspector, you had several calls this morning. First, the Commissioner, Mister Farrell—"

"That's fine, thank you. I can take it from here. You've got a lovely script."

She was tall and full with brown hair and a milk-white complexion, and several of the men smiled to see her color even more. She turned her back to them and caught her breath. "And there's somebody waiting for you in the dining room."

McGarr looked up. He wondered who it could be.

"A man," she went on, casting him a sidelong glance that made her brown eyes seem as big as buttons. "He was here when I opened. Bald, he is. And not young."

McGarr was glad he had worn his hat and would have liked to know if she considered him young or old. "What paper is he reading?"

"The *Times*."

Fogarty, McGarr thought, his nemesis. He wondered who had sicced the man on him. It could only be Ban Gharda Bresnahan, who was new to his staff. "Is there a phone in the bar?"

She nodded and smiled a bit.

"I'll take my coffee in there then, if you don't mind, and tell the missus where I am when she comes down, please."

The bar was empty, a dark room with a flagstone floor and old, wooden porter barrels stacked up behind the counter as decorations. Small stools and low tables made the place seem fit for faeries or Lilliputians, but McGarr knew better. It was a sing-song pub with a dais and a mike, but anybody wanting to be heard could just stand.

McGarr looked for the bartender and discovered, behind the bar, an open trap that led down a flight of stairs to a cellar. There a light was on. Rather than disturb the man, he poured himself a large whisky and carried the note pad to the darkest corner. He wasn't there a moment when Fogarty poked his head in the door, glanced around, and departed.

Striking a match to a Woodbine he read the messages: Farrell had rung twice, each time asking that his call be returned. It was urgent. Ballydehob. McGarr's office at the Castle twice as well, and McKeon from his home. Finally, McAnulty, chief superintendent of the Technical Bureau, had rung him only minutes before he came downstairs.

Carrying his drink to the phone, he called the Castle and found Ban Bharda Bresnahan on the desk. "I've told you before," he said, "your Sundays are your own."

"And your Sundays now, Chief Inspector, are they your own?" She was a massive young woman from Kerry, precise in her work and dedicated and not a little bit ambitious. She was also upright and quite religious.

"I'm in a lounge bar this minute with a smoke in me gob and a drink in me hand. I saw the insides of a church yesterday noon and it should last me 'til I die."

Bresnahan got right down to business.

O'Shaughnessy had detained a garage mechanic who had claimed to have been working on Sean Mur-

ray's yellow MG at the time of the Caughey murder.
The superintendent had met with a magistrate late
yesterday afternoon and had managed to obtain a
court order for the service chits of Ballsbridge Motors
Ltd., the concern involved. By the time he got back
to the garage the manager had dropped his opposition
to the request and willingly handed them over. Delaney then spent most of the night going through them
and the internal accounts of the firm, and he had determined that the mechanic, Doyle by name, would
have had to be working on three cars at once to have
serviced the Murray car. The bookkeeping balance
was short by the very amount that Murray had been
billed and had, by his own statement, paid. But
Doyle had kept to his story. He had a record, and
they were still sweating him.

"A record for what?"

"The superintendent doesn't say here."

"Could you check on that?"

"Yes, sir."

Then Ward had determined that Sean Murray kept
company with a group at Trinity who were suspected
of using drugs. He had checked further with other of
his contacts in Dublin, but it seemed that, if he was
a user himself, his source of supply was not Dublin-
based.

It wouldn't be, McGarr thought, for a young man
with money and doubtless friends who left and re-
entered the country often. He then thought of Murray's father's horses and wondered if that was the
means.

Otherwise, Ward had reported, the Caughey girl's
statement had been verified except for a short period

of time during which she claimed to have tried to visit the National Library that had been closed because of repairs.

At the R. D. S. Show Ground McKeon had made contact with a man who resembled J. J. Keegan in all particulars except for the mustache he now was wearing. McKeon couldn't be sure until he checked the man against the snaps McAnulty was developing. He wanted to know what he should do.

McGarr thought for a moment, tasting the smoky peat flavor of the whisky there in the darkness of the empty barroom. Keegan or Matthews or whoever he was calling himself now had not really committed any major crime. He could be questioned about the discharge of firearms at his residence near Drogheda, and then there was the question of his practicing veterinary medicine. But McKeon could be wrong and collaring the man would blow his cover, and McGarr thought it best to hold off for a while. Perhaps he had some idea about who had murdered his sister and would lead them to that person, if he were kept under strict surveillance.

"Have him continue according to my prior orders, but detail Delaney and Greaves to him. I want them to be sure of the man's whereabouts at all times."

He waited while she made the notes. "Anything else?"

"Ah—let me see—. Oh yes. Commissioner—"

"I've got that."

"And Superintendent Mc—"

"And that too."

"Well then, there's nothing more, Chief Inspector."

"Are you sure?"

"Well—you did have another call or two, but they weren't strictly official nor your wife, so I did as per your instructions."

"Good—" McGarr hesitated, almost having said "girl," a term which the young woman eschewed, "—job. And what did you say to Mr. Fogarty from the *Times*?"

"Only that he needn't be ringing here on the quarter hour, hour by hour since you were on the other side of the country with the missus and wouldn't be back 'til the morrow."

"And he asked if I was on holiday?"

"His very question. The man—he's remorseless."

"And you said?"

"I said, says I, I should hope not, with a murder investigation on his hands."

"I wonder," McGarr asked, touching the Woodbine to his lips and glancing toward the bar where the barman was stacking cases of bottled beer, "if you would know who might be sitting in the dining room of the place I'm now in?"

She let out a short, sharp laugh. "You must be joking."

"Oh, I'm not. Not in the least."

She paused. "Then I haven't the faintest."

For a moment McGarr considered upbraiding her, but didn't think it would do any good. She was from the country and only constant, daily exposure to people like Fogarty would make her any wiser. "I just thought you might have a spare vision, of a Sunday morning.

"Thank you, now." McGarr went to ring off.

"But wait—who!" she asked, a laugh in her voice.

McGarr sighed. "Fogarty," he said precisely and depressed the lever.

McAnulty said the blood on the towels was not J. J. Keegan's, a record of which they possessed because of his prior incarcerations. The cigar ash found near the windowsill in the upstairs bedroom was rare, from some handmade, all leaf, Cuban variety, and the bureau was still trying to identify it exactly. Given the firing-pin impression on the shell casings, the gun that had been fired most at Keegan's was a type of machine pistol. McAnulty wasn't sure, but he thought they might be from a Skorpion, a new and powerful weapon that had been developed as a hand gun for tankers in the Czech army. It could be fired comfortably from one hand in a single-shot manner, but could, in an emergency, supply suppressive automatic bursts as well. But it was an expensive, a rare, and also an illegal weapon. One casing, however, was from a .38. They had found it in the drain pipe of the kennel roof.

Return fire, McGarr thought, remembering Keegan's involvement with the I. R. A. He wondered if the "army" still meant anything to him and if he could count on support from others of them.

They had also gathered foot and tire prints.

About the booby-trapped car—standard gelignite that was practically untraceable. The device was artful, though, and had last been seen in the North during the spring. The prints on the screwdriver would also be hard to pin down: a partial thumb and index finger, but the left hand, which would narrow it down.

165

"What about the photos?"

There was a pause. "What photos?"

"From the Horse Show film. And the whistle."

Another pause. "For chrissakes, Peter—take it easy, will ya? First you've got a murder, next a near bombing, then a shoot-'em-up a couple hours later. That damn case is a year old."

"No, it isn't. They're all one."

Yet another pause. "You're coddin' me."

"I'm not."

It was enough for McAnulty, but not Farrell. "I don't know what you think you're running up there, a bunch of Blue Shirts or an Inquisition, but it's got to stop. I had some madwoman on the line yesterday afternoon charging you personally with harassment on two separate occasions. Then Fogarty with a complaint against Ward. And Michael Edward Murray himself wonders why you've unleashed O'Shaughnessy on his son."

McGarr only raised the glass once more and watched his wife pause in the doorway, an image— her silhouetted there against the sunlit window of the general store beyond, hand on the jamb, looking about for him, her expression expectant—that touched him. In an instant he seemed to call up all their days together from their very first meeting in her father's gallery on Dawson Street through all the flux of their lives together, abroad and in Rathmines, their hopes and aspirations and the trying times too, and he felt a poignancy—that the moment was over, that she'd seen him and now moved forward, that all those days and years now seemed to him to have gone by so fast, were over and irrevocable and dead.

"Well?" Farrell demanded.

"Well what?"

"Well—how in God's name did they get my number? Now I've got to call the phone people in again."

Ban Gharda Bresnahan, McGarr thought. "I think I can fix that."

"Then do it and fast. I don't know what the hell you're up to and I don't think I care."

"Enough said." McGarr began to ring off.

"But wait a minute—"

He paused for a moment, motioning Noreen to sit on his knee, but then he completed the movement. Farrell was an administrator and the less he knew the better.

The girl had realized that McGarr was trying to avoid Fogarty, and she carried their breakfasts in to them.

Paying for his drink, McGarr asked the barman, "How would I get to the Keegan farm?"

The man only eyed him knowingly.

"Or the Menahan place. Are you from these parts?"

"Indeed I am, Inspector." He laid the change down. "It's Bechel-Gore you're wanting to see, I gather."

"No, not exactly. First I'd like to see the Keegan house, if there's anything left of it."

The man, who was older—plump and rosy, like many in his trade—cocked his head and looked away, thinking. "A near ruin now, I believe." And he gave the directions.

"And the Caugheys, do they have a place around here?"

"Now that's a strange one, that is." The man pointed

at the whisky glass but McGarr shook his head. "I saw the news about Maggie Kate in the papers and it stumped me, to be honest. I grew up with her and Hugh Caughey, and I'd swear that she was still unmarried when he was long dead."

McGarr tapped the glass, and the man reached for the bottle.

"A sailor, he was. Lied about his age and entered the merchant marine just before the war. Ship went down somewhere in the North Atlantic. I saw in the obituary she left a daughter, nineteen. Now—that just doesn't figure, wouldn't you say?

"And then, Kate didn't turn many heads, good soul that she was."

"And Jimmy-Joe?"

"Older than me by," he raised his eyes again, "a good ten years. Wild, it was said. Trouble. But he had a kind of style about him, as I remember."

"Any others in the family?"

"Only one in the country that I know of."

McGarr waited.

The man's eyes moved from McGarr's to Noreen's and back again. "Married to Bechel-Gore. That's why I was saying—"

Fogarty was waiting for them at the car.

"But what exactly did he say to you?"

"He insulted my person in public." Fogarty's thick eyebrows formed a dark, knitted line.

"But the words, man—what did he say?" McGarr had opened the door for Noreen and now walked around the small car and got in.

"They're not essential." Fogarty tugged at his hat,

a tyrolean with a small spray of multicolored feathers in the band. His nose repeated the shape of the crown, a radical bend and large.

"I'd say they were." McGarr closed the door and rolled down the window.

"Well—" he looked away, his lips working, "he insulted me for being bald, and I call that cheap, very cheap. And low." He studied McGarr, waiting for a reaction.

"That doesn't sound like Hughie to me. And with me on the premises, it's a wonder he had to go afield."

"And then—" Fogarty's anger was nearly too much for him, "—then he called me . . . an innocent man."

McGarr placed a finger alongside of his nose and tried to keep himself from laughing. Noreen had looked out her window. "I'd say you'll have a job of it, proving that one in court."

"But it was the *context*," he insisted.

"I'm sure it was. I'm only sorry I missed it." McGarr began to edge the car forward.

"Where're you going?"

"For a little spin."

"You are like hell, you lying bas—"

But McGarr was away.

Bechel-Gore had awakened with a start. Somebody had been banging on his bedroom door. Momentary anger flooded through him, but he quelled it. Only his accident had made him realize the lesson he could have learned as a young man at Sandhurst—that one needed to modulate one's tone to command, and especially with these people. To shout, to swear, to holler elicited as much response as when one beat a balking ass.

He collected himself. "Yes?"

"Ah, sir—it's Kestral. She's got the colic. It's all we can do to keep her on her feet."

Bechel-Gore tossed back the covers and, using the grips on the stanchion over the bed, swung his legs out and tried to stand. He managed to raise himself up and lean his back against the bed brace, but his legs, wizened and slight compared to the rest of his body, wouldn't hold his weight, and he sank back onto the edge of the bed.

But in spite of the activity that was strenuous for him, he said in measured tones, "How do you mean, colic?"

The other man's voice was rushed, urgent. "Somebody's been feedin' her green apples. We found the spit-outs in the stall. She's in a bad way, sir."

"Has she gone down at all?" If she had, it was all over for the horse, as well as for his aspirations for the Horse Show, and perhaps even for his expectations of greater success for the farm at the bloodstock auctions there. Colic, especially from having eaten green apples, caused a horse such severe paroxysms of internal pain that it would throw itself down and writhe, thrashing about, tying its intestines in knots. The point was to keep Kestrel upright, keep her walking, and only then apply other remedies.

"I told them not to let her."

"Did anybody think to drench her?" Again the even tone. Bechel-Gore meant the old and very Irish technique of trying to force a purgative down the horse's throat by means of a solution in a long-necked, leather-covered bottle. Almost never did the gagging horse get all of it down its throat and into its stomach. Some nearly always got into its lungs and foreign-body pneumonia was the result.

And Kestral was Bechel-Gore's attempt to show the international horse world that horses bred and trained on his farm, even the mare who had crippled him, could be made into a first-class hunter or perhaps, as in her case even a premier show jumper.

"There was talk of it, but we remembered what you said, and I thought you'd want me to come get you up, beggin' your pardon, sir."

At least that was something. Fed her green apples, he thought. Somebody. He might have laughed, had he not pulled himself up again. This time his legs held him, and he took several shaky steps toward the closet. "Paddy, would you come in here, please. I'd like your help."

The door opened.

"Who's with her now?"

"The grooms."

"Which grooms, Paddy?"

"Will and Fritz."

The best of a bad lot, he thought, reaching for his pants. And he really couldn't trust them either.

But the man only stood there in the open bedroom door.

"Could you help me with these?"

"But, sir—you can walk."

"So I can, Paddy. But not very well, at least first off like this." He held up the pants. "Shall we try one leg at a time?"

"Oh yes, sir. Of course, sir." The man rushed toward him.

Bechel-Gore was well over six feet tall, and it seemed that his body—a barrel chest now covered with graying hair and a large but firm stomach—had been hung from shoulders that were rather too broad for his frame. With age they had become bony, and the reliance he had had to place on his arms, enlarging them, only emphasized the impression. His hair, like his mustache, was a light-brown color, almost chestnut. There was blond in the mustache but gray in the hair. His face was long and thin.

"Does my wife know about this?"

"No, sir. That's why I came myself."

"And the other matter. Has anybody been speaking to her about that?"

"Which other matter, sir?" The man glanced up at him. "Oh, that matter." He looked away. "No, sir." He helped Bechel-Gore into his socks, rolling them up from the toes.

Deaths and wakes and funerals, all their lugubrious interest in collapse—Bechel-Gore knew these people well, but his understanding did not make him any more sympathetic to them. All the woman had been was a blackmailer and a cheat, but he said, "I realize all this secrecy is . . . curious, Paddy, but please try to understand that we—all of us—have our livelihoods at stake, and you know how Grainne is. She's—" he thought for a moment, "—impulsive and uninhibited and the death would most certainly keep her from riding in the Show. Afterwards—that's the time I'll tell her."

172

Reaching for a boot, the man said, "But I don't see how you'll keep it from her."

Bechel-Gore did, however. Only there in Leenane was it known she was related to the dead woman, and the change of name—Caughey, wherever they had gotten that—was suitably remote. They'd be in Dublin tonight, if Kestral could be saved, and Grainne wasn't much interested in the . . . world.

"And it's only fittin' that she get a last look, I'd be thinking."

"I'm taking care of that, too, Paddy. The funeral, the wake—but in a case like this I believe a post mortem—" Bechel-Gore left off, as though the whole matter was too difficult to consider. "But I'm having it all postponed, and she'll be buried out here. With us."

The man's eyes shied.

With us, Bechel-Gore thought. He'd never be with them, not even if he divided up his holdings amongst them and allowed them to pursue the dreary, impoverished, agrarian idyll they cherished; they'd only think it was their due, that he and his ancestors and all of his kind were interlopers, that his having wrung cash from this barren soil was a passing wonder, luck, what have you, and they'd be content to let it go back to sheep and gorse. But that was acceptable to Bechel-Gore: letting them think of themselves as discrete. It took strength to bend events to one's will—his own ancestors had known that, perhaps too well—and in a modern world ethnicity, patriotism, and other atavistic ties were irrelevant, if not downright counterproductive. But he wondered about the child and how much she was like them.

"Now, if you could help me down the hall and stairs, like a good fellow, I'd be most grateful."

In the hall the man said, "Isn't it wonderful that you can walk, sir?"

"Well, thanks to you I can, my friend, and it's really not established. I'd like to keep it between you and me, if we could, sort of as a surprise for Grainne, for after the Show and after the . . . other matter. As a pick-me-up, so to speak."

"Ah—I understand. Yes, that would be perfect, sir. Grand. Not a word from me. Not one."

"I'm counting on you. You know how people talk."

"That I do. I do, sir. And I will—I mean—I won't, and that's a prmoise."

Across an expanse of tumbling, barren hills they could see Lough Nafooey to the south and Lough Mask to the east. There wasn't a tree in sight, and the breeze McGarr had noted in Leenane was a gale that pushed them back and made Noreen's skirt flap like a flag. But still, there in the blast, tiny, bright wild flowers grew with abandon, bobbing their yellow and violet crowns at a sun that thin clouds—more like a mist—only partially obscured.

It was bright and hot and, gaining the brow of the hill McGarr had to raise his hand to his eyes, having left his hat in the car.

Below them, back the way they had come, was the ruin of the Keegan farm, an old, formerly thatched-roof cottage of two big rooms and several outbuildings that had fallen to rubble. As McGarr had suspected, the front door had been removed. Now sheep were using the crumbling fieldstone walls for shelter during storms. The carving on the lintel said *Keegan, 1831*, and McGarr had been struck by the fact that the family had managed on such poor, if beautiful, land to survive the Famine and the attendant deprivations of a century—the nineteenth—that had been perhaps the hardest of any on the Irish, only to have relinquished it out of—what had it been? He didn't as yet know—torpor or ennui or disinterest during a period doubtless less severe.

And indeed the wind, soughing down the flank of the hill and through the chinks of the crumbling edifice, sounded like keening to him—a steady, low moan that rose to a chilling wail and died off, as though the mourners had paused for breath.

Noreen pointed through a gap in the ruin to a series of small stones that had been set away from the house, near a flat open space that had once been a garden. A graveyard. McGarr stepped over a low, wooden gate that a rose bush—stunted because of the wind—had obscured, and paused to help Noreen over.

And the nineteenth century had indeed been hard on the Keegans. Child after child—nine in one generation—had died either at birth or shortly after, and McGarr speculated that if any had managed to survive past the age of ten, he or she must have been made of tough stuff indeed. But still, life had been hard, and the only Keegans buried there who had lived to a ripe old age had been born either in the eighteenth century or the last decades of the nineteenth.

One of those had been Brieda Reid Keegan, wife of James Joseph and mother of seven, among whom were Jimmy-Joe, the oldest, and Margaret Kathleen, who had been next in line.

"And look at this," said Noreen.

It was an even newer grave, by a year. *Mairead Kehlen, 1960,* it read, *Infant,* and the relief pictured a little lamb curled up and sleeping in a bed of lilies.

"What do you think it means?" Noreen asked.

McGarr shook his head. "A namesake perhaps."

"If so, they're certainly predisposed to them—in this century. James Joseph, the father, and Jimmy-Joe, the son. Margaret Kathleen, one daughter, Mairead Kehlen, another but dead. And then the other one, the pianist, that's her name too, isn't it?"

McGarr nodded. Could it have been simply a lack of imagination? He didn't think so, and Noreen was right. It was only in the twentieth century that those names had appeared.

McGarr squatted near the back of the largest stone, that of the most recent Keegan family, and parted the grass so he could read the final child's name. Grainne —Bechel-Gore's wife—was the youngest in the family, born in 1935. An old cow's last calf, and by much. Her mother had been nearly fifty when she was born.

The father's inscription read, *James Joseph Keegan, Patriot, Soldier, 1881–1961.* Good stock, McGarr thought, perfected in a Malthusian vacuum. He only hoped that the man had indeed been a patriot and a soldier and had made the minions of the British policy of benign neglect suffer, and dearly.

But the graveyard had been a puzzle—not merely the names but the small, newest stone, the infant who had died in 1960. Whose child had she been? Certainly not the woman who had died the year before. She had been in her seventies; her husband in his eighties. Good stock, perhaps, but not that good.

Now, shading his eyes to look down the other flank of the hill, McGarr caught sight of the "great house" and its sprawling complex of outbuildings, stables, corrals, tracks, riding and jumping rings. It looked more like a secret research facility or a military installation than a farm, nestled there in a bowl which the hills made and many miles from any public road.

And McGarr knew the story of the house, having interviewed Bechel-Gore there concerning the incident that had crippled him. An elegant Georgian structure with monumental windows—an exquisite fanlight above the front door—it had been trucked (what was left of it) from Cork where, shortly after Home Rule, it had been torched. Bechel-Gore said he did not harbor any grudge against Corkmen, that he was only seeking open pastures and more land than was available there, but McGarr thought it passing strange that a man who was so outspoken in his advocacy of economic liberalism would abandon what had to be some of the finest and richest land in Ireland—deep topsoil, ideal for raising grains, and a limestone base that, some said, aided in the development of the strong bones so necessary to hunters and jumpers—for these bleak hills.

"What do you think they're doing with that horse?" Noreen asked.

A group of men were down in the stable yard with a tall, chestnut-colored horse that looked little different from the mare, Kestral, that McGarr had seen on the video tape the day before and on several other occasions. A long, somewhat flexible pole had been passed between both pairs of her legs, and two of the men seemed to be raising it, one on either end, as if to apply pressure to her innards, while the others led her forward at a steady walk. Another man had carried in several buckets of some solution that had sloshed into the dirt when he set them down. The final attendant stood near Bechel-Gore, who was sitting in the electric golf cart that had been modified for his use.

"Your guess is as good as mine."

"And that man, there!" Noreen pointed off, away from the stable complex toward the east where another man, lying prone on the top of a hill only somewhat lower than the one the McGarrs occupied, had lifted a pair of binoculars to his face, a lens flashing in the glare of the sun.

Or was it binoculars?

"The way he's hunched over there—" Noreen began to say.

McGarr turned to the men in the stable area. He cupped his hands to his mouth. "Hey!" he shouted. "Hello!" He pursed his lips and tried to whistle but he hadn't done it in so long the pucker was inexact and nothing came out but air. "Hey!"

Now Noreen began to shout, but the wind there seemed to stop their voices short and throw them back.

Finally the whistle sounded, sharp and shrill, and the horse pricked up her ears and looked up at them. The men turned toward them and McGarr pointed off toward the east, gesticulating, wanting them to see the danger that the man with the rifle there posed.

The man standing next to Bechel-Gore turned to see them better, and the first shot struck the cowling of the golf cart, knocking it askew.

The horse shied, rearing up, and felled one of the

men. Bechel-Gore tumbled out of the cart, using it as a blind.

Again the report sounded, a crack that was muffled by the wind, and McGarr pulled Noreen down into the grass. "You stay here. That's a bolt-action weapon, and he's not much of a shot." McGarr was thinking about the wind that had deflected the shot and the allowance the sniper should have made for it, and the way the road to the old Keegan place—just a cart path now, overgrown with brambles and gorse—had wound around the hill to the east, the one from which the fire was being delivered. And he had to have support, some car below there to get him out, since the only motor access to the Bechel-Gore property adjoined the road along Lough Nafooey to the south and the country for miles in every other direction was open, uninhabited, and wild.

"Where're you going?"

"Back to the car."

"I'm coming."

"No, you're not. You'll be safer here."

Another shot.

The horse had been led off, into the stables, and two of the men were crouched down behind the cart with Bechel-Gore, each one of them ahold of an arm.

And the golf car was smouldering now. In the shadows under the chassis sparks could be seen.

"But I want to come."

"You're not, and that's that." Running down the hill through the tall grass, careful not to step on a hillock or into a rut and twist his ankle, McGarr heard other shots, but rapid, as from an automatic weapon and coming from the stable yard, or so he thought from the direction. And another spurt, over the other, and several. Again and again.

Bechel-Gore must keep his men well armed, he thought, tugging open the doors of the Cooper. And illegally armed. He remembered his conversation with McAnulty and the cartridge casings he'd found near the window of the bedroom in the Keegan/Matthews place in Drogheda.

He jerked the Walther out from under the seat and placed it in his lap, starting the engine with the other hand.

He glanced up at Noreen as he swung it around, a dot of white and turquoise on the hillside, her red hair like a daub of paint against the burnished silver of the bright, lowering sky.

Get down, he thought, hurling the Cooper forward, the undercarriage grating over humps, the ruts nearly jarring the wheel out of his hands. He threw it into third and launched the car down a steep defile that then curved up around the flanks of a hill where, from the pinnacle, he saw a car or a van parked and two men running toward it, one high on the top of the hill and carrying something, the other close to the vehicle.

McGarr plunged the Cooper down the slope, but he was at least a half mile from the van and the first person had started it—he saw a puff of black smoke billow up from the rear—, a Land Rover, a diesel. He didn't think he'd have a chance to catch it, especially if the driver was acquainted with the area and broke out over rough ground toward the main road instead of staying on the cart path that followed the easy lay of the land.

But the other man, the one farther up on the hill, stopped, having seen McGarr approaching. He looked down at the Land Rover then back at the Cooper, as though trying to decide. But it was plain that if the Land Rover waited, McGarr would catch it, and the decision was already made.

The Land Rover jerked forward and then cut off the road sharply, jumping over hillocks and rocks, making toward the hills to the east that extended as far as the road to Trean and Lough Mask.

The man on the hillside looked about wildly and then veered off to the south where McGarr in the Cooper could not follow. Several times he stumbled and fell, looking back over his shoulder, and McGarr was again reminded of the video tape he'd seen earlier. It was either the noise of the wind, which was howling around the low car, or the treeless landscape that seemed to deny perspective, but it was as though everything had been stopped down, and the jouncing, lurching Cooper, and the stumbling man with the sniper's rifle, moved in a kind of slow motion, agonizingly slow, a snail's pace.

But when the man reached the horizon, there on the flank of the hill, and turned, raising the rifle to jack a cartridge into the chamber, McGarr switched off the Cooper and jumped out, letting it roll down the cart path toward the valley below, knowing it would follow the deep ruts, not wanting to get caught in a flammable box by a man with a high-powered weapon.

And it was McGarr's turn to test himself against the

wind which was blowing, it seemed, from every direction and no direction, now here, now there in a random way that staggered him and threw tangled, swirling patterns over the deep grass that concealed broken ground and caused him to fall.

And the man had seen McGarr but the shot carried wide, and he turned and fled, out of sight, down behind the flank of the hill.

By the time McGarr reached the ridge he was winded, and the man, having been availed of the easy descent, was distant, halfway at least to Lough Nafooey and headed, it seemed, toward a copse of tall conifers that clustered the bank of a stream there.

But McGarr pressed on, trying not to fall but falling, coming down hard on his elbows and chest, sliding over the wet ground and slick grass beneath him so that it was more like a long tumbling dive down a fair, grassy hill, the sort of thing he had done out in Howth as a child, than a downhill run, the Walther crammed under his belt, his pants and jacket now slick with grass stains and mud.

And he gained on the man, who now had boulders near the stream bank to get over. Off beyond the trees, miles in the distance, McGarr could see the glimmering, choppy waters of Lough Nafooey. If only he could get to the man before he struck the road there, he'd have a chance. In the trees he'd have the advantage with the Walther, and he was betting the man would not stop until the trees. There had been too much return fire from the stable complex for that. He had to be thinking that this pursuer had an advantage in firepower and that he was outnumbered, at best, fleeing.

And McGarr saw a break, a chance of cutting him off, a run of even ground on one side of the conifers where the needles had fallen and formed a soft bed over the rocks and rills. He wouldn't have to pick his way through the boulders where he'd be an easy target, and maybe he could get behind the man, cut him off, before he reached the road.

It was a gamble, but McGarr made the edge of the pines just as the man got beyond the boulders and raised the rifle to his shoulder. But he was puzzled and lowered it, looking around while McGarr kept himself concealed behind a wide tree.

He wasn't young, perhaps in his late thirties, with fine blond hair that the wind, less severe there near the trees, tossed about even more than the grass. He was wearing a black turtleneck sweater and an olive-drab field jacket, and with black boots he seemed almost military. McGarr wondered why the jacket—the many flap pockets—and if he was carrying other weapons. Why hadn't he dropped the rifle—because it could be traced to him or because it was his only means of protection?

Then the man was off again, now in the copse, on the bank of the stream and moving quickly. In order to get beyond him, McGarr had to guess—that he'd stick to the stream bank where there was probably a path made by anglers, that he'd try to reach the road.

And so McGarr no longer kept him in sight, only rushed headlong down the fringe of the copse and, when sufficiently away from the stream, he cut in, dodging the trees—some sort of spruce; Norwegian, he thought—wishing he did not smoke, pulling air into his lungs that felt more like fire, knowing his ankles and his knees would be sore for weeks, but wanting that man who, if caught, might be the key to at least several investigations.

The leather soles of his bluchers were slippery on the needles, and when he could see light ahead of him —the drop down to the road; the lake beyond—he angled back, going down on one hand, in toward the stream and the path, quietly now, wanting to make it clean.

Had the man gone by? No—he didn't think so. Birds were in the trees on the opposite bank where water of the stream tumbled off a ledge into a dark and deep pool. There in the shadows fish were plying the quiet water, and a heavy footfall would have frightened them.

McGarr glanced down the other way, a steep fall to the road—nobody. He looked around for the best cover but decided he had it there, in some brush on the lee side of a massive spruce. And then he heard the muffled clump of boots on the needle-strewn path.

He crouched and looked down at the Walther, making sure the safety was off, reassuring himself of its presence. And his heart was beating wildly now, he could feel it in his throat. It would be hard to take him like this, especially if—.

And then the man was almost upon him, limping but still moving quickly, one leg of his pants bloody, his pale cheeks red. He was winded and sweating, yet the rifle was still in his hands.

McGarr pivoted and stepped out on the path, going down into a low crouch, both hands on the Walther, arms extended, the muzzle pointed at the man's chest only a few feet distant. "Drop it. In the stream."

The man stopped, his eyes wide with fright but his hands still on the stock of the rifle, and then he looked off beyond McGarr, down the steep drop to the road.

Behind McGarr a car door slammed, and the birds rose up, complaining, wheeling off into the trees.

The man lashed out with the butt of the gun, striking McGarr on the side of the head, knocking him into the brush.

McGarr had seen only the swirl of his shoulders, then a flash—vivid orange and pink—and had felt the blow of the stock on his skull. Then nothing.

He came around slowly, his face and head in the brush and brambles.

"Get up out of that now," he could hear Fogarty saying to him but distantly, seemingly leagues away. "The bloody bastard stole my car."

McGarr tried to stand but couldn't. It was as though his head was heavy on one side and kept pitching him down. He was dizzy, and the side of his face—his head, one eye—throbbed with pain.

McGarr let his legs go and he slumped down, against the trunk of the tree. He was parched, but the stream was too far away. He tried to reach for the packet of Woodbines in his jacket pocket, but his hand wouldn't or couldn't grasp it, and he felt as though he might be sick. He was exhausted and his head—.

His flask. It was metal and intact.

With his teeth he prised out the cork and dropped it in his lap. As he raised the half-pint container, Fogarty turned to him, wanting to say something more, but the look in McGarr's eyes stopped him.

*　*　*

When had it started? Menahan asked himself, pausing before the door of the Monsignor's bedroom, the discontent with his . . . calling. With the transfer to Ballsbridge? Perhaps, but he couldn't be sure and he'd actually gone back to check in his diary.

It was all there, page after page of resentment—at the Jansenist implication, pervasive throughout Ireland, that God had made an aesthetic mistake when conceiving of the reproductive functions of the human body, at the guilt one was made to feel at becoming cognizant of any "attachment," however vague, to the flawed and repulsive body.

And he hadn't hesitated when he received the phone call from Jimmy-Joe. "You know, some chemist in your parish. Somebody with a . . . Fenian bent. He'll understand." It was a wound and was becoming infected.

The body again, Menahan had thought. Festering. And of course he could help Mairead's uncle, almost his own cousin, his former neighbor whose family had shared with his nearly—how many?—two hundred years of known history and probably more as well. Did that matter? Months ago he would have thought not—only God's law, as proscribed in vivid "Thou shalt not's," would have guided his actions. But all that had changed for Menahan.

"Be happy to. Do you need anything else?"

A pause. "I could do with a bit of money. I've got a good amount in the bank, but that's not something I could put my hands on. Now."

"How much do you need?"

"A couple hundred quid, if you could manage it, Father."

"I think it could be arranged."

Keegan had been surprised. "You're a . . . prince. I hope you don't mind me sayin' that, Johnny."

Not at all, not in the least.

Menahan now girded himself with his new mantle of worldliness and rapped on the Monsignor's door. The knock was louder than he intended, but maybe it was better like that.

"Yes?" The voice was thick with sleep.

That was good too. He had caught Kelly napping. "Father Menahan here. May I speak to you?"

"About what?" He was awake now and angry. There was an edge on his words.

"A private matter." Menahan glanced down the hallway, noting the other doors, each the quarters of another priest. He heard a floorboard squeak. Gossips, he thought, worse than old women. "I'd prefer not to speak through the door."

"You would, would you now," he heard the old man mutter as he moved to the door and tugged it open. "What is it?"

Menahan surveyed Kelly—the full shock of white, bushy hair, the florid complexion; the thick glasses that made his eyes seem bulged and pugnacious, like headlamps on a machine—and he thought of the bit of Joyce doggerel, the lines that spoke of the militancy of the Catholic Church in Ireland. How did it go?

> O Ireland, my first and only love,
> Where Christ and Caesar are hand in glove.

And in truth the discipline imposed on priests—unknown in its severity in other Catholic countries—and the innate, reactionary bent of the Irish hierarchy was quasi-militaristic. Even the rectory here with its severe, carpetless hall reminded Menahan of a barracks—soldiers in Christ, and not merely the Jesuits, and Kelly himself the colonel, hitching up his black suspenders over his black shirt, in black pants and the shoes. Army issue.

"I'd like to speak to you."

Kelly only glared at him, even allowed the maddened, goggled eyes to work down Menahan's body, making no attempt to conceal his dislike.

"All right—here then."

Kelly's ears—large and red, like twilight sails—pulled back, but he kept his hand on the jamb.

Menahan smiled, noting that the trepidation Kelly could instill in him and others had left him completely. In its place was a kind of contempt. The man standing over him was nothing more than a bully, plain and simple. "I have urgent personal matters to attend to, and I shan't be able to say last Mass or give the mathematics seminar at the convent either." It was only the latter, really, that had held Menahan's interest throughout the long, drear months of his "priestly" submission to Kelly's command—that and Mairead, of course. In many ways mathematics was the only sure knowledge over which one could exercise near total control, and being the basis of music, Menahan had given the field long study and thought. It pained him not to be able to attend the meeting, at which he had been scheduled to read a paper on Descartes, but he supposed the situation required some sacrifice. "As well, I might be gone for a day or so."

Another creaking floorboard in another room.

And Kelly heard it. He stepped aside, allowing Menahan to enter the room. Kelly closed the door, but kept his hand on the knob. "Is that a request?"

"Yes."

"Request denied."

"Well, then—." Menahan sighed; in his own way Kelly had not treated him unfairly. He had demanded obedience, but he had dispensed assignments fairly, never giving Menahan, as the most newly arrived priest, an undue share of the early masses, even saying a few each week himself, but there was only one way to approach the man—straight on, a confrontation. "It's my intention—"

"To leave the priesthood?"

Menahan chuckled. He had known it would come to this. But Kelly was vulnerable. He had a record to preserve, of taking on all the hard cases—the young and prideful priests, the intellectuals, like Menahan, or the willful, like some others—and bending them back into the fold. And that he would not jeopardize. No renouncements, not one in—how many years had Kelly told him?—thirty some, and there had been pride in his voice. It was a posture that left him much less free to match wills—or "prides," Menahan thought ruefully—with a young priest who had no record nor any real desire for one of any kind.

"Oh, no you don't, Monsignor. You can't and won't call my bluff. If it's going to take a renouncement for me to attend to this matter, then you'll have it forthwith—when I return. I've never asked you for something like this. Others have, and I've filled in for them. And this is . . . vital."

"Yes, but others—"

"Are no different from me. They're human beings too and have needs."

"And yours are?"

"Tending to a sick friend."

The old man walked to the desk where he selected a pipe from the rack. "I don't believe you."

"You think I'd lie?"

Kelly looked up and cocked his head. "No, but we have a parish full of worshipers, people who need your particular services. This is Sunday, and there are doctors, nurses, hospitals for sick people."

Menahan wondered if he could trust the man and decided he could. "Not in this case."

Kelly paused in reaching the match to the pipe. "Will your actions embarrass us?"

"I don't know. I don't think so."

Kelly drew in the smoke and let it out. It was thick and hung in the heavy air. He batted it away from his head. "Tell me, Father—what do you think it means to be a priest?"

Menahan had turned to the door; Keegan had said he needed the antibiotics fast, and that had been early the day before. "It means being God's minion, here on earth. It means—" he opened the door, "—being good. And that's an active state too, Monsignor—doing good."

"And you can assure me that what you're about to do is good?"

If advancing those persons and things which were preeminent was good, then what Menahan was about to do was certainly good. Keegan wasn't by any stretch of the imagination such a being, but he was Mairead's uncle and almost the only relative and familial pro-

190

tector that she had. And Keegan had proved his role over the years and proved it well. Certainly it was God's will that he should be helped and allowed to carry on the task that He had assigned him. "It is good." Menahan opened the door.

"It has something to do with this Caughey thing, hasn't it?"

Again Menahan paused. "It has."

"Then good luck to you, Father. God bless."

"Thank you, Monsignor."

Menahan closed the door, and walking down the dark hallway he thought of the quote he had read when leafing through his diary. Descartes again, but an aspect of his thought that was little known or ignored.

I shall consider that the heavens, the earth, colors, shapes, sounds and all other external things are nothing but illusions and dreams.

I shall consider myself as having no hands, no eyes, no flesh, no blood, nor any sense; yet falsely believing myself to possess all those things.

If, by this means, it is not in my power to arrive at the knowledge of any truth, I may at least do what is in my power, namely, suspend judgment and thus avoid belief in anything false, and avoid being imposed upon by this arch deceiver, however powerful and deceptive He may be.

Menahan paused on the stairs and said it over to himself. It was like a poem or a hauntingly modern prayer or a special sort of occasionalist mantra.

And there Descartes was hedging his bets. What if

the business of knowing was cruelly unequal? What if human beings had been presented with neither the perceptual accoutrement nor the capacity for knowing the real? Then, Renatus wouldn't play. To hell with God and his silly little game. He's nothing but an arch deceiver.

Menahan shook his head and smiled to himself, before continuing down the stairs. It was a nice point, a twist, and indeed a worthy consideration.

The library was massive, perhaps even too large, and extended across the entire back of the Bechel-Gore house. The windows were towering, wide, and elegantly paned in a proportion suited to their dimensions. But McGarr had the feeling of being in a school or a public building, and the dark wood, the books lined to the ceiling, the catwalks of pegged mahogany with a two-tiered ladder on brass rollers, the map and atlas tables and reference books, and especially the writing desk with the globe and quill pen seemed like relics from a former, more leisurely and doubtless a more totally exploitative time when the purpose of such an estate had been to support a man of letters.

But the desk, up to which Bechel-Gore pulled the wheelchair, seemed little used, and beyond the sweet smell of old paper and leather there was the mustiness of a room that had been all but abandoned. And the man had said, directing McGarr in there, that he would prefer that they not be overheard. "Especially by my wife. She's . . . sensitive, and we have the Show coming up. I want her to be relaxed and ready and not distracted."

They could see her from the window in back of the

desk, standing in the stable yard and watching the grooms lead Kestral, the mare, around. Noreen was standing near her.

"You don't suppose your wife will say anything?"

McGarr had turned to the man, only able to see him with his right eye. The other was swollen shut, and the entire side of his face was hot and aching, as though he had several severe toothaches at once.

They had been served cold ox-tongue sandwiches with horseradish and pickles. McGarr was hungry but he hadn't been able to eat. Lager was offered as well, but the pain had made it taste hot and insipid. He had lost the sniper, and the appendages of his body were sore from the long, difficult run over the broken ground and the fall into the brush. His suit was ruined, a soggy and torn mess, and a last in one of the bluchers had burst. McGarr was tired, exhausted, and now the man in front of him was intending to play games.

McGarr pulled out a Woodbine and lit it. Even drawing on the cigarette hurt his face and his lips and his lungs—. "You mean, you hope my wife won't mention to yours the fact that her sister, Margaret Kathleen, was murdered."

Bechel-Gore reached for the quill pen and twirled the stem in his fingers. "Well, yes . . ." his voice was a throaty drawl, characteristic of his class, and normally McGarr would have tried to dismiss it as natural, a part of the man's background and nothing else, but now it seemed affected and nearly histrionic, and with everything else it taxed McGarr's patience. ". . . we were hoping to inform her after the Show."

The Show, McGarr thought. It was everything for

him and for Murray, for the horse and for the wife—
he wondered how much it mattered in all of this.
And then he remembered Ward's report—that the girl,
Mairead, was a rider; and he thought of the little
gravestone in the next valley and of the infant who
had died in 1960. "You'll be there yourself?"

"Yes, of course." Bechel-Gore had a way of twitch-
ing his bushy, light mustache before speaking like a
man hiking up his pants.

"To watch?"

His brow knitted. "Yes—to watch and oversee matters. This is the most important event of the year
for the farm. And this year particularly."

"Particularly what?" All pleasantness was gone
from McGarr's voice.

"Well—we're hoping that Grainne and Kestral
might come away with a trophy or two."

To prove what? McGarr almost asked the man, but
it was pointless really and he wanted to conserve
whatever strength remained. It was pride, but something else too. He wanted to spite Keegan or whoever was responsible for his injury. McGarr wondered
to what lengths the man had gone or would go.

And there were many questions that McGarr could
have asked—where he was at the time of the Caughey
murder and during the raid on the Keegan/Matthews
place; how the barnyard dirt had gotten wedged
under the instep of his boots that were propped on
the struts of the wheelchair, an encrustation that
could have been caused only by somebody who had
placed his weight on the boot; about his having purchased the copy of the R. T. E. video tape of his accident and why, about Keegan's letter, "Sis, Get out.

He's onto me. Jimmy-Joe"; and about the Keegans themselves, to whom he was related by marriage, whose land he now owned, and how he had come by the land—the price, the circumstances, his feelings—but McGarr didn't think those queries necessary.

He had been staring down at his left hand, which he now opened. In it was a bright bit of metal. He tossed it toward Bechel-Gore. It bounced off the desk top, ringing like a chime, and struck Bechel-Gore in the chest. He waited.

It was a rimless, 9mm short cartridge casing, seemingly identical to the ones McGarr had found near the bedroom window of the house in Drogheda. This one, and dozens like it, he had noticed in the stable yard, where Bechel-Gore's grooms had fired from.

"Well, yes, of course—I suppose the Skorpions are illegal. I was given them as a sort of gift from the Czech army. They rather fancy my horses, you see, for dress parades and the like. After my injury and the other . . . problems my family has experienced in this country, well, I thought they'd come in handy in case of just the sort of situation you witnessed today.

"I mean, I certainly intend to protect myself.

"Why—it's not against the law to use them on my own property, is it?" His eyes, which the weathered skin of his face made very blue, were too wide, the brow too furrowed.

"Tell me what you were doing in Dublin on Friday afternoon."

Bechel-Gore looked away. It was just a guess, but McGarr was now certain the man was concealing something. "Attending to certain of the Show details."

"And in the afternoon, say four-fifteen?"

"At the Show Ground."

"You can prove that?"

Again the glance to the left. "I believe so."

McGarr looked away, out the window. "Your horse has gone down," he said in a low, matter-of-fact voice.

"Didn't catch that."

"I said your horse, the big chestnut mare—" McGarr gestured with his hand, "—she'd just gone down."

Bechel-Gore's hands fell on the arms of the wheelchair, not the wheels, and he began to raise himself up. His eyes met McGarr's and he eased himself back down. "She's not down, is she?"

McGarr turned toward the door. "You should clean your boots. You've got shit on them, mister."

"Where're you going?"

"To talk to your wife."

"Don't do that." Bechel-Gore stood up and pushed the wheelchair away from him. "I'll make a trade. What I know and all of it, for your understanding of what the Show means to us. It's taken me years to get Grainne and Kestral and the farm to this point. I can't ride myself anymore and we're only a few days away from—" his voice trailed off.

McGarr turned. "From what?"

"From proving ourselves."

"To whom?"

"To ourselves, to . . . the country and—.

"Look, let me show you what I found in the post box yesterday." With a key he opened the top drawer of the desk.

The clouds had burnt off and sunlight flooded

through the tall windows, making the library seem dusty and stale and an unnecessary refuge.

Bechel-Gore pulled out two thick envelopes. "These were obviously Keegan's. They were sent to me, but not through the mails. There isn't a mark on them.

"He'd been blackmailing me, you see."

McGarr hadn't moved away from the door to the hall.

Bechel-Gore had to raise his voice and seemed to speak across a distance, his voice echoing down the long room.

"I . . ." he turned and looked out the window, at his wife and Noreen and the horses and grooms.

Other mounts were being led through a cavalletti in a farther ring, and workers were leading horses into one of five vans that were parked beyond the stable yard.

". . . had an affair with Grainne, you see, before we were married." It was difficult, McGarr could tell, for him to speak of the matter, privacy in personal matters being yet another characteristic of his class. He began pacing in front of the window, his steps long and seemingly firm, the heels of the boots coming down hard.

"She was twenty-five at the time, and it was unconscionable of me, given her other . . . disabilities."

"Which are?" To McGarr the woman had seemed only a handsome person who appeared to be much younger than her forty-four years. Her body was lean but not thin, and she carried herself in a lanky, easy manner that had in fact reminded McGarr of the Caughey girl.

And with that thought it became clear to him how the Caugheys had supported themselves in such style, the reason for the warning note from Keegan to the dead woman, and perhaps for even the murder itself.

"She's not quite right. It's not that she's feeble-minded, really, it's that she's just not apt with words—reading and writing and such. And those are things which don't interest her.

"Well, I'm not trying to excuse myself, but she only lived over the hill and she was a natural with horses and beautiful—" he glanced out the window "—if you could only have seen her then, McGarr. The raven hair and dark eyes and the way it seems that with her frame she couldn't be so . . . full.

"I got her pregnant," he blurted out, coloring.

"How old was she?"

"As I said, mid-twenties."

"And you?"

"Oh, Christ—in my forties. Three, four." He paced a bit more, wringing one hand in the other, behind his back, unable to look at McGarr. "And I was married too.

"Then—" more pacing, another pause, "—there was the difference in our . . . class, and I hope you can understand that McGarr—I'm not class conscious myself, but the difference was real, then—and our religions, and her people too posed a difficulty.

"Her mother had just died, father a few years before, and Keegan," he said the name between his teeth, the vehemence obvious and undisguised, "was—well—not a man I could exactly talk to."

"Did you try?"

"Not really. I never got the chance. He and that

sister of his took her away and that was the last I saw of those two. Grainne returned to live with a neighboring family more than a year later, saying that the child had died. Keegan and the sister even put up a marker over there," he moved toward the window, "where they had lived.

"At the time I was relieved, not just because of the problems but because she wouldn't have made much of a mother, I'm afraid. Her—what shall I say? —debilities. They were, they are, hereditary. Mind you, I researched the history of the family thoroughly—idiots, incompetents, every generation had its share. Ask anybody around here. They have the reputation of being somewhat . . . queer, the lot of them.

"You see, I'd really never got along with my first wife and she'd sued for divorce in England and I was —well, unattached, but after—*after* Grainne returned.

"I offered her a job because . . . because she was utterly destitute and horses was all she knew, the only thing she could do. Well—I thought she'd be an asset to my venture here.

"No, that's not the truth. Grainne is special. And I realized she was . . . special to me.

"Anyhow, we were married."

"Where?"

"In London."

"When?"

"1962. January."

"She was judged competent?"

His ears pulled back. "Of course," he snapped. "She's not an idjit. Speak to her yourself."

"And that's when the letters began."

"Yes." He stepped to the desk and picked up one

stack. "Snapshots, doctors' bills—London, Rome. Demands for money. Threats that they'd tell Grainne, and I knew what that would mean—disruption, unhappiness. Believe me when I tell you that Grainne could never bear all the pressures and demands of being a mother. She's too . . . fragile. And I was just beginning this venture. I know that's selfish of me, but do you quite understand the risks, the capital I've got—.

"In any case, they weren't about to give the child up. When, at first, I balked, they threatened to kill the child and send it to me in a box."

"Keegan threatened that?"

Bechel-Gore nodded, but McGarr did not believe him. There was something he wasn't being told.

"Not once but several times. I destroyed the letters, of course, in case something happened to me and Grainne—.

"But the child was, or I believed she was, a part of me, my own flesh and blood, and I went along with the demands, engaging at the same time several agencies to look into the matter, but they came up with nothing. Keegan, with his I. R. A. contacts—whenever any of them learned that, they told me they were no longer interested in pursuing the matter. Too dangerous. One man was dumped on the doorstep of his firm, beaten to a pulp. Around his neck was a card. 'Next time the knees.' "

"Where did that happen?"

"In the North."

The man McGarr had chased had been tentatively identified as an I. R. A. fugitive whose last residence had been in County Tyrone.

"So I paid them off."

"You have other children?"

Bechel-Gore shook his head. He paused, looking down at the stack of papers—letters, photos, record books—on the desk, then glanced up. "Have you met her?"

"Who?"

The mustache twitched, he blinked. "Mairead."

McGarr nodded.

"What is she like?"

McGarr really didn't know beyond her appearance and the reports. "She's . . . beautiful, like your wife, but more so. And talented, so it's said."

Bechel-Gore waited.

"She's a pianist. Prize winner at the conservatory in London. This year. And a horsewoman. It's a wonder you haven't bumped into her. She rides the Murray horses and well, I'm told."

"Caughey," Bechel-Gore mouthed and smiled. He had seen her. "Well," he continued with renewed force in his voice, "what are you going to do?"

"My very question to you."

"I don't know. Whatever it is, it'll have to wait."

Until after the Show, McGarr thought. The Show again. He reached for his packet of Woodbines and another cigarette. "Smoke?"

"No, thanks. I don't."

"Ever?" McGarr glanced at a pipe rack.

"I used to. A pipe once in a while. A cigar after a good meal or a . . . victory."

Out in the stable yard, Bechel-Gore's wife had said little to Noreen. "Do you know horses?"

"No."

"What do you know?" Her voice had the mild lilt of that part of Galway, to Noreen's ears perhaps the pleasantest of the country's many brogues.

And Noreen had had to think about it, noting the woman's long and thin muscles that a knitted jersey and tight riding pants outlined. She knew nothing in a definitive sense, in the manner that one would or could say I know woodworking or battleships or—but she said, "Art. I own a shop," if only to make conversation.

"I know nothing about art," the woman replied. "I only asked because you look—" the glance of the dark eyes was particular and all inclusive, as though she were judging a mount at an auction, "—like you can ride."

Noreen was moved to say she could, but she knew what the other woman meant and in that way she could not ride.

It was upon her again, the feeling. She wondered, as she had in the past, if it had something to do with a phase of the moon or atmospheric pressure or her diet or how she had slept, something . . . extraneous, but it was probably silly to question it. Still, like the headaches she got, there was the flashing in the periphery of her vision, the giddiness, the feeling of lightness as though she could float away, and the pounding heart. But there was the concentration too, and she knew when she sat down at the piano she'd be able to be outside herself and hear herself, almost like another person.

She was on the stairs with Inspector Ward, whom she'd bumped into at the stables. He had said he had just been driving by and decided to stop in on the off-chance she'd be riding, but she'd seen him earlier, talking to the guard who patroled the neighborhood, and later on at Neary's, conversing with a bartender. Perhaps he had merely been going about his tasks, but she thought not.

She now remembered her mother and thought she should feel guilty for being so insensitive, but she felt too good for that. "Damn—" she looked up from the purse in which she'd been digging for the latch-key, "—where is that key? It's not necessary to keep it locked, now that Mammy—" Now she really did feel guilty. It sounded so . . . blithe and callous. "I mean, it's only she who insisted—. I didn't mean it as it sounded."

"That's all right," said Ward, "I realize why you think it should have sounded differently, but it sounded just fine, as though you're going to get over it." The landing was narrow and Ward had to brush by her to try the door. In the shadows she glanced up at him and smiled.

And she had an effect on him, there was no denying that. Maybe it was because of the fact that he had met her under official circumstances—that he wasn't able to pursue her—which made her special, like forbidden fruit, but he thought not. It was more the impression she gave him: of being extraordinary and not just in her dark, good looks, something precious and fragile but at the same time strong.

But he found the door open, and his head turned

into the apartment. There was a smell of smoke but scented and—. Without waiting for her to enter first, he stepped toward the sitting room.

There, seated in a tall, wingback chair—smoke rising through a shaft of early evening sunlight and seeming very blue—was Sean Murray.

"A police escort no less. How nice of you, Inspector, or are you off-duty now, on another sort of chase?"

The girl's expression was pained. She tossed her jacket and handbag into the mother's chair. "Oh, Sean—don't be a boor, and put that thing out." She moved to the bay windows and opened the tops and bottoms of those on either end. Silhouetted against the direct sunlight, her dress became almost transparent, and Ward caught a glimpse of her body— trim but full enough, lithe in an athletic way, tall and thin and balanced.

"Ah, have a toke and relax." Murray's speech was a bit slurred, and he seemed to be shaking or moving slightly, the ankle of one leg, which was crossed over the other, spinning quick circles, jerking, like a pendulum marking some internal time.

He was wearing a white linen suit, a violet shirt that was open at the neck, heavy-framed sunglasses, and shoes, which seemed to be made of plastic, that matched. In all, he looked like a clown. "Or one of your pills," Murray went on. "You're too tight—I've told you before. Learn to live.

"Inspector—" On a bent wrist he offered Ward the cigarette, the smell from which Ward couldn't place. Hashish? No, something sweet and not as scorched. Cocaine? Ward wondered if Sean would have enough money and the access to cocaine in such quantities that he would consider smoking it, even if it only laced some other substance. Perhaps it was just a variety of marijuana he had never smelled before. "A hit? Hell, I won't tell. Not me." He began laughing foolishly.

Ward only stared at him.

"I'm going to get us some wine," she said, hands on her hips, looking down at him. "When I return, I expect you to be gone." Her pose was interesting, Ward thought, militant and poised and almost like a boxer's with one foot forward, one fist in the palm of the other hand.

"Oh, be nice. Be nice, now, or I won't let you near me pretty horses.

"Do you know she's going to ride for us in the Show? Papa's orders. She's got a line on him too, you see. I'd watch yourself, if I were you, Inspector. Got some witch in her, she does."

At the fridge, she became suddenly furious—with Sean, with being suddenly thwarted in her intention to play while the mood was on her. She grasped the neck of the wine bottle and slammed it down on the counter. And, dammit, there was hardly any left. She stormed into the pantry and tossed things around until she found the case, down below where the pots were, and another bottle.

"Temper, temper—" Sean shouted to her. "And she's got one, you know. Mairead gets what Mairead wants, if not—" he smiled foolishly at Ward, "—she could strangle you. I think Mammy" he said derisively, "spoiled the bitch. Poor, dear, *dead*, darling Mammy."

Ward himself now felt his gall rising. He wanted

to snatch the butt out of the young man's hands and haul him outside, seeing to it he had a rough trip down the stairs, but he was interested in what was being said too, in a professional way.

Still he said nothing, only stared.

"A shame, isn't it?" Murray went on. "That only now can I sit here with you, of all people, relaxing like it was home." There was an off note in that too. "A pity. I bleed for her, honestly I do."

And he had for somebody else as well, Ward thought. There was a stitch in his upper lip.

"Yes, Papa thinks Mairead's just the cat's pajamas, as he puts it. Or maybe it's just that he prefers her *in* pajamas."

She moved back into the sitting room quickly, carrying a tray with two glasses and a bottle of red wine.

"Quaint expression, isn't it? Dates him, so it does. But Mairead isn't anybody to hold age against a person. How old was that lover of yours, Meg? The randy old one in Rome? You know, Giuseppi di Pizza Pie."

She set the tray down on the back of the piano and turned on him. "Get out!"

"Well—maybe he wasn't exactly your lover, but you can dream, can't you?" He turned his head to Ward. "Lots of imagination in Meg. She pictures herself with some Prince Valiant type, or at least a prince of something or other—older, loaded, somebody who can launch her 'career,' and she's got several in mind." He turned to her. "An ambitious girl. Imaginative, as I was saying. But don't touch her, don't *dare* touch her. Oh, no—"

The girl took a step toward him, but Ward reached

out and pulled her close. To Murray, he said, "Go. No talk. Just go."

The ankle stopped spinning. The hand with the cigarette came down. The head quivered and the stitched mouth opened.

Ward only shook his head.

Murray stood, unsteadily at first, buttoned his jacket and stepped toward the door. Ward behind him.

At the door he turned and opened his mouth but thought better of it.

Ward followed him down and examined the catch, which was on.

She was waiting for him at the top of the stairs.

"Wasn't that door locked?" he asked her.

"I don't know, I can't remember. Is it important?" Her smile was strange, heightened, her eyes slightly glassy.

"And this one?"

She didn't move out of his way, only stared down at him as though she expected something from him. "I don't know. I can't remember."

She played for him for nearly two hours, mostly pieces that he didn't know and hadn't heard before, but she had a command over the large, black instrument that could not be denied, driving and checking it, making it sing at one moment and whisper the next, but never letting it get out of her grasp. In hand, he thought, remembering how she had treated a horse that had refused a gate at the jumping ring earlier, staying with it firmly until she bent it to her will. Her fine features, the wispy clothes she wore, her almost too feminine demeanor were deceiving.

There was iron in her touch. It was well concealed, but it was there.

Afterward, she went into her bedroom and changed into a lounging outfit that reminded Ward most of pajamas, but special pajamas made of dull gold that clung to her hips and made them seem fuller than she had felt under his hands when he had pulled her to him. Only one button closed the jacket under her breasts, which were emblazoned in the light from the lamp on top of the piano.

She waited. Ward could see her heart pounding, sending tremors down the taut shape of her golden, shimmering chest. It wasn't that he was calm himself, but he had been in situations like this before, and he knew what was expected of him and what he wanted to do, but he was torn between that urge and his duty. Granted they were alone, but he had met her in official circumstances and the investigation was continuing.

But perhaps—he told himself as he placed his arm behind her and turned on the couch so he was facing her—it would be worse to disappoint her, and what harm could one kiss do.

She looked up at him, her eyes dark and glassy and not just from the wine, and he lowered his face to hers slowly, watching her lips tremble and then open to accept his.

She wasn't practiced at kissing, of that he was sure, but it was as though their touching set off something uncontrollable in her. Her body rose up into his—her chest, the small area at the base of her spine that he could feel under his hand—and she was suddenly torrid. The skin on her cheeks, her forehead, her neck was hot to his touch. "Stay with me tonight," she said into his ear, pulling his head down on her chest where the tan line stopped and the skin was smoother on his lips than Ward had ever felt. Already his hand had slipped beneath the waistband of her slacks and he could feel her hand on his thigh.

But he broke from her. "I can't and you know why and you don't want that either." He turned her and rested her head in his lap. He brushed back the hair on her temples and stroked her forehead, which was damp.

And tears. She felt angry and frustrated, but she felt like a savage too, a beast; her personality was so . . . furious there was no controlling it, sometimes. And her mother—.

She closed her eyes.

Later when he suspected she had fallen asleep, Ward heard a noise on the stairs. The door opened and the priest, Father Menahan, stepped in.

What he saw at first startled him, but he composed himself, smiled, and left as quietly as he had come.

6

LOVE AND A BOTTLE,
A KIP,
JIBES, DEATH, THE TRIBE
AND CODDLE

McGarr was the last to arrive in his office at Dublin Castle, well past ten, which was unusual.

The others turned to him.

One stopped in the act of slipping a sheet of paper into a typewriter. Another scanned McGarr's face—the puffed eye, the large bruise that had turned a mottled blue-green, the scowl. His ears pulled back and he looked away.

It was McKeon, however, who summed up their sentiments. He wrinkled up his nose and let out a little howl, high-pitched and humorous, but McGarr wasn't having any of it.

He had a newspaper rolled up in the fist of his right hand. He slapped it on Ban Gharda Bresnahan's desk and said, "Coffee." He then trudged through the rows of old wooden desks into his cubicle, where he flicked the door shut behind him.

A patch of red had appeared under each of the woman's cheekbones, and she turned to McKeon, who had recruited her as his assistant only a month before. She was handling the job and well, as far as he was concerned, and he wanted to keep her.

"Whoy," she aspirated in the distinctive brogue of her native Kerry, "—who the hell does he t'ink—"

"Ah now, Ruthie—" McKeon began trying to calm her, noticing the flush that had spread to her broad forehead, her ears.

She was a big, red-haired woman, and the dark-blue uniform, buttoned across her chest, made her seem even sturdier. "Imposing" was the word McKeon himself had used after they had settled an interoffice jurisdictional dispute and not to his favor.

She stood and leaned toward Delaney. "Why didn't he ask you, mister?"

She turned on Greaves, jamming her hands on her hips. "Or you, mister?"

Greaves cocked his head, as though to say it was a good question.

But Bresnahan was not in a mood to listen. "It's because I'm a woman, that's why.

"Well, we'll soon see about this, we will. Who-miliatin' me in my work place."

McKeon stood, but she brushed past him and reached for the knob on McGarr's cubicle door.

Greaves lowered his head, as if ducking. Delaney slipped the piece of paper into the machine and pretended to busy himself with a report. Even Ward turned his back and looked out the window. There had been a time, and not long before, when on such a morning it had been he who had been sent to the tea station up the hall, but that was when he had been the most recent appointee to McGarr's staff.

McGarr thought he had never felt worse. He wasn't injured enough to remain in bed, but he didn't feel

capable of being up and about either. It had most to
do with his vision, that was still only partial on the
left side, and made it seem as though he was looking
out through a slit in a bunker.

He hadn't even glanced at O'Shaughnessy, who was
sitting in a chair to the side of his desk, a pearl-gray
homburg on his head, the *Press* in front of his face.
McGarr had opened the lower right-hand drawer of
his desk for the bottle he kept there.

He had then raised the window and looked out,
hands in his pants pockets. He hoped the fresh air
would partially revive him before his coffee arrived,
but he knew the overall ache in his arms and legs—
somebody rapped on the door—and his chest and back
wouldn't leave him for days.

Again the rap.

"Yeah?" Out of the corner of his eye he saw only
the bright-red hair and the general shape of the
woman, before he turned back to the window. "Put
it on the desk." A moment passed and then he remembered. "Please."

O'Shaughnessy hadn't lowered the paper.

"I—if I could have a word—"

Oh, Christ, McGarr thought, noting the militancy
of her tone, having heard it before when she'd had a
bone to pick with McKeon. McKeon—it was the last
personnel decision he'd ever handle.

McGarr drew in a deep breath. Every aching muscle in his body, every iota of his flesh hoped that she
had brought him the large Styrofoam cup of thick,
black coffee with the plastic lid on the top to keep it
piping hot. He exhaled and turned around slowly,

both hands still in his pockets where he was jiggling some coins.

There she was, he thought, that mountain of red flesh and—he glanced at the desk—*without* the coffee.

O'Shaughnessy lowered the paper. Only the creased crown of the light-gray hat, then the brim, and finally the eyes appeared. They glanced from her to McGarr. O'Shaughnessy raised the paper again.

She opened her mouth, but before she could speak the door popped open and McKeon appeared, craning his neck around her to see McGarr. He had something in either hand. "Coffee," he said, "and tea." He jerked a thumb at the newspaper.

O'Shaughnessy mumbled something and McKeon, without glancing at McGarr again, closed the door.

McGarr moved toward the desk. He prised off the lid, raised the cup, and took a long, slow sip, closing his eyes. The coffee had been on the burner all night, and it tasted like thick, bitter and delicious mud. He put down the cup, pulled the cork from the bottle, and topped it up. Only then did he glance at her.

At the sight of McGarr's face—swollen, the one eye seeming to be locked in a pugnacious, brutish squint—her features softened. She had enjoyed Fogarty's description of the bungled arrest attempt and the theft of his car, and perhaps all the more for having spoken to the journalist only the day before. His plain, hard-hitting style had made it clear what had gone on, but maybe he hadn't told all.

McGarr placed the bottle back on the blotter of his desk, but he did not recork it. He glanced at her again, picked up the coffee, and carried it to the window.

There he drank for a good long time, letting the hot liquor burn down his throat. The effect was almost immediate. He set the cup on the sill.

Again the azure skies with only fine, cirrus clouds high above, looking like the mottled highlights in a turquoise stone. Yet another hot day. An eighth floor of girders had been added to the office building since he had last looked. Somebody in an old biplane, the engine of which blatted when it dived, was up over the Bay. The plane was bright yellow and glinted as it bellied over and climbed past Howth Head.

When McGarr turned around, Bresnahan was gone.

Keegan placed the *Times* down on the one dry area of the narrow table. On it were four pint glasses and fresh, the yellow, creamy collars hardly touched. He glanced up at the others. Lag mates—he had helped them all at one time or another, but what was it he read in their faces? Consternation, indecision, fear? "What's this lot then?"

"Ah, Jimmy—this thing," with two stiff fingers he tapped the newspaper, his voice hardly a whisper, "it's as good as dashed, the whole bloody business, and make no mistake about that."

Keegan tried to ease his back against the cushions in the snug, but even the slightest pressure made it hurt too much. The antibiotics had arrested the infection and the drugs helped too, but he knew he'd need further medical attention and soon. And he was getting weak.

"They'll have every feckin' bluecoat in Dublin on

him now. We're not trying to break on you, mind—it's all equal to us—, but they'll make a show of us, so they will."

Another said, "Are you sure you didn't set him up, before you got hit and all? I remember, before the raid on—"

Keegan only shook his head and considered them—all old men, like himself, who belonged here amid the noise and clutter of the pub, knocking back a few jars and reminiscing, not out on the job and a hard one at that. And this was a private matter, his own.

Hadn't the bastard as much as tried to annihilate his family? First he'd tried for the land with a lawyer's trick, the business about no proper deed, and when that didn't work somebody had shopped him, Keegan, even told them where he could be found and at what hours and how he should be taken. They caught him like this, having a pint in a snug. Ryan's, it was, in Kingsbridge.

Keegan now looked out and caught the barman's eye. The man raised his brows; the bar was packed, but there was a certain deference to age and Keegan knew he looked ancient—without the mustache and tweeds, but with the sallow, sickly complexion and the old coat and cloth cap.

He held up finger and thumb, measuring off the size of a ball of malt, then indicated he wanted one for each of them. The others would wonder where he'd gotten the readies, but he was beyond caring. He went back to reminiscing.

And then—when he was gone—getting Grainne, who was young and simple and was home alone with Maggie Kate (another innocent), fat with child, and then swearing her to secrecy so that he, Keegan, had had to beat the truth out of her . . . he could hardly bear to think of it to this day.

By then the farm had been all but abandoned and Maggie Kate and Grainne's child had to be provided for, and Grainne herself, who'd gone daft because of it. The offer was there, a low offer. Through a solicitor Keegan had accepted. He'd been in Birmingham, having been fingered again and having gone to ground.

He'd gotten drunk for three days. His farm, the family's land—it wasn't much by any standard, but it had been theirs, and to sell it for next to nothing was anathema to Keegan. And it had been then, on the jag, that he had thought of the way he could make Bechel-Gore pay. And he had gotten support too, from the people who knew how to do things. His people, after a fashion.

But now should he ask them again? He didn't think so. They'd walked the extra mile already. And there were young ones who'd do what he wanted for a few quid and a chance to use a weapon.

The malts were delivered.

"Lovely chat, this," one of them said, raising his glass. He looked this way and that, bending close to them. "To the bloke and his mates who tried it. May their aim improve betimes."

The others muttered and they all drank but Keegan. He had taken the drugs and didn't want to chance it, not while he still had things to do.

"But then, Jimmy—if it wasn't you, who was it?"

"Sure, he's got a Republic full of enemies," another said.

"Yes—but in particular."

Keegan kept still, looking up at the three dull globes that shone over the bar.

"There's Murray. No love lost there, I've heard it told. Both into the big foreign sales market, you know, and Butcher-bleeding-Gore having the lead and all. Way out in front, it's said, and gaining all the time."

"And the army too. Something like that would put all the horsey set on notice—that we haven't forgotten, that they've been allowed to remain here at our sufferance.

"Well—wasn't he from the North, your man? Didn't he have a history and all? Not a proud thing, I grant you, but all the same it's there and definite." The man tapped the newspaper again. The sniper was a known Provo and suspected of several bombings in the North.

Keegan placed his hand on the table and tried to stand. The large man to his right helped him.

"Off now."

"What—so soon? Ya haven't even touched—"

"The back. I've some pain-killers in me. Have it yourselves." He'd left the change on the table too, and the paper. He couldn't bear to look at it.

"How is it now?"

"On the mend, thanks."

"If there's anything—"

"No, no—you're right. I'll bide my time awhile."

"Do that and we'll settle him, the lot of us, when everything sorts itself out. Quiet like."

As he departed, Keegan heard one of them say,

"He's a generous bugger and always was. I wonder who put the bend on him."

"It's as plain as the nose on your face. Bechel-Gore's got money, and money is power, and there are those of us with short memories and long thirsts."

"Why you filthy son of a . . ."

Drunk on a couple of rounds, Keegan thought. He was better off without them.

But out on the hot pavement, waiting for a break in the traffic, he felt a hand on his arm.

"You're going through with it, aren't you?"

He looked up. Dick, the big man who'd kept with him from the start of his trouble out in Slane. His face was battered and scarred from boxing and stints in British nicks where being large and rebellious didn't count for much. He looked away, down the Merrion Road where a long line of cars was queuing up to pull into the Show Ground parking areas. "There's only so much of that," he motioned to the bar, "I can take and what's left for us now?"

He was a bachelor. He had a small horse farm, raised some donkeys, but his heart wasn't in it anymore.

Keegan knew how it was and he was better off. He had Mairead . . . after a fashion.

"Will we lift him?" McKeon asked McGarr, cupping his hand over the phone. "He's just left the Horse and Hound with the other bloke, Boland. The other two they met are still inside."

McGarr thought for a moment, looking down at his desk. On it was a cheese Danish, the shiny, nut-brown crust hot to his touch. He broke it open just to see what was inside. The golden dough was rich and the sour-sweet cheese steamed up. Bresnahan had gone out for it herself, and it was a vapor that he couldn't resist. He cut a slice and pushed it across to the others who were sitting on chairs or leaning against the cubicle walls around his desk.

The fingerprints that the sniper had left in Fogarty's car matched those on the handle of the screwdriver that McGarr had found under Keegan's Daimler at the garage in Ballsbridge. They belonged to a certain Jack B. Frayne of Armagh, a Provo activist.

But what interested McGarr most about the man's dossier, a copy of which had been rushed down by the constabulary in the North, was his earlier training in the British army. He had become expert with four types of weapons, including a target rifle of the sort he had struck McGarr with. Then why had he missed Bechel-Gore? Although a good shot, McGarr was no expert, and he was willing to bet he could have placed a slug in Bechel-Gore's heart at twice the distance. Of course, the wind had to be a factor, and it hadn't been steady, rather blustery and changing. And one of the grooms might have been in the sniper's line of sight.

But after what had happened to Keegan—the raid, Maggie Kate's murder, Pegeen, the lot—could Bechel-Gore have thought it wisest to foment an incident in order to surround himself with police protection? The apples and the horse and walking her in the stable yard, the sniping—it went awry, of course, but he could easily have heard that McGarr was staying down at the inn in Leenane. It was a small country place and people talked.

But then the cartridge casings—the 9mm short

rounds he'd picked up out in the stable yard—hadn't matched those found at Keegan's place in Drogheda. They had been fired from the same type of weapon, a Skorpion, but from none of the three that Bechel-Gore had owned and were now impounded. The tire tracks of the Land Rover, however, and the bootprints left on the hillside matched those found in the soft earth near the kennels. But if Bechel-Gore had commissioned that attack or even taken part in it himself, would he have wanted McGarr to know about the Skorpions?

McGarr didn't know and he was getting far afield. "No, Bernie. We don't want to scare either Frayne or Keegan off, if there's a connection between them. It's Frayne we want, and there's more than the murder at stake here. Just have them stay on Keegan and close. I'll be out there myself, later."

McKeon spoke into the phone and rang off. "Like I was saying, Chief," he went on, consulting his notebook, "Boland, his name is. Same background as Keegan—patriots," he raised his eyes to the ceiling, "in and out of the drum, here and on the other side. Two phone calls and from the way he dialed them— Dublin area.

"While they were away from the horse lorry last night, we went through it. No weapons, unless they're packing them themselves. Put a nice, fat bug in the bunk space. And—let me see, oh yeah—Delaney reported that the father stopped round about nine-ish last night, carrying a packet about so big." He indicated a small carton, about the size of a shoebox.

"Menahan?"

McKeon nodded.

"A *Bible,* I bet."

"Nope. Drugs for the wound and two hundred quid. They talked about the dead woman. Usual stuff that's said about them that's gone, but Keegan's convinced it was Bechel-Gore who killed her."

"He say why?"

McKeon shook his head. "Delaney says your man was watching what he said. Later, when the priest left, him and Boland yakked a good couple of hours, old times mostly, but at one point Keegan wondered if it'd been Menahan who'd tipped off Bechel-Gore. It seems he knew, or at least Keegan thinks he knew. Interesting, what?"

McGarr thought about the discrepancy he'd noted between what the girl said about studying in London in the transcript of her interview with Ward and what Menahan had told McGarr: the girl—that the mother had to convince the priest that studying in London would be a good thing for her; the priest—that he was for it, but the mother was not. "Let's see what we can dig up on Menahan's finances. He seems to be able to throw around a good bit of cash. But discreetly."

McKeon glanced at Bresnahan, who noted it down. He sat.

"Liam?" McGarr asked.

O'Shaughnessy removed his hat and placed it on the knee that was crossed over the other leg. "I'll begin with Menahan, since there's a tie-in. Showed up at Murray's about ten forty-five."

"Murray's . . . where?" McGarr asked, easing the chair down.

"The house. It's in his parish, don't you know, but

221

I've been wondering what could have prompted the visit. I called the rectory, got the pastor—"

"Monsignor Kelly."

O'Shaughnessy nodded. "The man. He said he didn't know where the hell—his very words—Menahan was, and was he going to be arrested? I asked him why, and he went sour. Rang off right after.

"Now, with Murray himself I've got another tie-in."

"Father or son?"

"Father, Doyle—he's the garage mechanic we've been sweating—he's stuck to the story about often working on several cars at once, and, checking it, I've found it's pretty much so. Only the service shops of the big garages turn a profit from their custom. The others have to fiddle.

"All well and good, but—" O'Shaughnessy's temper suddenly squalled and his lips turned white. Through them, he said, "—that little gobshite is a lying son of a—" He glanced at Ban Gharda Bresnahan. "Beggin' your pardon, young lady."

"I think I've got something on that," she said, brightening and perusing her notes.

But O'Shaughnessy raised a large hand. "You'll get your turn, girl.

"In and out of the shovel, this Doyle. Six kids, the missus due again. I figured he had to have been paid a smart sum or . . . well, we did some checking, and who should turn up as the principal owner of Ballsbridge Motors Limited? Our Mister M. E. Murray, T. D."

McGarr, who was leaning back in the seat, began rocking slightly.

"And there's a solicitor waiting for me in the day-room with a court order to remand Doyle into his custody."

"Murray himself?"

O'Shaughnessy shook his head. "Junior partner. Free of charge, he had me tell Doyle, who didn't want him. At first."

McGarr looked up, over the cubicle wall to the ceiling that needed paint. "Amn't I right in thinking Murray has an I.R.A. connection?"

"You are, but a safe one that, of course. All mouth it is. His riding spills over into Irishtown and Ringsend. He makes the trip to Bordenstown. The second wave, he's in."

The first two places were Dublin working-class districts in which several factions of the I. R. A. found some support. The last was the site of Wolfe Tone's tomb where on his birthday, once a year, officials of the Republic place wreaths to honor the man who founded the United Irishmen, the forerunner of all the later Home Rule organizations.

In the afternoon, however, another army—and perhaps more the one Tone had envisioned—assembles and to the wailing of bagpipes places other wreaths on the grave.

McGarr often found himself posed against that guerrilla army, but he respected its goal—a united Ireland—and for Murray to march with them was shameless and cheap. Doubtless he contributed to their cause, but, after what others had given and continued to risk, money was not enough.

And McGarr remembered the way Murray had looked getting out of the limousine—bloated, flushed, sweating, harried. "I wonder how M. E. Murray, T. D., is doing on the whole. Can we check that?"

"We can." O'Shaughnessy's light-blue eyes were avid.

McGarr glanced around at the others. Bresnahan brightened and looked down at her notes, but he said, "Hughie?"

The young man stood away from the wall and buttoned his khaki blazer, which was obviously new, across his chest. He was also wearing dark slacks, a buff-colored shirt, and a paisley ascot. "The priest showed up at the Caughey place about midnight. Popped his head in, saw me, and left. I got there about eight. Sean Murray had let himself in. Mairead had said in her statement that he didn't have a key to the place, so either he had one made or he's adept at picking locks."

Bresnahan again opened her mouth, but McGarr stayed her.

There was a third possibility, of course—that the girl had lied.

"Murray was loaded. I took the ashes with me. McAnulty's chemist says it's marijuana laced with an animal tranquilizer. Powerful and dangerous stuff. There's the story of the kid who took it over in America. He got lifted and next morning they found him in the cell with his eyeballs in his hands."

"His what?" Bresnahan asked.

"Eyeballs," Ward said tonelessly. "Dug them out with his fingernails, he did."

Her hand went to her mouth and she blanched. Given her great size, the gesture seemed comical to

McGarr, like an elephant being frightened by a mouse.

"Impressions?" McGarr asked Ward, who nodded. "Well—" Ward turned and moved toward the window, "—Murray, the son—he's unpredictable and in trouble with . . . himself, if nobody else. I don't know what he was like before, but now he says whatever comes to mind, it seems. Right off the top of his head. Mairead doesn't respect him, that's plain, treats him like a . . . convenience, I suppose—when it suits her, she lets him take her here and there. Shopping, the horses."

"Does he know that?"

"She makes it obvious. Chucked him right out when we got there. Sort of cocked her body like she was going to throw a right cross.

"Now, Mairead—she's a curious woman. She's not a woman, really, although looking at her—the clothes, the way she moves—you'd think so. In many ways she's . . . childlike and . . . simple even. But she's not simple, she's . . . complex."

" 'Mairead'?" McKeon asked McGarr. "And at midnight, no less. The witching hour. The mot's turned the poor boy's head, I think. It's as simple or as complex as that."

"No, really—" Ward complained.

"*Really*," McKeon insisted. Bresnahan handed him the notebook. "We've got you coming out of the apartment at two thirty-seven this morning, dabbing at your lips with a hanky. Was it a little gargle you were after having or a few crubbeens?" They were a variety of pig's trotters, and Greaves, who was just slightly older than Ward, began to laugh.

"Whatever it was," O'Shaughnessy chimed in, "he's well prepared for it this morning with that napkin tucked into his shirt."

McKeon howled.

When they had quieted—watching Ward, who with his body turned to the window had taken a fat cigarette from a blue packet and lighted it—Bresnahan said, "If we can proceed now, Chief Inspector. I've reports coming in and work to do, and frankly I can see no great smack in a murther, the shooting of a poor, harmless ass . . ."

McKeon began chuckling again.

". . . an attempted assassination and a savage attack on an officer of the law." There was a self-righteous purse to her mouth, and she waited for McGarr to react.

He moved forward in the seat and cut himself another slice of Danish. "Bewley's?" he asked, meaning the cafe and carry-away bakery on Grafton Street.

She nodded.

"Quite good. I must tell the missus about it."

"Thank you, sorr. I'm glad you like it." She waited a while longer while McGarr broke off a piece and put it in his mouth.

"May I proceed?"

"Tally-ho, Ruthie." A bit of bun fell on his lapel and he batted it away.

"Fuhrst things fuhrst," she said officiously, folding out the notebook. "Your requests of the day past: You asked for Doyle's record. Three counts, all the same—accused, tried, and convicted of violations of the 'Offenses Against the State Act,' in particular, importing

226

weapons for use by an illegal organization. Total time in prison, six years seven months."

"Which prison?"

Her eyes flashed at McGarr. "I was getting to that, sorr. Kilmainham and Portaloise."

"Do we know what drums this fellow Frayne has rattled?" Speaking the name again reminded McGarr of the release of that bit of information, which he would have preferred kept quiet. Somehow Fogarty had got hold of it and without clearing the matter with Phoenix Park had put it in the *Times*.

"It should be in the dossier the R. U. C. sent us, sorr."

"Would you—" McGarr discarded the word ferret; she was anything but a ferret, "—dig that out for us, Ruthie?"

She nodded. "Presently, sorr. Now—the ashes from the bedroom of the house in Drogheda were the product of a cigar produced by the firm of Blodgett and Zinn, London. A list of customers is being mailed to us.

"Blood type on the towel found in the bathroom, type O. Mister Keegan's is type AB. Sir Roger Bechel-Gore's is O, but negative, or so says the Coombe Hospital where he was taken last year after the accident."

McGarr raised an eyebrow. She had made that inquiry on her own initiative, without being asked.

"Lastly, the photographs of the man at the Horse Show have arrived. It's Keegan, all right. They're the stack to the left side of my desk. To the right is the artist's rendering of the man who attacked you, Chief Inspector."

McGarr colored a bit. It was not an apt choice of words. The R. U. C. mugshots of Frayne had been taken when he was still a juvenile, and the British army photos were dim.

"Now then, yesterday—Sunday—without the usual distractions I consulted the records, specifically those stored on the computer." She glanced at McGarr. Her knowledge of computer science had been the reason McGarr had consented to McKeon's adding her to the staff. Nobody else knew anything about them and didn't seem to want to learn, although Ward was taking a course, and a good showing on the machines would allow McGarr to turn a blind eye to her other foibles.

"I ran much of the hard information we've culled so far in this investigation through the system, but unfortunately," she paused dramatically, her dark-brown eyes surveying the group under the red eyebrows, "I could find but two correlations.

"First, the license plate eight, haitch, oh, bee, t'ree, zed, which is the number of a certain yellow Morris Garage roadster belonging to one Sean Murray of Herbert Park, Ballsbridge, was ticketed for illegal parking on Sandymount Avenue at four ten P.M. Friday."

McGarr placed both elbows on the desk and folded his hands. On them he placed his chin and watched her.

"I then tried a number of other tacks and came up with this detail. Property loss entries—especially those due to burglaries—have been numerous in the Ballsbridge area of late. I asked the computer if the times listed on the Murray tickets correlated with the times of the break-ins and the places. Well, they did and they didn't. The times were roughly the same, and the places were always a block or two apart.

"So I dug further, into the reports themselves. One complainant reported having surprised a young man in her flat and foolishly she gave chase."

McGarr shook his head slightly, not knowing quite how to interpret that.

"She followed him until he entered a yellow roadster. She only caught sight of the final three figures on the plate." Again she waited. "Bee, t'ree, zed," she intoned. "And your father called."

"What?" McGarr was putting it together—the drugs, a habit, the need for ready cash and more than his father allowed him.

"Your father called, sir. I didn't know whether to say if you were available or not."

"When?"

"A half hour ago, when you first came in."

"I'm always available to my father," he said absently, clasping his hands behind his head and leaning back.

"Well, well, well—" said McKeon, crossing his arms and beaming at Bresnahan, "—a kettle of fish, the Murrays, the Doyles, Ballsbridge Motors. The whole bloody bunch. Pounds to pence Frayne's in there somewheres with them."

"We don't know that really," McGarr said. All it proved was that young Murray was in the neighborhood at the time of the murder, that he'd lied to them, that his father was sufficiently knowledgeable of his son's problems that he would choose to sponsor the lie.

But still, Ward's report that young Murray had the

capability of entering the Caughey apartment at will disturbed him, but he remembered that the murdered woman had taken off her apron. Would she have done that for young Murray? McGarr didn't think so, given the daughter's statement that they hadn't gotten on. She probably wouldn't have let him in, if she could have helped it. "Was there a burglary reported in the immediate neighborhood at the time of the murder?"

"No—not that's been put into the computer, least-wise."

O'Shaughnessy caught McGarr's eye. His expression was questioning.

"Ah—not yet, Liam. And release Doyle without any fuss. See what he does. What we have is circumstantial, and even then it's not much. I don't think young Murray is . . . ambitious enough to have begun with the raid on Keegan, then the murder and the sniping. And if he's having to steal himself, where would he get the money for the others or for . . . contingencies or supplies?" He reached in his pocket and pulled out one of the cartridge casings. "This stuff isn't available in the West, and it costs, especially the way it was used up in Drogheda."

"Could it have something to do with the I. R. A?" McKeon asked. "Some internal struggle?"

Could be, but again McGarr didn't think so. "I can check on that." McGarr thought of his father's call.

"Or maybe his old man and him are together in it."

McGarr couldn't see Michael Edward Murray trusting in any person with his son's problem.

Said O'Shaughnessy, "It could be that none of the violence is related."

McGarr again thought of the note from Keegan to the dead woman, his sister. "I'm going to assume that it is, Liam, for the moment."

"So, everybody stays put," McKeon said.

"For the moment."

"Read the papers?" he asked, a twinkle in his eye.

"All the time."

"Get much out of them?"

McGarr shook his head. "Nothing ever seems to happen anymore, and the writing—it's inflated."

Before Bresnahan could leave, McGarr asked if he could have a word with her.

"When's Sinclaire due back?"

He could see the anxiety his question caused. She had been led to believe her services would be required only for the duration of Sinclaire's holiday. It was McGarr's way of softening the blow, if she should prove unsuitable.

"Tomorrow, sorr."

"Australia, is it?"

"Yes, sorr. If you remember the postcards he—"

"Flying back?"

"I should imagine so, sorr. The trip—"

"I wonder if he could have left yet?"

"I don't know, sorr, but I could check."

"Better, Ruthie—see if you can get him on the line for me. We have his wife's family's number down there, don't we?"

"Yes, sorr." She turned to go, but he reached for her elbow.

"And you're doing a fine job for us here, do you know that?" He walked her toward the door.

She glanced at him, not knowing if he was putting her on. And she could only see his eye, the one that was swollen.

"Everybody's entitled to a few mistakes, and I like the way you dealt with the evidence we've gathered here. It was deft and inspiring to the lot of us, I hope.

"Did you find the computer course difficult?"

"Oh, no sorr. It's a snap. You can just breeze—"

"For some," McGarr said, easing her out of the cubicle, "for some as bright as you. Are your studies finished?"

"No, sorr, in fact I've been thinking about sitting for the examination for a degree."

"Here in Dublin?"

She nodded.

"Nights?"

"Yes, sorr."

"I'd do it, if I were you."

She waited, expecting him to say more. Finally, she asked, "Does that mean you're going to keep me on?"

McGarr remembered the problems she'd had with McKeon. "That's up to Sergeant McKeon. As far as I'm concerned you're a big plus, but, of course, it's he who must work with you." He turned to her. "You wouldn't happen to be going for coffee, would you now?"

Color had again risen to her cheeks, but her expression was joyful. "Straight away, sorr. Oh—" she turned back, "—would you mind if I called my mother? She's been waiting to hear."

"You'd better clear that with your boss."

McKeon was reaching for his hat on the pegs near the door, and Bresnahan made straight for him.

Back inside the cubicle, McGarr picked up the phone and carried it to the window. There he dialed Dermot Flynn at R. T. E. and asked him if he was interested in a scoop.

"Something to do with the murder?"

"That's right."

"Will we—I mean, I—will I be getting an exclusive?"

"It's a promise."

Another pause. "What do you want from me?"

"Well, seeing you asked. . . ."

Frayne looked down at the toilet sink and wondered what the hell he was going to do about that. The stain was black from the dye he'd put in his hair and indelible, it seemed; streaks had seeped into the porous areas where years of steady dripping had worn away the enamel.

He'd been a fool to take a room in the kip, but O'Rourke knew the place and assured him the old "army" men would keep their mouths shut. But a good job it was that he couldn't sleep and had gotten up early—the dye, the clothes, only a whim had made him buy *all* the papers, and thank God for that. He'd only been trying to make a few quid on the side—Christ, the others had jobs, the most of them—but he knew what they'd say. No orders had been given, and when they found out who he'd been working for and why, he was as good as dead.

What to do? He didn't know. There were just too many possibilities, and Frayne had never been much for planning.

He leaned against the wall and felt for the Skorpion in the sling under the new tan suitcoat. "It's too big

233

for you, sir. I'm telling you that, sir." Jesus, he'd felt like blasting the bitch, her making a stink right there on the floor of Clery's with everybody carrying a paper under their arms. But, forget it—Christ, he had to think.

He looked down at the stain again. If they shopped him—no, they wouldn't, it wasn't their way. Could he be sure of that? He could. A kneecapping—he flexed his legs—a bullet in the back of the head, but knowing who he was they'd probably take him any way they could. Yes. Could he count on that? He could.

But could they justify it, here in the kip? He kept his eyes on the stain. They could. It was in all the papers, wasn't it? The old man could say he saw the papers and came up to ask a few questions, taking a gun along just to be safe. The police, of course, would know he was lying, that he'd been sent to—but he'd get off with excessive force, if they gave him that.

But Frayne didn't get that sinking feeling he'd known when he'd gotten into tight situations with the others. He was alone here, and he didn't have to worry about bumblers. The bastard had money and he'd squeeze him, so he would. Frayne had never cared for orders, and the little money he'd seen from all he'd done for them up in the North had been pissed away on expenses. And the way they had handed it out to him in dribs and drabs, like he was a beggar boy—.

And it stank, the dye—sulfurous and chemical—and the color it made his hair was wrong, some blue-black tint, phony and wiglike.

He stepped to the mirror, which was cracked and spattered. The whole place was filthy smelling like the city, ages of dust and exhaust and industrial fumes. My God—he had shadows all around where he'd tried to brush it on his eyebrows. It wouldn't come off his skin completely, no matter how hard he'd scrubbed, and his hands—he looked down at them— had outlines around the nails of the first three fingers of his right hand. Frayne felt the wrath rise in him. Dirt. He hated dirt and filth and—.

He turned away from the mirror and the image of his face—dishlike, the nose long and thin cheeks hollow; a face that was not uncommon, though, and that was something—and took a cautious step into the bedroom.

O'Rourke, he'd been gone too long.

He stopped. They'd send O'Rourke first, not the old man. And O'Rourke could get back with them that way.

Frayne looked around the low bedroom, the floor that heaved toward the one window, wide but looking right out on the street, and he wondered if he had left anything and if it would matter. No—not now.

And he heard the floor creak.

"Jack?" a voice called out.

O'Rourke.

Frayne's hand moved inside his coat and came up with the machine pistol. Silencer? It didn't matter much either, but he had three floors, and the others had probably been tipped off. He fitted the sleeve on the muzzle and tightened it down.

"Jack?"

Had he forgotten anything? he again asked himself, a sort of calm coming to him, now that he had decided. He'd squeeze him, sure. He'd squeeze him good or kill him. There was always England and the drug racket, if he couldn't come up with anything in the trade. He put in a stroke or two that way before. There was money in drugs, and the scum—.

Not in the hall. O'Rourke was cautious. He'd have somebody backing him up out there, or on the stairs. How many could they have gotten together on such short notice? The old man. The barman too; Frayne had seen him around before when they'd taken a shipment. And that other bloke, the one from the kitchen. Four, tops. He had to take at least one of them there in the room.

Frayne moved around the bed so his back was to the window and knelt, placing the gun flat on the bed where his left arm would conceal it, his right hand still on the grip and the trigger

"Jack, for chrissakes, you've got a phone call."

"Who is it?" he asked the door.

"It's him, I think. Says it's urgent."

"Tell him I'll call back. I'm busy."

"You know he doesn't want that."

O'Rourke was very near the door, and Frayne knew he wouldn't try to kill him while he was at his prayers. O'Rourke was religious. Weak. And Frayne suddenly hated him for that weakness. He'd shopped him, hadn't he? And yesterday—he could have waited. He had a weapon in the Rover. He could have—.

The knob turned and Frayne lowered his head, still able to see the door out of the corner of his eye.

It swung wide. "Jack?"

Ah, he was right. O'Rourke had one hand behind his back. "Can't you see I'm busy, Billy. Give us a moment's peace, for God's sake."

O'Rourke took one cautious step into the room. He

was a short man, young and stout with a full black beard that made his face seem stolid and imposing, and his eyes—some hazel shade, like a pig's—were agog, unnatural, frightened. The coward, Frayne thought, even dressed as he was, as a priest, a guise nobody would question, and him without his description in the papers.

Frayne didn't have to look up. He jerked up his right hand and squeezed. The pistol popped thrice, each time higher—the chest, the throat, the upper lip to the side of the nose. Like those jewels Frayne had seen Indian women in London wearing on the side of their nostrils, but this one snapped O'Rourke's head back and splattered the wallpaper above the door, and he fell forward onto his face, his fat body coming down hard and dead and sliding over the slope of the floor. Dust from the filthy carpet puffed up from under him.

Frayne opened the folded butt, a brace that was made of aluminum tubing and fit over the barrel and the sleeve of the silencer. He had seven rounds left in the ten-round clip, but he pulled it out and inserted a twenty-round magazine.

That was one thing about the bastard. He wasn't cheap and he knew guns. The Skorpion was a blowback weapon with a high rate of fire, but there was an inertial mechanism in the grip that delayed the bolt and reduced the rate of fire to a controllable cycle. Weighing only three and a half well-balanced pounds, it was an ideal weapon for a situation like this. Frayne wondered how he'd gotten them. Jesus, with a couple thousand of these—.

Frayne wasn't nervous or jittery, he wasn't even

thinking of the others that he knew were there, the fact that he was three floors from the street, that if they had heard the shots and knew O'Rourke had taken some they'd send up maybe more than he could handle, and he'd heard another footfall on the stairs and then in the hall. Whoever it was, he stopped.

There was quiet for a while there inside the kip. Out on the street he could hear cars, lorries, and Frayne wondered if those other people could know that here was where it was happening, the news, what they'd be reading about in the papers tonight and tomorrow, and really how much it differed—what he'd read, for instance about himself and the cop in Galway—from the way he felt going through it, what he saw. And did it matter? Yes and no. Yes, that he had savored every word, every letter; but no, he preferred it the way it was, like this, in a quiet and calm that made it all seem like a special kind of child's play, but dangerous and bloody.

But Frayne was good at what he did, and he knew it.

"Billy-boy?" He heard the old man's voice on the stairs. "Somethin' happen up there? We heard a clump like the ceiling fallin' in.

"Jack?"

Frayne said nothing and remained where he was, kneeling at the side of the bed. He thought of the dusty carpet and how it might smudge the knees of his new tan trousers, and he was filled with loathing for the kip and the old man who owned it and those other old roustabouts who could live—.

He heard the board creak again, the one out in the hall, and again. Two of them, one to decoy, the other to fire. Frayne had seen it used before, but not by him.

He again laid the Skorpion alongside his left arm and bent his head.

"Billy?" the old man asked again, his voice heavy with fear. "Jack?"

Frayne then saw him in the doorway, nothing in his hands but a bulge to the side of the tattered cardigan he wore, and in this weather. His eyes, like O'Rourke's had been, were bugged and fearful and false. "What happened to Billy-boy, Jack?"

Frayne kept his head down, waiting for the old man to step away from the door and for the other one to appear with the—.

The old man's eyes shied to the left, and he stumbled as he stepped back, so that Frayne, snapping up the Skorpion with both hands, caught the other man as he walked into the fire.

The burst drove him—bloated and fat, like O'Rourke, a barstool warrior full of all sorts of tripe about the Troubles—back into the hall, nailing him against the wall, a cluster that tore bright red pennies in the white smock and seemed to hang him there for a moment, his eyes bulging, his mouth with only a few teeth as yellow as that donkey's in Drogheda gaping.

The first one, the owner, had fallen and he scrambled up and tried to flee down the dark hallway, but the doors were locked.

In that same great calm Frayne watched him for a while, as he clawed at the doors, then fished in his pocket for a ring of keys that he dropped at his feet, looking with horror over his shoulder at Frayne. Then he left off and turned around, his hand moving inside the cardigan. But he stopped. "Ah, Jack-boy," he whined. "Ah, Jack—"

The slug seemed to take off the front of his head, like it was charged and exploded, and the door into which he was driven cracked.

Frayne moved down the stairs slowly, keeping the butt of the weapon in the crotch of his arm, grasping the long housing of the magazine in the other hand.

And everything seemed more real to him—the sunlight flooding through the begrimed stairway windows, stuck shut with grease and dirt; the stench of the latrines at the end of each hallway; voices from the other rooms, the sweat-sour reek of bacon and eggs and tea that wafted up from the dining room.

Frayne lowered the weapon as he turned the corner of the landing to the street floor, keeping it against the wall and his body.

Two men came out of the dining room, farmers by the look of their windburned faces, trying to save a few quid in a kip before the Horse Show, no doubt. Frayne hated that sort of niggardliness. They probably owned half a county between them. One of them glanced up at Frayne and nodded.

Frayne smiled.

"See your man about?" the farmer asked.

Frayne stopped and put his body between the man and the gun. What was two more? he thought, but he had to use the phone before he left. He hated those little kiosks; they were traps, and he wasn't going to get caught in one.

"He stepped out to change a note for me. Maybe you can catch him. The bank's just up the street."

"Thanks."

"Don't mention it."

The two men went out, and Frayne waited for the door to close on the sunlight again before he moved down the stairs, across the hall, and into the bar.

The barman was alone there and, looking up, he was surprised to see him. And frightened, there was that too.

Keeping him in sight, Frayne closed and locked the door.

The man was tall and thin with craggy features and gray hair cropped short along the sides, the rest of it a bushy spray.

Frayne didn't raise the gun, only said, "Both hands on the bar and keep them there."

The man complied, and his eyes watched Frayne move by and pulled the phone onto the bar.

Frayne folded the struts of the gun butt back over the silencer and the barrel and laid it on the bar pointing at the man, his hand still on it.

With the other hand he dialed the number. When it answered, he listened for the sound of the voice. Satisfied, he said, "I'm here. I want the money."

He heard a laugh that was deep and wet and winning. "Relax, Jack. I've got it, boy, and it'll be in your pocket before the day's out, just like we agreed."

Then the voice dwindled to a near whisper. "Listen, Jack—they're at each others' throats, they are, and I'm only after leaving the Show Ground myself. The place is swarming with police."

Frayne liked that even less. He'd dealt with finks before, and the bastard was trying to pull out on him. And after what had happened upstairs Frayne would need all the help he could get and money—more than he'd been promised by far—and a way out of the country. "Then you don't want the horse either?"

The barman's body was trembling now. He wasn't looking at Frayne but out across the tables to the two windows that long, yellow shades covered. The sunlight made them brilliant. And Frayne could hear something like water dripping.

"Ah, Jack—she's weak, so it's said. We've done enough."

"*We've* done enough?" Frayne roared into the phone. "You don't know the half of what *we've* done."

The barman was whining now, shaking all over. Frayne looked at the man's trousers, which he could see down the length of the bar. They were sodden. The coward had pissed in them. Frayne had no use for cowards, not here, not anywhere.

"Listen to me now and listen good," Frayne went on, not taking his eyes off the barman. "You set this thing up and it's not done, not by half. You'll be reading about what *we've* been up to while you've been out at the feckin' Show Ground and all, and now I want double, cash, small notes, and a way out of the country or you'll find yourself among what *we* can do.

"Do you get me?"

The man on the other end smiled. Frayne was predictable and thus controllable. He'd be stopped, of course, and that would be all to the good. "It can be arranged."

"Double."

"That too."

Frayne didn't care for the way he had agreed so quickly.

"I might be needing you again, you see."

Nor that either, but he said, "Then be there with everything."

"But it'll take—"

"No buts, just be there." Frayne dropped the receiver into the yoke.

The man on the other end paused before hanging up. Even so, he thought, perhaps it would be wise to take precautions, in case of contingencies. Only Frayne and one other could tie him to the whole, bloody mess, and Frayne was too close, too available.

But it was nice the way he was playing Frayne. Dicey, to be sure, but with a certain control. It was that which he enjoyed most.

Back in the kip Frayne turned to the barman, who was wilting, head down, body shaking, tears streaming from his eyes, only his hands on the bar keeping him from falling.

Frayne walked by him toward the door. "You dirty, filthy, cowardly man, you. You probably cacked in your britches as well," he muttered.

At the door he shouted to the man, "Did you?"

The man broke down, nodding his head, and something spluttered from his nose.

From the other end of the bar Frayne gave him a burst, all up and down his back, aiming at the pants.

The man fell softly, crumpling down into his own filth.

Frayne waited to hear if the shots would bring some others. He then placed the Skorpion in the sling under the jacket, put on the sunglasses and cloth cap, and stepped out of the bar, locking the door behind him.

Out in the street he dropped the key in the gutter and began walking toward the library.

Watching the girl step down the stairs of the funeral parlor, Ward wondered how much love had to do with loneliness, the wanting to have a personal, an inviolable touch with another person and the . . . life force—children, family, a generational perspective, back and forward in time, one that helped you understand the process of birth, growth, aging, and death.

And he wondered how much it had to do with feeling a certain lack in oneself that the other person could and would fill. Take the way she moved—easily, fluidly—or the way she had been when she'd played for him, carried away, or her talent itself, the . . . artiness in her approach to the world that was so different from his own. She was everything that he was not, but there was a trap in that too—she'd be a concert pianist, traveling here and there, and he'd be a cop for the rest of his life, that much he knew was certain. And if she gave in, she'd be unhappy. And if he allowed his feelings to carry him away, he'd be unhappy.

But perhaps it was just the impossibility of the situation that made him watch her legs all the more closely, the narrowness of her waist in a pleated, flower-print dress that swayed with each step, her smile from under the flounced hat—full, holding nothing back. She swung the pocketbook like a little girl.

Ward forced himself to look away. Christ—.

He stepped out of the car, buttoning his jacket.

"You make me feel better already," she said, lifting her head so the brim wouldn't get in the way as she kissed him, full on the lips, their teeth colliding. Her cheeks were cold.

"It must be difficult."

They were on St. Stephen's Green, and she took his arm. They began walking under the shade of the tall trees that grew over the sidewalk and shadowed most of the street. And they had company, tourists mostly, who stared, seeing in them—Ward imagined—a young, handsome Ireland far different from the worn Georgian row houses, most now converted to offices, around the Green.

And she had pulled him close, her breast against his arm, their legs together, stepping down the patterned blocks of the sidewalk into the park.

"Not really. The coffin is closed because of the—" she looked away, squinting because of the patch of bright sun they had walked through, "—post mortem. But I'm not sure I'd want to see her again as she was in that chair or in some funeral director's idea of high fashion.

"I know it's callous of me, Hugh, but once you're dead you're just so much flesh and bone and it's barbaric to have people linger over you.

"The old people had the right idea—to put the person away by sundown of the next day. But the waking, the sitting up the night long with the . . . cadaver, and the relatives who hadn't given a tinker's damn for you when you were alive, coming hither and yon to thank their lucky stars you went before them, it's . . . savage, uncivilized."

Ward had the urge to slip his hand around her waist, but he kept himself from it. Yes—he could love her, and—dammit—he probably already did.

"Can you imagine . . ." With one hand she reached up and slipped out the pin, removing her hat. She tossed her head, and the fine black hair struck the side of Ward's face.

He was staring down at the rolled clay of the park path, ostensibly concentrating on what she was saying, but really watching her narrow legs and ankles and her feet, which were long but remarkably narrow inside Prussian-blue shoes with low heels.

". . . a man called the funeral director purporting to be my Aunt Grainne's husband. He said that as the nearest relative his wife wanted the body sent to Galway where the funeral and burial would be arranged."

And there was a certain way she put down those feet, the oval of white flesh at the top of the shoes flicking out, turning slightly and seeming to pause before she set them down. Softly. Ward wondered if she ever wore out a shoe.

And for her part, she enjoyed his quiet confidence. He was intelligent without being a bore, young without all the inane problems and aspirations of the others she knew, like Sean, and he was quite handsome. And last night she had gotten the feeling that he knew something about women and had had experiences with them, and that alone, in Ireland, was to be prized. But it was rather disturbing too and she wondered who they had been and what he really thought about her, in comparison.

"I had thought that Aunt Grainne was—" she glanced at him; should she tell him? "—insane . . ."

He didn't look up; he had known.

". . . and not really marriable. At least Mammy always told me she was a 'lost soul.'" She turned to Ward and smiled, seeing only the dark curls on his temple. "In Mammy's inimitable way, best left forgotten, that whenever she saw any of the family it only made things worse for her. And now she turns up with a husband."

Again she looked straight ahead. "What do you know about this, Inspector? And how is it coming along, the investigation and so forth?"

Ward smiled. "It's progressing. Of course, I'm—" he hefted her arm, "—handling the most interesting aspects."

"If indeed 'handling' you are." She pretended to tug her arm away. "But continue."

He glanced down at her legs again, pulling her close to him.

It wasn't his place, as a detective, to reveal any information, and from what McGarr had said about his interview with Bechel-Gore, the girl was ignorant of her origins. "It's known to us, of course, that you have an Aunt Grainne, but, as I said, you're my area of responsibility. I'm to concentrate on you."

He flashed a smile that she knew was self-consciously shy. His teeth were even, spaced rather far apart, and seemed very white against his dark skin. "How did the father respond to the—was it a demand?"

"Concentrating, are you?" She had noticed how he had been staring at her legs. Over Sean—who in many little ways, such as that, had made no pretense of his affection for her—she had felt a certain power, but with Ward it was different. He gave her the feeling that he was always in control, and she liked that. Control—something she herself could use a little of, now and then. "He told the man that I was Mammy's closest relative and a legal adult and arrangements had been made to my wishes.

"They had a bit of an argument, it seems, and the man said he was going to take the matter to the courts, or so I gathered."

"What did Father Menahan say?"

And her not being certain how much of his attention was because of her or his duty made Ward even more appealing to her. If he was making a pretense of his affection, he was very good at it; if not, she was flattered and could admire him all the more. For his reserve. "That he doubted it."

"Doubted what?"

"That the matter would or could go to court."

"The father's very good for you."

She wondered what that intended. Father John had been acting rather differently since—. Eager or something. "Yes. Our families have always been very close."

"And what did he say about your aunt?"

"That he didn't believe she could have a husband."

"Then who could the man have been?"

"I don't know." It was that which had troubled Mairead most, but she put it out of her mind.

There was a man selling ice cream from an HB cart near the fountain, and Ward stopped. "Your favorite is chocolate on chocolate," he said, remembering McGarr's report of the contents of the fridge in her flat.

"How did you guess."

"I'm a detective, amn't I?"

McGarr felt a swell of pride in what he was seeing—the long reception room, all glass with a deep pile carpet, the low marble-top tables and designer lamps, the bustle below them in the work yard that stretched down to the quays where winches were lifting stacks of Norwegian and Finnish timber from the holds of two ships onto tall, fork-lift trucks that then scuttled the booty into warehouses—that the Michael Edward Murray he had known as a child, a friendless, disheveled kid and very poor, could have put the complex together, employing—what?—hundreds of people and providing the country with the building materials that were necessary to carry it into the twenty-first century.

Granted, the carpet was a red so bright that McGarr could scarcely look at it directly, and the designer of the lamps and tables had communicated but one thing —that a small fortune had been squandered on the materials—but McGarr imagined some concession had to be made to Murray's abilities in commerce. Whatever way he had assembled his mini-empire—by pay-offs, political favors, and ruthless undercutting of competitors, some said—and whatever way he expressed his new wealth, it was impressive, and McGarr had a soft spot in his heart for the people he had grown up with.

O'Shaughnessy, though, had scanned the room with unconcealed distaste. He had stared down at the material of the emerald-green couch before sitting down and hadn't touched the tumbler of malt Murray had had sent out to them after McGarr had announced himself. "Colorful, isn't it?" he had observed, and when McGarr had raised his glass, the Garda superintendent had only said, "Ice," his expression as frigid.

"Peter!" Murray bellowed from the doorway to the offices. "And Liam. Sorry to keep you waiting." He too had a glass in his hand, but also a fat cigar protruding from between his fingers, and his complexion was an alarming red, nearly purple. His eyes were bloodshot and he seemed to have a tic or a muscle spasm in one lid. It fluttered uncontrollably, and he had to put a hand up to stop it.

He proceeded to show them what he called the operation, much of which was visible from the top floor of the tall building. But it wasn't all of his activity, he put in. There was the Blackrock complex, the Limerick concern, the Ballinasloe plant, and so forth. "And then there's the horses too."

"In a way," McGarr cut in, "that's why we're here."

Murray's head quivered, and he blinked several times. His bulbous nose was veined and raw. There was a drop of mucous on it, which he wiped away with his hand. "Yes—well, why don't we step into my office."

It was all that McGarr had expected, a somewhat smaller version of the reception room but with one wall covered by framed photographs of his family, friends, his political associates, his business operations, horses and riders. Two were of Mairead Caughey looking . . . noble, a derby on her black, bunned hair, a mud net over her face, which was set in concentration. In a hard, determined way she was as striking as McGarr had ever seen her.

"She does something for a horse, wouldn't you say?" McGarr asked.

"I would. I would that, but it's what she does *with* a horse that I admire."

"Almost as skilled as Grainne Bechel-Gore on Kestral, I'm told."

Murray looked down at the top of his desk and seemed to sigh. He slumped into the tall, leather chair. "You've got a bad source there, Peter. She does much more, and you'll see if you go to the jumping tomorrow."

"That good, eh?" McGarr kept staring at the picture. There was something frightening—or was it intimidating?—about the way she appeared, as though she were wearing a modern-day equivalent of a medieval knight's battle helmet. And the expression in her black eyes and on the clean lines of her face was sinister, threatening. A kind of brutal and hard but feminine centaur.

"On the proper mount."

"And you have that?"

"Several. I only wish she could have torn herself away from that blasted piano to have competed overseas for me. Now, with the mother dead and all—" He looked away.

McGarr turned to him and walked past O'Shaughnessy, who had not accepted the proferred seat but stood at the glass wall, looking out at the city. "Don't mind me saying this, Mick, but you look terrible."

Murray's eyes quavered. "Up all night. The Show and—"

"Your son, Sean."

The eyes fixed McGarr's. The man was sweating, although the office was air conditioned. "Is that what brought you?"

McGarr nodded and pretended to search his pockets for a smoke.

"Cigar?" Murray offered.

"Love one."

O'Shaughnessy shifted his weight.

When McGarr had it lit, he sat. "Sean's got problems, Mick."

"I know."

"How long have you known?"

Murray swiveled in the chair and looked out the window. "For longer than I've wanted to admit to myself, but now he's gone off the deep end. I'd thought —what the hell is a little hemp? Smoked it myself, to no effect." He raised the whisky glass.

"Maybe . . . maybe I made too many demands on him, pushed the business on him, the law, Trinity. I'm not one to believe that any cause is ever really lost, but I hear it's like booze—you never really come back from it a hundred percent, there always seems to be something missing.

"Sean and me, we had it out, and . . ." Murray looked out the window, over the work yards and the Liffey and toward the city in the distance. "But I suspect you're not here, talking to me like this, just because Sean has a drug problem."

O'Shaughnessy moved again.

McGarr cocked his head. Surely he *would* have come

to him, an old acquaintance, with precisely that information, had it been all that he knew of the son's recent activities. "Are you still representing him?"

"I don't think he'd want me to, now."

"Mind you, Mick—I'm not interested in making an arrest, but there's been a rash of break-ins in the Ballsbridge area."

Murray turned to him, but he said nothing.

"Around the time of several—four to be exact—Sean's car was ticketed in the vicinity." McGarr waited. There was no reaction from Murray, but McGarr hadn't expected any, him being a solicitor and a good one.

"In another case and recently, a young man was chased from a woman's flat. She described a fellow very much like Sean. He got into a yellow roadster. The last three figures on the plate correspond to Sean's."

Still Murray remained as he was, the stream of cigar smoke rising up pale blue and sinuous.

McGarr waited.

The cigar moved toward Murray's mouth. The end was gluey.

McGarr looked down at his own—all leaf tobacco, a maduro wrapper, a light, white ash that held—and drew in on it. Cuban filler, top leaf, a first-rate smoke, expensive. "Blodgett & Zinn?"

Murray nodded.

O'Shaughnessy moved once again.

"But that's not why you're here, the break-ins."

McGarr was again surprised by the question. Wasn't it enough? "Do you mean the cover-up, your getting Doyle and Scanlon to lie for you?"

Murray frowned. It wasn't that either.

"And then, his car was tagged a block from the Caughey house at the time of the murder. He had the means to get in, he's proved that since."

"Motive?"

"He and the mother didn't get on. Your son's a jealous sort, Mick, and he rather fancies Mairead, I believe." McGarr turned his head to the photos on the wall. "Not that I can blame him."

"Circumstantial evidence. You couldn't make it stick."

"Wouldn't have to. The drugs, the other break-ins, his violent temper. I hear he's all banged-up right now. And then there's the questioning—I understand he's not one to put up much of a front."

O'Shaughnessy was pacing in front of the window, hands in pockets, hat on head, head down.

Murray watched him for a while, hating the culchie bastard. Little did he know, less could he care, what it had taken to build all that Murray had out of nothing. And he was jealous—Murray could almost feel it. A civil servant, a leech.

"He's my only son, my only child. I thank you for coming here like this, Peter, but I must tell you that I'll fight it tooth and nail with everything I have, fair and foul."

"I thought as much."

"But between us—" he paused, his eyes suddenly filling with tears; he swallowed and looked away, "—I guess I'm as much to blame as Sean or Bridie. No—" He shook his head. "Not Bridie. She's a good woman, the best. And Sean, he's been like day and night since he's been to that bloody college of his. It's there, I'm sure, that he got in with them muckers and gobshites. I should have sent him to a Catholic university. I—" his voice broke. He reached for the drink.

It was an embarrassing moment, but McGarr had been with many people in such situations and was content to watch the smoke drift up from his cigar.

Not O'Shaughnessy, however. "Where were you at four-fifteen Friday afternoon, Mister Murray?"

Murray looked over at him and blinked away the tears. He turned to McGarr. "Is he included in this conversation, Peter?"

"It would seem so."

"Do *you* want me to answer that question?"

"Well, I wouldn't want you not to answer it, Mick." McGarr placed the cigar in his mouth, drawing in the rich, musky smoke that tasted of the dank earth in which it had been grown. Spicing it was the aroma of the cedar humidor. He tasted the drink. It pleased him as well.

Murray considered McGarr—always was a little gouger, that one, he thought. Small and tough and fast. He never got caught. Had he been a fool to think he could play along with him, like this? He had, but it was too late for that now. "I was in my office."

"Here?"

"No, my law office."

"Where's that?"

"In Kildare Street."

"Where in Kildare Street?"

Murray snapped his head to McGarr. "Why him and all these questions, goddammit? Kildare Street isn't very bloody long, or doesn't he know?" He turned back to O'Shaughnessy, muttering something else under his breath.

"Near the library or away from it?"

"Every bloody thing on the entire bloody block is near the bloody library, you fool."

O'Shaughnessy remained unperturbed, staring out the window, hands now clasped behind his back, his tall and wide figure shadowing the room. "When was the last time you were in the library?"

"Is he serious? Years!" he nearly shouted. "Years and years ago!"

"You'd make a statement to that effect?"

Murray sighed, pushed himself back in the chair, and drew on the cigar. They'd gotten to him, they had. He must be slipping. Tired, he was, dead tired, but with Sean having as much as dropped the Show in his lap, and the other thing that was bothering him, he couldn't have slept even if he'd tried. He smiled wanly. "Sure. Why not?"

"And sign it?"

"Je-sus." He pushed himself forward, picked up a pen, and scrawled on a pad. "I," he said, "M. E. Murray, T. D., have not been in the National Library in five years.

"Here you go. Have a happy day, my friend." He held it out.

O'Shaughnessy did not move. "And Father Menahan—is he on your payroll?"

"Yes, from time to time, although I wouldn't call it payroll. He comes to company dinners, banquets, the like. The man is a brilliant speaker. He plays the piano like . . . like Rachmaninoff."

"He came to your house last night. What for?"

"A personal matter, having to do with my son. I need advice, Superintendent. It's not every day one discovers that his son is a dope addict."

That was too quick, too defensive, and McGarr sat up, pushing the drink away from him. O'Shaughnessy went on.

"Are you aware of the real antecedents of Mairead Kehlen Caughey?"

"What?" Murray turned to McGarr. "What's he talking about?"

McGarr only kept his eyes on the cigar, listening closely to Murray's tone. He didn't know the man well enough, but if asked he would have bet he was lying and had been for the last several minutes.

"Now then," said O'Shaughnessy, his tone somewhat didactic, teacherly, implying that he had in fact caught the man lying, "this 'operation' here, all that I can see down there in the yard—is it going well?"

"You have eyes, man. Everybody's busy enough, aren't they?"

"I've been led to believe you're nearly bankrupt, over your head in debt. The Ulster Bank called in a ninety-day note last Friday and you were unable to meet it."

"Then you've been misled. I've never been overly fond of the Ulster Bank. They've just had a change in upper management and one of my—shall I say?— adversaries has come to the fore. He called in that note."

There was a pause.

McGarr asked, "Did you cover it, Mick?"

The eyes, bloodshot and rheumy, shied. "It's being

done now. The horse sales at the Show ought to cover it easily."

The Show again, McGarr thought. "Do you have many . . . adversaries, Mick?"

"Of course." He heaved himself up from the chair. "Every man in public life does. You yourself—you've got that character on the *Times* on your arse, and I've got my—" he glanced toward the window, "—O'Shaughnessys and Maloneys," the name of a competing building materials firm, "and—"

"Your Bechel-Gores," said O'Shaughnessy.

"Yes, but the difference is, Superintendent, that Sir Roger Bloody Bechel-Gore is a *worthy* adversary." He was sweating profusely now.

"Really, Peter, I'm up to my neck in work here, and can we—"

"Just a moment or two more, Mick. We could have asked you and Sean down to the Castle for this, rather than waiting until after the Show."

"Is that a promise?"

"Yes."

Murray was relieved. "I appreciate that."

"I thought you would." McGarr stood. "But tell me about your I. R. A. connections. Your Mercedes showroom—how many on the payroll there?"

"Ah, now Peter, if I can't give a break to some fellows—"

"How many?"

Murray thought for a moment. "Four—but I'm a silent partner there."

"Don't cod me, Mick. You're not a silent partner anywhere.

"How many here?"

"A good number."

"Ten, twenty?"

"Twenty some, I'd say, though it could be more."

"What about Jack B. Frayne of Armagh. Ever employ him?"

"Never heard of him until I read his name in this morning's papers."

McGarr offered his hand. "I hope, Mick, this is all I'll have to be asking you for a while."

"I don't know why you have."

McGarr waited until the eyes moved toward him and then he fixed them with his own. "Because I don't believe your son has a violent nature—drugs or no drugs—and because the death of Margaret Kathleen *Keegan* Caughey, the raid on Keegan's place in Drogheda, and the sniping incident at Bechel-Gore's place in Galway are connected in some way that seems beyond Sean's . . . purview, at least as I understand things at the moment.

"And by saying this, at least one of us—" he glanced at O'Shaughnessy, "—thinks I'm putting you on notice, so don't expect any further concessions from me."

"Then you're not going to lay a charge against Sean? I mean, you yourself."

Was there a note of disappointment in the question? McGarr searched the man's rough, formerly handsome features—the short, wide nose now veined, the slack jowls, the silver waves that flowed to curls at the back of his head—but he couldn't tell.

"No. Not yet anyway. I'll keep you informed."

"Well—that's grand of you."

"What are you going to do?"

A door opened and a secretary said, "Begging your pardon, Mister Murray, but Commissioner Farrell is on the line for Chief Inspector McGarr. There's been some sort of tragedy. It's urgent."

But McGarr didn't turn to her. Murray's seeming ambivalence toward his son intrigued him.

"Get Sean the most competent criminal solicitor I can."

"And who would that be?"

"Handelmann. He's new to my firm."

"The I. R. A. lawyer?"

"He's done a bit of that, but we've covered that ground, I think. He's good, but he's poor. He wants to change that and I'm giving him the chance."

McGarr went in to the phone.

There had been a time when Bechel-Gore had enjoyed his wife's childishness, the contrast between her striking and womanly appearance and the delight she took in a world that was a continuing mystery to her. But not now, not with all that was facing him. What was now required was competence and good sense and not a little bit of luck, if they were to get through the crisis.

"Would you look at that, Roger," she said, as Paddy, the driver, pulled the Bentley up before the marquee of the Shelbourne Hotel on St. Stephen's Green. "What are they, tinkers?"

A group of students or, he supposed, "troubadours" with beards and unkempt hair and guitars and penny whistles were camped on the sidewalk near the large, fashionable hotel. A uniformed guard was watching the singers from afar, making sure they didn't disturb the hotel's guests.

"I don't think so, dear," he said evenly. "When was the last time you heard tinkers making music?"

"There're some fine musicians who are tinkers, though I can't remember their names."

Musical—Bechel-Gore thought—like the girl, who certainly hadn't gotten her talent from him. But he missed grasping his wife's arm when she opened the door and stepped out. She made straight for the music, reaching into her purse for a banknote. Was it blue? It was.

"My God! Stop her, Paddy, will you?"

Bechel-Gore watched in a sort of fascination, noting the contrast between her well-turned-out elegance —she was dressed in the yellow silk suit he had ordered for her in London the year before, the white streaks in her black hair making it look more perfect; the long muscles in her legs and arms well-toned and hale—and the flaccid and unkempt and sickly-looking rabble on the sidewalk. Then he saw the priest, Menahan, waiting under the canopy of the hotel.

"No, Paddy! Get me out of here!" He was still in the back seat, the collapsible wheelchair at his feet.

But with the music and the street noise of cars passing around the Green he wasn't heard.

She stopped in front of them, one foot forward, poised, the ten-pound note in her hand, and, although the music was raucous—some war chant, she imagined, with tambourines, *bodhrans,* the click of spoons, and the wail of bagpipes—she surveyed them calmly, her black eyes working over each one of them, noting the long ringlets of dirty hair, the scraggly mustaches on the men, the shirts of plaid flannel on the women that concealed their breasts and made them seem like boys who'd never grown up.

And she waited for the music to stop, the driver in his gray suit and cap at her arm.

But Bechel-Gore had his eyes on Menahan, and when the priest stepped out of the shadows and began to walk toward her, he hesitated for a moment, then slid his legs out of the car and used the door to help himself stand.

"What are you going to buy with this money?" she asked the first player, an older fellow with graying hair like her own, but curly and oiled.

"Whis-ky," he said through bottom teeth that were bad and discolored.

"Why whisky?"

Paddy had taken her arm now, but she knew he'd not lead her away.

"Because it makes me feel good."

She blinked, then looked at the others. "It always makes me ill." She dropped the note into the tambourine that the player held out, and a shout went up from the others.

Somebody stepped in front of her. A priest.

"Do you remember me, Grainne?"

"Get out of here," Paddy said, the pressure on her arm suddenly firm.

"I'm John Menahan from the next farm, Bill and Moira's boy."

"Johnny?" she asked, her voice rising oddly, trying to connect the stout man in front of her with the dim recollection of the little boy who'd been full of fun and mischief and who had played with her as a child.

"Yes, Grainne. Johnny."

"Get out of it now, Father, or I'll—"

"Easy, son. Easy!" said the player on the sidewalk. "Don't disturb the lady when she's got philanthropy on her mind."

Bechel-Gore let go of the door, hoping his legs would carry him after the long ride in the car.

Paddy tried to pull her away, but the silk of the sleeve was glossy and slick and she slipped her arm free.

"Maggie Kate is dead, Grainne. She died Friday. She's being waked just across the Green there. At O'Brien's. I know she'd like to see you."

"You bastard!" Bechel-Gore shouted, hobbling toward them. "Stop him, Paddy!"

The player stood. He was tall and rangy.

The driver reached for her again, but the player, thrusting out the palm of his hand, struck him in the chest and knocked him back.

"And the child is there too. I know you'd like to see her. It's remarkable how much Mairead Kehlen resembles you."

"Child?" she asked, looking away and cocking her head, like a bird listening to the sound of a familiar call. "Mairead Kehlen?" Just the name alone brought up such bitter, painful memories. "Maggie Kate?"

"But Roger told me—" She turned to look at the car and saw her husband *walking* toward her. She felt suddenly weak and faint and confused.

"Yes," Menahan said in a soft voice, almost a whisper. "She was murdered, Maggie Kate was. Last Friday. And Mairead Kehlen—"

Again the driver launched himself at the priest, but this time the guard restrained him.

"I'm the lady's husband, guard, and I want to get her into the hotel." Bechel-Gore's voice was commanding, certain of the prerogatives that went with the Bentley, his tweeds and long face, the chauffeur, the Shelbourne, and the ten-pound note.

"O'Brien's?" she asked the priest. "O'Brien's what?"

"Funeral—"

But Bechel-Gore had her by the arm, and he and Paddy led her toward the canopy where hotel personnel assisted them.

In the lobby one of the managers moved toward them. "Sir Roger—good to see you. And Lady Bechel-Gore." Then his smile fell. She appeared dazed or stunned or—. He turned to Bechel-Gore. "And *walking*. My word, that *is* good news."

Bechel-Gore only nodded and pushed by him. But he stopped short.

Sitting there was Keegan himself, another man in the chair next to him. Keegan had one hand under his coat. Their eyes met and Keegan smiled, his eyes hard.

Bechel-Gore moved Grainne toward the desk and the elevator. "I'll register later. Have it brought up to me."

McKeon, who was sitting by Keegan, also had a hand concealed—in the side pocket of his jacket. "Know him?"

Keegan said nothing.

"That's Sir Roger Bloody Bore," said McKeon reaching for a cigarette. "Horses.

"How about that drink you promised me?"

They went into the bar.

McGarr didn't arrive at his father's flat until nearly midnight, and he didn't bother to switch on the hall lights on his climb to the fifth floor. The circuit was attached to a timer and only as a child had he been able to sprint up the flights of long, narrow stairs and make the door before they went out. And anyhow, the climb in the dark was rather reassuring —that in spite of events which he seemed powerless to control, other things (the daily, homely details of Dublin) were in place:

The smell of a hot iron on wet clothes on the Birmingham landing and the bawl of a baby beyond; cabbage and fish stew, with the inevitable two cases of empties after the weekend where Missus Magowan, who was a fishmonger with a cart, and her sister still lived; a telly and flute music out of the third floor, a family who was new by ten years or so and not known to McGarr; silence at Keatings, since he was a bachelor and a barman and would be closing up now; and at last the smell of white burley pipe tobacco that had always been a part of his house but had grown stronger over the many years—nearly twenty now— since McGarr's mother had passed away.

And another smell, something cooking and good.

And laughter, a woman's voice—Noreen. He could hear his father too—high and weak now with age—as he related some story in the sing-song pattern of his native Monaghan, his voice wandering up at the end of a breath, no matter the sense.

McGarr paused before stepping in, wanting to resolve at least some of the questions that he'd been mulling over since leaving the Castle ten minutes before.

—Frayne: a killer for hire, first by the I. R. A. and then by somebody else. The affair at the kip on Eccles Street was only Frayne breaking away from the I. R. A. connection, but the bloodiness of it all, especially the thirteen slugs that had been pumped into the barman, who had been unarmed, made McGarr realize that he was dealing with a psychotic. The man liked to kill and he was skilled at it. McGarr had found the hair dye, the Clery's packet, the sales slip. They now had his description, and he hoped that would help, but Frayne was well-armed and whoever was employing him had money to burn.

—Bechel-Gore: the gun alone was a connection. He'd gotten three Skorpions from a Czechoslovakian army general as a present, or so he had said, after a big sale of horses to that country. McGarr's staff hadn't been able to reach the general, but the consulate in Prague was working on it. Why three? Why not two or four or a half dozen? Or five or ten, if the gift was going to be in multiples? And Bechel-Gore certainly had motive enough for the attack on Keegan and the murder of his sister. Would he have the I. R. A. connection? Could he have developed it early in life, say, when he was a student at Trinity? And all the horse sales to the foreign jumping teams, the British army stint he'd done, the studiously wrought Horse Ascendency demeanor, the "great house" and the Bentley, were they only a blind—? No. It was too elaborate for the I. R. A., who fought more like a tribe than an army and whose organization had never been known for its precise and long-range planning. But Bechel-Gore had been in Dublin the day of the murder and he had motive and was duplicitous—the legs spoke for that, perhaps so did the story about receiving Keegan's records in the mail as well. And the cigars. McGarr had thought he'd had something when Murray had admitted that the cigars he smoked were produced by Blodgett & Zinn, but Bechel-Gore was on the list, as was Fergus Farrell, the Commissioner of Police.

—Sean Murray: McGarr had enough to lay a charge against him. They had him under surveillance, and for his own sake he should have been picked up that morning. He'd since pawned an expensive camera—his own—for next to nothing, tried to have a spat with the girl, Mairead, in the lounge bar at Neary's, then exchanged what money was left for a small packet from an unsavory character well known to the vice squad. Could the murder of the old woman and everything else be unrelated? McGarr didn't think so.

—Murray, the father: he had motive. His businesses were not as sound as he made them out to be. Ulster Bank had had no vendetta against him; the loan he'd taken had simply fallen due. He had entered the bloodstock business when he was overextended, and for the first several years he met with little success. He had I.R.A. connections of sorts, or at least he'd been good to them. The cigar. The knowledge that a horse fed green apples would kill itself would be his too. But mostly McGarr thought of the interview in Murray's offices that morning, and the bathetic tone of voice when talking about his son. It had been like— McGarr thought of the television on Mrs. Brady's kitchen table—a soap opera, almost as though he'd been wishing the murder on his son. And the trembling, the bloodshot eyes, the boozy sweat. And it occurred to McGarr then that they still did not know M. E. Murray's blood type.

—Keegan: he was a victim too, but certainly he'd had the connections to have employed Frayne, and the money, given the information in the files McGarr had gotten at Bechel-Gore's. And he too had knowledge of horses, evidently in depth, since he'd passed himself off as a veterinarian for more than a decade. There were those who swore by him, the Drogheda barracks superintendent had said. And then the incident at the Shelbourne. McKeon had reported that Keegan had planned on being there at that hour, as if he'd known in advance Bechel-Gore's activities.

—Menahan: he wasn't at the rectory and hadn't been for two days and nights. He'd visited Murray twice since, however, and had been "hired" by him before. And why had he accosted the unfortunate Grainne Bechel-Gore like that? McGarr was an optimist, and it was difficult for him to conceive of a purely evil person or act—the web of circumstance, personal history, and causation being a complex weave—but that had been evil and cruel. But, then again, was Bechel-Gore's having kept the knowledge of her child from Grainne all those years any less so? No, but it hadn't been . . . violent in intent. Menahan's act was as much an assault as if he had struck her.

—The girl: McGarr didn't know what to think of her yet. She, like her mother, was an enigma, and he wondered how wise it had been to have detailed Ward to her. McGarr had watched her training out at the Show Ground only several hours before, and she was deceivingly strong—hands, arms, legs—and would have been able to have—. No. He didn't think so. He didn't want to think so. What motive could she have had? And how could she have affected the connection with Frayne? Would she have had the kind of money to pay him?

He didn't know and he was tired.

He opened the door, and the pleasant warmth of the turf briquettes that his father kept burning in the stove winter and summer greeted him along with the aroma of coddle, a sausage-and-bacon stew that was peculiar to Dublin and best late at night like this.

McGarr helped himself, ladling the coddle over some spuds that had been simmered in their jackets and which he cut into the bowl. He took off his coat and placed his hat alongside his father's on top of the fridge and walked down the hall toward the sitting room from where he'd been hearing the voices:

Noreen—cheeks flushed, green eyes sparkling; she had a drink in her hand, not the first. McGarr's father —his long face, all nose now, it seemed; and another old man. What was his name? Tierney. Jake.

"Ah, Peter—" his father said, having to bend over to stand up, "—we were just talking about you, how a few years ago you would have caught the bugger on the run in them fields—"

"Or plugged him after—" the other man put in.

"Or plugged him after," his father echoed, nodding to Tierney. "But, as it stands, you didn't and he did a good job of dirty work for you. Rid the country of a tough and three old bowsies. Good planning, that. Ill luck you had to get a shiner for it, but I'd say it

269

gives his sorry puss a little color, wouldn't you, Noreen?"

"I'm used to color," she retorted. "Every other night it's lipstick."

"Him?" His father's walk was more a shuffle now, all on his heels, and for the last few years McGarr was always surprised on seeing him—how it appeared that he was shrinking down, even his bones. He was small, tiny even, compared to his days as a smithy at the C. I. E. (the national transport board) works, three blocks distant. Then he had never looked bullish, but he had been strong. He still had much of his hair, which was gray, and he enjoyed company, something that happened all too seldom.

On the mantel was a stack of Yachtsman cut plug, a holder of old briars, and a newspaper, which he picked up. "After Fogarty's done with him he'll not get a peck from a politician, I'll lay odds."

The others laughed.

McGarr smiled and nodded to Tierney. He sat near Noreen and spooned up some coddle and potatoes.

"It's this that brought Jake around," his father continued in a more serious tone. "He thinks he's got something for you. Works at the library, he does. The National on Kildare Street."

McGarr looked up, savoring the porky sweetness of the stew, which his father had labored long to degrease and spice. There was a leek in it, he guessed, and a few sprigs of parsley, and some thyme, and a clove or two of garlic. "Military history, isn't it, Jake?"

The man turned his head a bit, agreeing. He'd worked as a ticketman on the trams, and later the buses, most of his life, and he had a nickname, "Two-t'rees," which for a long while had been the minimum fare and much requested. But like many Dubliners his avocation had been the real center of his life, and in retirement he had landed a job cataloguing at the library.

"I saw the piece in the *Times*. It mentioned that this Frayne bloke had been in Paras. I thought it a bit odd that later he'd go over to the other side without some cause, so I got a hold of a friend of mine in London." Tierney was small and bald and wore thick, octagon eyeglasses with narrow gold bows. "Came in right around supper." He reached into his jacket for a slip of paper. "It says—"

"Jack B. Frayne, corporal," said McGarr. "Released from service for insubordination, brawling, and striking an officer. Considered unfit for further service because of psychiatric reasons."

Tierney looked up surprised and adjusted his glasses.

"We were sent a summary of his British army records too," McGarr explained.

"But do you know who was his commanding officer for most of his career?"

McGarr thought for a moment. The only principal in the case who had a history of service in the British army was Bechel-Gore. "Why, Sir Roger, right?"

McGarr's father smiled.

Noreen looked down into her glass.

"You knew?"

"No, just a lucky guess, and I thank you for the tip, Jake. We've been trying to make a connection between the two, and there it is."

"But that's not all," said his father. "There's more."

"About the library itself?" McGarr asked.

Tierney nodded.

"The girl, is it? Mairead Kehlen Caughey?"

Tierney passed some air between his lips and looked up. "The kid's smarter than he looks," he said to McGarr's father, "and no thanks to you. Let's see if he can get the second half of it."

"She has an admirer," McGarr went on. "An older gentleman friend. He uses the library regularly in the afternoon. His special interest is horses." McGarr took another spoonful of coddle, thick with sausage and bacon.

His father handed him a mug that had taken two bottles of lager to fill. McGarr drank from it and rejected Bechel-Gore. He had his own library there in Leenane. McGarr had perused some of the volumes and a whole section, it had seemed, had been devoted to horses. Horse periodicals, veterinary magazines, farrier's journals, and work books were on the long tables.

The others waited.

McGarr lowered his glass, dipped his spoon into the stew, and raised it once more. He looked at Tierney. "Michael Edward Murray, T. D., our old and mutual friend from down the street."

"Bingo!" his father crowed, but put in a Dublin denial. "That Frayne fellow must have slapped some sense into him."

Tierney looked deflated.

"But tell me this, Jake. Does he actually go into the reading room?"

"Him? Hell, no. There's too much of him for that. He cuddles up in the librarian's anteroom."

"Alone?"

"Mostly—but that son and the girlfriend stop by, and more her than him."

McGarr smiled and took another spoonful of stew. Noreen said the telephone at their house in Rathmines had been ringing since six. It had been the same at the Castle—reporters, Farrell, the family of one of the slain men—, but there were cars parked in front of the house too. A newsman had asked her if she thought her husband was going to get the sack.

"And who would they put in his place?" she had countered.

"There must be hundreds of capable men who could fill his shoes."

"Then give us a name and not Fogarty."

They spent the night at the flat and his father was delighted.

7

A NASTY SMILE
AND A GOLDEN SHOE,
SLINGS, ELEVATIONS, GRACE
AND VIEWS

The westering sun seemed to follow Sinclaire's plane up across Europe in a perpetual sunrise that became full only as the plane banked over Dublin and swung back into the blinding yellow-gold beams.

As the plane landed and taxied toward the terminus, Sinclaire checked his watch, a massive, eighteen-karat-gold Rolex oyster shell that a jeweler friend in Sidney had lent him as part of the guise: 7:30 A.M., Irish time. He had expected that somebody would be sent to meet him, but not in the Mercedes limousine that had been pulled up in front of the debarking stairs.

Sinclaire stood and allowed the stewardess to help him with the gray seersucker suitcoat, a Savile Row item, and he smoothed back the sweep of his dark hair before fitting on the Cavanaugh hat. Good job he had thought to bring them along on his holiday in Australia. His wife and kids would be taking another flight later in the day. For the present he would be known as Holohan, a scion of a wealthy Australian cattle-raising family. He wondered how McGarr had arranged the identity on such short notice.

He had been the only passenger in first class after

the London stopover, and he tipped the stewardess, a brunette with curves and nice legs.

"Thank you, Mister Holohan. I hope you enjoy your stay in Ireland. To the Horse Show, is it?"

"Yes, but only for a day or two. I'm here for a purpose."

"Are you in horses?"

"Well—let's say I'd like to be. I've come to buy, if your animals suit me."

At the foot of the stairs a large man with a red face and silver-gray hair was waiting for him.

"Bechel-Gore?" Sinclaire asked, having cabled the Bechel-Gore Farms from Australia saying he was coming and interested in purchasing several horses.

"Not on a bet. Holohan, isn't it? I'm Mick Murray." He even came up a few steps with his hand out. "Thought I'd drive you in myself." He pumped Sinclaire's hand enthusiastically. "And this is my son, Sean."

McGarr had filled Sinclaire in by phone, and he knew the reason for the sunglasses.

"Political privileges," Murray went on, explaining the reason for the limousine being allowed to meet him at the plane. "In addition to our horse farms and my other businesses, I'm a T. D., you see—a member of the Irish parliament."

Once they were seated in the expanse of rear seat of the limousine and safely off, speeding through the still empty streets of Swords, Sinclaire asked, "I hope my credit has come through. I wonder if *Bord na*—" he pretended not to be able to pronounce the Irish.

"Yes, of course. *Bord na gCapall* received it, I'm told, and you're quite a good risk, I must say.

"What is your business, Holohan?"

Sinclaire frowned. "I'm not really in business," he made it sound like a dirty word, "per se. At least I want to keep away from it, if I can.

"I'm glad the credits have come through, but I'm curious about how you came to meet me here, Murray. When you didn't return my calls I rang up your competitor."

"You called me, personally?"

"Yes, on Friday last. Several times throughout the afternoon."

Murray's son turned and looked at him.

"Perhaps you didn't try the right number. I've got—"

"Well—" Sinclaire took out his pocket secretary, "—I tried your concerns in Dublin—Hibernian Building Supplies and your office. Then the Blackrock number. I even rang your home. I wonder, did you get my messages?"

Murray bit his bottom lip and shook his head. "No —I must say I did not, and that makes me damn mad. Only this came." He showed him a copy of the telex message that Sinclaire, on McGarr's orders, had sent to Bechel-Gore alone. The only difference was the address, which named Murray's bloodstock firm in Ballsbridge.

"Oh, *Friday* afternoon. Yes—now I recall. I slipped out to the library. I like to think of myself as a—" he turned to Sinclaire and flourished his hand, "—literary man. I'm just a dabbler. Irish, it is. The language, God rest her soul." He winked at Sinclaire ingratiatingly and reached for the console at the back of the seat. In it was a small bar.

"Holohan. That's Irish itself, is it not?"

"Yes, but the record is dim, I fear. So many came out to Australia wanting to forget the past, and I've been content to respect the original Holohan's wishes."

Murray chuckled and poured two drinks, but his son was staring at him, smiling, and the smile was nasty, no question about it.

Murray's hand was unsteady on the decanter and he fumbled with the stopper. After handing a glass to Sinclaire, he turned on the son. "What the hell's wrong with you?"

"Nothing. Nothing at all. Everything's just marvey, Father. Super. Far-out." He waited a while, watching Murray drink from the tumbler, the last finger of his right hand, fat and hairy, raised like a salute.

Then he said, "The library was closed on Friday afternoon." His voice was almost too low for Sinclaire to hear. "All afternoon. Repairs."

"What damn bit of difference does that make: I was out, all right?" Murray turned to Sinclaire. "You don't always need a library to study in. In fact, the damn place gives me the chills sometimes." He shuddered and drank from the glass, finishing it.

The son leaned across the father to speak to Sinclaire. "Do you know that my father is musically inclined, Mr. Holohan?"

Sinclaire cocked his head. The boy's expression intrigued him. With the protrusive lower lip, the bent nose, and the sweep of black glasses he looked maniacal, and his features seemed swollen and rounded, like those Sinclaire had noticed in cadavers. The lip jumped toward the nose once, in a sort of tic, before he spoke.

"All we Irish are, of course, but my father, being wealthy, is enamored of young performers, people whom he can help get started. He likes them especially if they're young, sleek, dark, and female."

Murray turned to Sinclaire. "Sounds like a good prescription for horses," he said easily, reaching for the decanter again.

The young man said something under his breath and looked out the window, and Murray left him in the car when they went into a hotel near the Show Ground for breakfast.

Frayne awoke in a bed upstairs in the hotel. Next to him was a German woman he'd met in the bar the night before. In spite of the years he'd spent with the British Army of the Rhine, he hardly knew two words of German, but she had been drunk and no other Irishman seemed to be taking an interest in her.

And she had told him that too—it was her first time in the country and she'd read the literature and it was, "So hard on the Irish man. He just can't be that bad—" she had glanced up at him, "—in bed."

She was getting old, but she was pretty in a scrawny way, and Frayne had bent her under him, like a barrel stave, until she said, "Enough, please. You're hurting me," and slept.

He got up before she did, showered, dressed, and left her without a word, although he knew she was awake and only pretending to sleep.

Waiting for the elevator with a bunch of other people, he asked himself if he'd thought of killing her. He had, sure, while he was showering, but only if it seemed she knew. And it made him feel good, sure that the garbage in the papers, what Bechel-Gore, the bastard, had put down about him being a misfit and needing the shrink was wrong. If only he hadn't missed when he had him in his sights. Why had he turned the gun away? Orders. And then the other one, Paddy, the fool, he'd kept himself between them. And the cop. He should have plugged him too.

No—he was a soldier, pure and simple, and a good one—the best, goddammit—and he felt a kind of thrill that he was standing up for nobody but himself now: one person, a country all by himself.

Walking out through the foyer he glanced in the long mirrors that covered one wall. A shame the bleeder hadn't been a bit bigger, he thought, noting the way the puffy cap sat on the top of his head and the loose jacket—some modern Continental design in a kind of shiny stuff, like vinyl—pinched his shoulders.

But the pass into the Show Ground wasn't questioned, and the DAF with the Dutch plates was parked where he had left it, the horseshoeing equipment— the leather bib apron, the goggles—were still there alongside the body that Frayne barely glanced at.

"I'm here to observe the farriery competition," the young man had said in precise English.

"Farriery?" Frayne had asked, hardly able to pronounced the word himself and hating the sonofabitch, the way he had hated the Germans, for being able to speak his language better than he did.

"Horseshoeing, you know. The hammer, the anvil." He had laughed, a bit drunk, like the woman.

"In Holland?"

"Sure—we're backward in Holland, just like you. We've got all sorts of horses there."

"Where's the competition take place?"

"In Simmonscourt Hall, same place as the horse auctions. It's right next to the jumping enclosure. To tell you the truth—" the man had looked around the parking lot, "—I couldn't give a damn about the competition. It's the horses I've come to see."

"You mean, they won't make you compete?" Frayne had glanced around the dark car park. They had been looking at a gold-plated horseshoe that Vanderhoof —his name—would present to the grand champion from the Dutch Horse Board, in hopes he would come to Holland and give a demonstration.

"Oh—" he had looked away, the blue eyes trusting and kind and seeming even weaker behind the heavy shaded lenses of his foreign-looking glasses that Frayne thought were just right, "—they might ask me to show the winner a thing or two," he said jokingly, "but I'll refuse. I'm on holiday. A few drinks, a few of your Irish girls maybe, this trifle, but I've come mainly for the horses."

There was nobody around, and Frayne judged that the cover was good. If he'd only not dyed his hair and the man had been a bit taller, it would have been perfect.

"But it's got a chip in it, the shoe itself."

"Where?" Vanderhoof bent toward it, where it was lying in a velvet-lined case on top of the tools in the box.

Frayne had done it before: grasping the jaw in one hand, the back of the head in the other, and laying his knee into the small of the man's back. A quick twist, the heavy snap he felt right through his leg, and that was all. He released the body, shoving it forward with his knee, and it fell into the space beside the box. He removed the man's passport, glasses, watch, and the cap. He found the coat among the other clothes in the rear seat. The wallet contained travelers' checks and a small amount of Irish money, which came in handy. The identity and money he'd arranged for earlier in the day hadn't yet reached him. In short, a smart job of work.

Now Frayne climbed back into the car, the windows fogged with morning mist that glared in the bright sun. No sense showing up too early and taking a useless chance. Later, when the crowds got thick, he'd get something to eat. But it had to be today, he decided. The longer he stayed the greater the risk, and he'd been assured he could get out tomorrow or the next day at the latest.

Over the steering wheel he folded out the map of the Show Ground, and on the front seat the map he'd bought of Dublin.

O'Shaughnessy was standing in a long and cavernous trailer that was parked near the number board of the jumping enclosure. In front of him were three banks of television screens, the cameras of which were focused on more than thirty different areas of the sprawling Show Ground, and only in the enclosure itself were horses not to be seen.

Everywhere else, it seemed, in Rings 1 and 2, where the judging of medium and lightweight hunters had begun, in the practice rings, the Simmonscourt Pavilion where hacks, cobs, and ponies were being put through their paces, ridden mostly by children this early in the day, in the stables and yards and outside the bloodstock sales concerns—horses were pictured, their coats glistening in the full, early morning sun.

Horses. O'Shaughnessy's own father had been killed on one, trying to jump the front gate of their farm late at night after having taken a drop, and to O'Shaughnessy they were as familiar a sight as rocks in a pasture. But here they were special, not only the best the country had to offer, but a type of art—their care and training—to be revered and encouraged, and anything that would mar the course of the remaining six days would be to him anathema.

But there were other events and exhibitions too, and several cameras were working over the trade stands in Main, East, and Industries halls and the farriery competition that had begun a half hour earlier; the men and boys with goggles and bib aprons and gloves on, hammering away at the white-hot metal that was scarcely visible on the color screens; an apprentice keeping the forge fires hot; grooms watching, holding the horses to be shod. In bleacher seats a large crowd for such an early hour was looking on.

"I don't see how this can help him much," said Dermot Flynn, rubbing at his bushy hair. "He hung his arse in a sling and now he's as much as hung mine." It was hot in the caravan and he tugged at the turtleneck collar of his jersey, his movements quick and nervous. "If I can't justify the cost someway, I'll—" He glanced up at O'Shaughnessy, who was standing with his hands clasped behind his back, unperturbed. "Aren't you hot? The way you're dressed you'd think you were going to a funeral."

He looked back at the screens. "Half the bloody cameras have been assigned to other departments."

"Didn't you clear it with the director?" O'Shaughnessy asked, his eyes flicking over the screens, concentrating on one whenever it focused on the faces in the crowd, trying to establish in his mind where exactly in the Show Ground each was located. Clustered on stools around him were two squads of eight, uniformed Gardai, each of whom had been assigned two screens to watch, after having been given photographs and artists' renderings and all the information they had on Frayne to peruse.

"Like hell I did. He'd've taken the thing over for himself, sure he would. This is my show," he thumped his chest, "here."

Flynn turned back to the cameras, rocking from foot to foot. "But, Jesus, how do we know he's here? And did you see the papers?"

O'Shaughnessy had. Even the *Press*, which was usually very much in McGarr's corner, had noted in an editorial that it was unfortunate that the killer had not been apprehended in Galway, which would have prevented the bloody scene in Eccles Street. It hinted, however, that all had not been told of the incident.

Fergus Farrell had asked McGarr to issue a statement making clear the circumstances surrounding the Galway arrest attempt. McGarr had refused. Once he began justifying himself like that, he had said, he'd end up spending more time thinking of the public reception of his actions than getting on with the job, and it was incumbent upon Fogarty to clarify the matter. O'Shaughnessy agreed.

"And where the bloody hell is he anyhow? He set this thing up and now he'd run out on me."

O'Shaughnessy kept his eyes on the screens.

McGarr had slept fitfully the night before, more because of the case than because of his injuries. They had every class of tantalizing evidence and information, it seemed, but one fact seemed to negate another, turn him in one direction and then lead him back.

For instance, earlier in the evening he had phoned Bechel-Gore at the Shelbourne about Frayne. "Is he the same Frayne I cashiered? I thought the name seemed familiar. If you check the records you'll discover I showed him no mercy. A low, violent type and utterly unsuited to the military, as he's since proved."

"What about the Skorpions? General Ztod says he sent you six."

There had been a pause. "That's odd, I only received three. They came by post when the Czechs returned our tack. If *three* are missing—" he had left off.

McGarr had been thinking the same thing. The apples—how had they gotten into Kestral's stall and how was it that Frayne and whoever had been with him had been so familiar with the Leenane countryside. Perhaps somebody on Bechel-Gore's own staff—? If Bechel-Gore was telling the truth.

"I'd like to know why you thought you needed the Skorpions?"

"I should think that's obvious, or at least should be to you."

"You knew you were breaking the law?'

"How much did the law help you yesterday, Mister McGarr?"

But then Frayne had missed Bechel-Gore and why had he missed? And if Bechel-Gore had set about to put an end to Keegan's blackmailing, to exact a modicum of retribution, to retrieve his daughter and only child and perhaps in so doing put the blame on Murray, a competitor (and no doubt ruthless) in the bloodstock trade, did Menahan and the incident at the Shelbourne fit into it too? Another device to cast suspicion on the others, like Menahan's having visited Murray's residence over the past several days? Could all of that have been staged?

And it had been with those thoughts about Menahan that McGarr had climbed out of bed and padded down the carpeted stairs to the kitchen. There in a pot he had brewed coffee, simply sprinkling the ground beans into water he had brought just to the boil. He covered the pot and glanced up at the clock, an antique that had been found in a tobacconist's shop in Eccles Street, of all places. 3:37. He'd give it six minutes before straining the brew into his cup.

McGarr sat at the table, the white enamel of which the light bulb overhead made seem yellow. He hadn't turned the handle of the tap off tight, and a steady drip of water was syncopating the ticking of the clock.

What was it Menahan had said to him the other day outside the church? The method, Descartes's method, something McGarr had had to study in school but had forgotten.

He went over it, counting the steps off on his fingers.

Accept nothing as true which you do not clearly recognize to be so; accept nothing more than what is present to your mind so clearly and distinctly that you can have no occasion to doubt it.

Divide each problem into as many parts as possible.

Commence your reflections with objects that are the simplest and easiest to understand and rise thence, little by little, to knowledge of the most complex.

Lastly, make enumerations so complete and reviews so general that you should be certain to have omitted nothing.

In regard to Menahan himself, what did it mean? McGarr thought back.

By his own admission Menahan had been in the apartment until about an hour before the old woman was murdered. Menahan had been the girl's piano teacher. He had realized her talent was such that it required further training, which he was unable to give her, and he had arranged for her to sit for the prize at the conservatory. He was from the same area as the Caugheys, Keegans, and Bechel-Gores. Leenane, County Galway. He had been in touch with the Murrays ever since the murder. He had accosted Grainne Bechel-Gore with the news that the baby she had thought had died at childbirth was alive, and that her sister Maggie Kate had been murdered.

McGarr then divided the problem into Menahan's relations with Bechel-Gore, the Murrays, and the Caughey-Keegans.

He had sold Bechel-Gore his family's farm. He had

been born and raised in that area and would know it and the locals as well. He had accosted Grainne Bechel-Gore at the Shelbourne.

He was the Murrays' parish priest.

He had taught the young Caughey girl and had arranged for her to sit for the prize at the conservatory in London. He had been generous to them. He admired the girl very much.

McGarr then tried to make sense of each proposition. Was each true? What motivation would Menahan have had in every instance?

McGarr glanced up at the clock. Six minutes. He pushed himself out of the chair and shuffled toward the cooker. Placing his hand on the lid of the pot, he stopped. What was it he remembered? Something in Ward's report of his interview with the girl, the official statement, the one taken back at the Castle? McGarr seemed to remember that the girl had said that the priest was against her studying in London. Could that be? He didn't know and he'd have to check.

And then the incident at the Shelbourne.

McGarr carried the pot to the sink, taking care not to jar it. He held the strainer over the cup and poured off the clear, mild liquid. Late at night he preferred his coffee like that. He still had hopes of sleeping.

He raised the cup to his lips and breathed in the dark, rich aroma. Java beans. Noreen had gotten them in Bewley's.

The Shelbourne. The priest and the poor, simple woman. McKeon had explained the way she had cocked her head, like a bird listening to a special call, unable to understand what was being said. And then the shock, the way she had had to be led into the hotel.

No—McGarr could not understand that. And from a priest.

McGarr was now sitting in his Cooper, down the street from the Caughey apartment. Ward had reported that Menahan was staying there and had, in fact, bought himself a number of "civilian clothes—suits, shoes, and so forth.

Murray, the son, had already picked up the girl and left for the Show Ground to prepare for the Equizole and Thibenzole stakes, both of which were the first of the international jumping competitions of the show.

"Perhaps he's not going," Noreen said. She was sitting beside him.

If he didn't, it wouldn't surprise McGarr. The case was a continuing enigma to him, and it was Menahan who bothered him most. Was he working in concert with Bechel-Gore or the Murrays, or was he on his own, just the unknown in the equation, the vice, as it were, the meddler? McGarr didn't know.

And other reports from Bresnahan had proved no more availing. Murray's, the father's, blood type was O, the same as the blood on the towels that had been found in the bathroom of the Keegan place in Drogheda, but that too really proved nothing. There were thousands of people in Ireland with type O blood.

Then Doyle, the garage mechanic at Ballsbridge Motors Ltd., and Frayne had served stints together in the Longkesh internment camp in the North, having been in the very same barracks for a seven-month period.

Finally, Bresnahan had managed to put the computers to further use in determining the condition of Menahan's finances. With a court order she and Delaney had visited the records departments of the nine major banks over the night. Scattered in six of them were accounts totalling over £53,000.

Menahan—was he the key to the whole matter? McGarr hoped so.

"Mother," said Noreen, "get the full of your eyes of that one." She was looking up the street. "Blazer, ascot, and all, how are you, and him out taking confessions from sinners for the good of their souls!"

The engine ignited with a turn of the key, and McGarr pulled up the street to the curb.

The priest was wearing a blue blazer, light gray slacks, and soft moccasins with tassels, and the light-blue silk ascot matched the color of the crest on the pocket.

"Give you a lift, Father? ' McGarr asked.

Menahan smiled, looking almost handsome with his glossy black hair combed back. "You know, I was in Missus Brady's just now, hard at trying to raise a cab, and I chanced to look out the window and there you were. 'Here it is,' says I, and she thought it a blessed miracle. Hadn't I only me hand on the phone!"

What was it McGarr was hearing? Menahan was at once playful and acting beneath himself.

"Aren't you the nobs this morning, Father," said Noreen, sliding out of the Cooper and into the back seat.

"In full bloom, girl, and without the pale, hunted

look your man here was expecting." He dropped his bulk into the seat and jarred the machine. He slammed the door and turned to McGarr, offering his hand. "Janie, Inspector, you look a sight, so.'

McGarr accepted the hand and glanced down at the crest. "You're a Trinity man, I see."

"Why, yes." Menahan's jowls flattened against the ascot, as he tried to see it himself, his heavy beard showing blue in the grooves. "But—" his eyes met McGarr's, "—Cambridge. It's something that's appreciated at the Show, I'm told. Not that I'm out to salve every lingering scald in a horsey heart, mind."

"No," McGarr said, turning the car back down the street. "You seem more like a man who takes care of his own, Father."

Menahan's brow furrowed. "I suppose you're referring to my 'chance' meeting with the Bechel-Gores at the Shelbourne. Is that what's brought you round?"

McGarr said nothing, only concentrated on driving down the tree-shaded street, the gray stone-and-brick houses set well back and neat behind hedgerows and iron fences. The day was again sunny but cool, with patchy clouds and gusts off the Irish Sea that would bring rain by evening.

"I thought it would," Menahan went on. "That and my role of bank notes."

Yes, thought McGarr, turning to him again. Fat enough to choke a bull, and McGarr was hopeful.

"Prudent investments, the latter."

"In Hibernian Building Supplies Limited, I suppose?"

"In part. But I'm also in horses."

"You can prove that?"

"I can, if I have to."

"Oh, you will. You certainly will, Father. Count on it. Now, about the other matter—"

Menahan paused for a bit, then said, "Think back on our last conversation, Inspector. We discussed the truth, I believe, and the impossibility of knowing it in all its particularity. Well, let's say that I wasn't really playing devil's advocate with you and, lo and behold, my concern for truth in all its forms is no less than yours.

"Now," he had raised his head, talking with his left hand, and he appeared didactic and smug and very priestlike to McGarr, "none of the . . . anomaly of the Keegan/Bechel-Gore situation, which was allowed to fester until it issued in the deaths of Maggie Kate and those four poor souls in the kip in Eccles Street, would have occurred, if our Mister Bechel-Gore hadn't lied to Grainne about his marital state before he got her with child; if Maggie Kate hadn't lied to her and him about the child who was placed in her care by the nuns at the hospital; if the nuns, having been misled about Grainne's mental health, hadn't lied to her about the child; if Jimmy-Joe and Maggie Kate hadn't propounded that lie themselves; and then proceeded to extort—for only the very best reasons, of course—a livelihood from Bechel-Gore for the child, and so forth."

"You knew about that?"

He nodded once, scanning the panorama of Ballsbridge, his hand around the back of McGarr's seat, the other on the dash, like some minor potentate or . . . . god, McGarr thought.

"I did. I did that."

"And I suppose you didn't tell me because I never asked."

"I don't hold that against you. You could not have known to ask."

"But you did understand the nature of my commission when I spoke to you, as a representative of the police arm of the government, investigating a murder."

"I'd be a fool if I hadn't."

"And you, as God's representative here on earth, didn't feel compelled to inform me of all you knew?"

"Ah, now," he held up a hand, "when you asked about Keegan I told you, and our conversation wasn't very long at all, at all.

"And then," he sighed, and looked out through the windscreen and the side window as they approached the Show Ground. " 'Tis a fine line between representing the right, as it has been perceived down through the ages, and becoming ignorantly righteous oneself."

"But telling Grainne Bechel-Gore of her sister's death there on a public street was not self-righteous?"

"God—less so than his keeping from her the death of her sister and the earthly existence of the child of her womb. I only succeeded in the first, since he trundled her away."

"And you thought her capable of absorbing such news easily, readily, without any untoward results?"

He cocked his head. "The truth is sometimes difficult." There was an off-note in that, and McGarr was put in mind of Murray's remarks concerning his son.

McGarr lowered the visor with the Dublin Municipal Police pass on it, and a guard, recognizing him, saluted as they rolled to a stop at Gate II.

"Being such a lover of the truth, Father, I suppose you discussed the essential truths regarding the Caugheys, the Keegans, and Bechel-Gore with your business associate, Mick Murray?"

Menahan opened the door. "I suppose I should lie now, really I should," he said, almost in a sort of an aside, "but what's the point? I might have, yes."

"Was that before or after your investments in the Murray concerns?"

Menahan's brown eyes were as clear and as bright and as healthy as they had been the few days before. "I should think there was a reasonable degree of—I'll appropriate your word, Inspector—congruity in that." He looked down at his watch. "And, God—I must rush. Mairead and Grainne are expecting me."

"Shopping more of the truth, are you?" Noreen asked in a hard voice from the rear seat.

"And did you tell somebody at the Bechel-Gore farm about the 'lies,' as you call them?"

"Well, Mister McGarr, if they're not lies I don't know what they are. Let's say I consider the Bechel-Gore *farm*, as you call it, home. I might have mentioned something about it, my former neighbors being their former and present neighbors and being interested in the people they know."

"But don't you feel some responsibility for the deaths of five persons?" Noreen again demanded. In the mirror McGarr could see the flush that had spread up her neck and onto her cheeks.

Menahan had slid his legs out of the car, and now he turned to her. "I pondered that, honestly I did, but then it occurred to me that not only was that beyond any control that I would want to have over the destinies of others, but also—" he furrowed his brow and shook his head slightly in a manner that was histrionic and designedly so, "—think of it this way: in a sense they've all succeeded in ridding themselves of their gross corporeality, a—shall I call it?—*gesture*, which in a very direct way satisfies the strongest urges of this culture."

Menahan waited for a reply, assessing her.

Her green eyes flashed once. "Just look at yourself, for Jesus' sake, all tarted up like a castrato." Her voice was low and icy. "You're not codding anybody, *Mister* Menahan. You're an ambitious and quite a corporeal man. And tell me this—are you still a priest, or have you made the leap and 'elevated' yourself?"

Menahan stood up.

McGarr was out of the car.

Menahan's smile was forced. He glanced at him. "Can you see what I said about a fine line? Tightrope-walking, it is. It's hard to keep yourself from falling off.

"For her information, I no longer consider myself a priest. Haven't, really, for a long while now. And, yes —I *have* elevated my gross, physical being. It's the least I could do for this—" he stretched his hands to the side and looked down at himself, "—body, while I'm in it.

"And one more thing—I don't know how to put this any more delicately—but I'm not a castrato, decidedly not." He turned and, stuffing one hand in the blazer pocket, began to amble off, his stride jaunty and forced.

"One moment . . ." McGarr didn't know what to call him, "one moment, John, please."

294

Menahan slowed his pace, but he did not stop.

When McGarr caught up to him, he asked, "Tell me what you thought of Mairead's wanting to study in London?"

Menahan stopped. "I've told you once already. As a citizen I have certain rights and one is not to be harassed by the likes of you." He started forward again, flashing a member's pass at the gatekeeper, who stopped McGarr until he could show his identification.

The crowd was thick now, especially there where the two main sections of the Show Ground met, and people were passing back and forth. But McGarr caught sight of Menahan and pushed and shoved his way toward the priest, who was walking down the length of Simmonscourt Road toward the exercise area in Ring 6.

He grabbed the man's sleeve, but Menahan, turning, pulled it away. "I'm warning you—" the dark eyes were hooded, "—I'll lay a charge against you, and it'll not go unnoticed, along with your other blunders."

McGarr motioned his head toward two uniformed Gardai who were standing at the entrance to the exercise ring, watching them. "Shall we give it a go? Say the word and we'll put it to a test. I'm sure I can come up with enough against you to avoid a harassment charge, and I think I'd enjoy seeing you sweat a bit, my friend. Now—you were saying?"

Menahan apprised the guards and tried to read McGarr's pale gray eyes. He did not want to miss the jumping, and he could see Murray standing by the rail of the exercise ring.

"I was for it, of course."

"Why?"

"Because Mairead is in need of an extraordinary teacher."

"And you are merely ordinary, I take it."

Menahan's eyes flashed, his lips blanched. "Yes—for her."

"And what now are Mairead's needs besides money?"

"I don't know what you mean."

"Bullshit, Father," said McGarr, fixing his gaze. "Like her real mother—but in a different way—she required a manager, amn't I right? And this . . . transformation of yours is all to that end.

"Or could I be wrong and your aspirations in her regard are somewhat more intimate?"

Menahan forced his eyes away from McGarr's, but he said nothing.

"I'll be speaking to you again, Father, and soon, down at the Castle. It'll be your first stop on the way to the shovel."

Menahan stepped toward the exercise ring. "You'll have the devil's own time of that, man."

McGarr smiled and, imitating the humbly insouciant tone Menahan had adopted earlier, said, "Say it you, so," but knew it was a hollow jibe, for there was not one law that Menahan had broken.

Ward had been standing by the exercise ring for nearly an hour. He had watched the girl enter the ring on the first of the four horses she planned to ride in the afternoon competition.

Like many of the other riders, dozens of whom were working their horses in preparation for the early afternoon event, she was dressed simply in a dark green sweater, fawn-colored riding pants, and boots, her black hair loose on her shoulders. And yet, he thought, the aura she projected was undeniable and had little to do with his own feelings. Others seemed to make way for her, to stare, to watch the way she guided the dark bay over the jumps, moving with the flow of the horse, how she concentrated on her charge in spite of the photographers and reporters who lined one side of the rail.

And Ward was so taken with her and the moiling scene, lit as it was from the east by the low morning sun—a rich, yellow light that caught in the dewy grass around the ring and made everything seem brighter, more lively, and somewhat unnatural—that he only noticed the Bechel-Gore woman when she reached the gate to the ring.

There she paused, the trepidation plain on her somewhat gaunt but still handsome face. She too was dressed plainly, in black that contrasted sharply with the white markings of the piebald gelding she had mounted. Her graying hair was clasped in a bun at the back of her neck, and she sat easy on the horse, hands gathered almost as though praying, following every movement of the girl and only entering the ring when Fogarty himself and his cameraman approached her.

And it seemed that she was preoccupied and that the horse went through its paces—walking, then trotting and cantering around the ring to warm up before taking the low gates—out of habit, changing its leads in the turns, taking her along. She kept staring at Mairead when she passed, and the horse, sensing her disinterest, slowed to a walk and stopped.

Bechel-Gore was there too, his groom by his side. He seemed nearly distraught, shifting his weight on his thin legs, but he said nothing.

When the girl approached her, she turned in the saddle and followed her and held out a hand, asking her to stop.

Her heart was beating wildly, and she felt sick to her stomach almost, not having slept the night long. Everything seemed so out of place—Roger's walking, the appearance of Johnny Menahan, the priest, the things he'd said that had made no sense to her, and what she'd thought about since then, and her, the child who—she moved past, but turned the horse and trotted back—looked so much like she had when a girl that it had to be true.

When the girl stopped, facing her, she couldn't bring herself to speak. She only searched the dark eyes, the long thin nose—Roger's nose, she was sure of it—and his shoulders, wide and thin. The girl smiled—her own smile, the very way she turned her own head. "Mairead?" she asked, scarcely able to say the name, the light seeming to go dim all around her.

"Yes. I believe I'm your daughter."

She had been right, but she didn't understand—how it could be, how the child would know and be so certain, how suddenly after all the years—.

A passing rider made the horses shy, and they moved together, and she reached out and stroked the girl's hair. "How—?" She shook her head.

At the closest section of rail the men were gathered and one shouted, the others aiming their cameras at them.

But neither turned.

"I'm not sure that's important now, really. Are you going to jump this afternoon?"

"I—" she faltered and looked toward Roger where he stood, watching them, his face anxious and intent, "—I don't think I can. I'm—"

"I'd like you to. Where's Kestral?"

Her hands jumped toward the girl, and she seized her wrist and then her hand, long and thin—she looked down at it—again like Roger's, and all the thoughts she'd had carrying the child, the hopes and fears that she'd damped down, that had taken her years to forget came welling up, and her eyes grew blurry and she felt the wetness on her cheeks. "In the stable. She's still . . . weak." Her voice cracked. "Forgive me."

The girl had reached over to her, and she felt a strong hand on her shoulder. "From what I know of it, Mammy—and it's all too little—there's nothing for you to be forgiven for."

She buried her face in the girl's shoulder and sobbed once—a sound that was deep and agonized.

"But we'll sort that out." The girl glanced back at Ward. "And soon."

Farther down the rail Murray watched them embrace, not knowing what to think. She was beautiful, the girl, no question about that, but, like the mother, she was a bit off and who knew how much, capable of anything, unpredictable and—.

Menahan moved alongside of him.

Murray regarded the clothes he was wearing and wondered what it meant. "You've made a balls of this, Father. Just look at them."

Menahan had regained his aplomb after the run-in with McGarr.

"On the contrary, my friend—what you see there is just what you were hoping for. Mairead is—" from his jacket pocket he removed a cigar and lit it, "—a performer, a superior performer, and having her—" he paused to pierce the nib of the cigar with the point of a gold penknife, "—folks looking on, well . . ."

"And the other one, she's gone to pieces. You can see so yourself." He looked up at the woman whose face was still on the girl's shoulder, her back hunched. "She won't be out of it for months, if that."

"I hope you're right."

"Of course I'm right. They're my—" he turned to Murray, his smile thin, his teeth clamped on the cigar, "—people, aren't they?"

Another man was approaching them, but Menahan continued, "You know, Mick, I hope you haven't planned anything for today. I don't want to know, of course, but it would be stupid, now."

"And you don't look well. How's the shoulder, still bothering you?"

Murray turned on him. "Listen, Menahan, and for Jesus' sake the last time, shut up about that."

And then to the other man Murray said, "Ah, Holohan—I'd like you to meet an acquaintance of mine."

Keegan had watched Murray and Menahan conversing, and he had wondered what it meant—the help he'd gotten from the priest, right down to the automatic weapon he had strapped under the greatcoat. That in itself had been strange, coming from a man of the cloth, but Keegan understood intrigue, and their low tones and glances had been collusive, he was sure of it.

And now the cop—what was his name? Something British, though he was Irish and had gone to Australia more than twenty years before . . . Sinclaire. It probably didn't matter, really, since the johnnies were as thick as he'd ever seen them in one place, bluecoats and plainclothesmen, like the man at his side. McKeon, he was, though he'd said different.

But they'd given him this much rope already, and it was just enough for Bechel-Gore. Keegan didn't care what happened to him after that.

Mairead and Grainne had parted now and were walking their horses over to the rail where Bechel-Gore and Paddy were standing. Keegan saw Bechel-Gore's hand reach for Mairead's, and his heart could have gone out to them, but there was so much history in the way, and him a dying man himself.

8

MOTHER AND DAUGHTER, A CLEAR ROUND AND SAVVY, CHAOS, WEAKNESS, A PUG AND A NAVVY

From the R. T. E. announcing booth that was situated in a perch near the number board above the jumping enclosure, McGarr looked out on the sweep of green field bordered by clipped hedges, walkways, and grand-stands filled with people. It was a vast crowd and rather quiet. All were watching the figure of a lone rider passing slowly through the field of gates, check-ing the course, and getting the progression of the fences fixed firmly in his mind, even though he and the over two dozen other riders had walked it only moments before.

Then the jumping ground had been a field of color: the British and Germans in traditional red jackets, the Italians and two of the Irish entrants in military uniforms, the sole American in a quiet, blue-gray coat, and the other Irish riders in dark green. Mother and daughter had been among them, walking together with their black velvet caps and their dark hair clasped behind their heads, twins even down to the way they moved in stride, that same big-shoul-dered gait McGarr had noticed before.

And it was as though they were conscious of their

perfection and the eyes of the multitude, which were upon them, but he suspected, from what he had learned of them, that they were not.

The mother had stopped at the fourth gate with the water hazard beyond it and pointed out something to her child, then again at the double oxer of two high fences right together.

Bechel-Gore, who was standing next to McGarr, had stirred, and McGarr had wondered why. Was he that hard a man that only the winning was important to him? No, he wasn't, but it was what he had in mind and the importance of the Show to him was obvious. McGarr wondered what Bechel-Gore's financial situation really was, and if his large holdings in Galway, all his recent wins with Kestral and other horses, and his supposed brisk trade at the bloodstock auctions were only what met the eye. McGarr made a mental note to find out.

A bell now rang and the crowd quieted yet more, as the rider, an Englishman, and his horse broke into a lively but collected canter and proceeded back to the first fence, both eyeing it carefully, judging it— the height, the speed necessary to clear it, where they should come down and how, in regard to the next fence.

The horse was a big animal and gray, muscular and firm in the way it trod the earth, almost in a dance with its rider as they approached the fence and picked up speed briefly and vaulted, the rider's hands still loose on the reins, his body thrust forward in the saddle, head up, back arched, feet splayed in the stirrups, grasping the horse only with his thighs, looking toward the next obstacle even before they came down. The horse changed its lead naturally, they charged forward and cleared it easily.

"Yes," said Bechel-Gore. "He's going well. That's a good mount."

McGarr glanced at him. There was pride in the assessment, and McGarr knew that the horse had been raised on Bechel-Gore's farm in Galway.

"Can't say as much for the rider, though."

McGarr waited.

"The hands. That fist is a bad sign. He's tense. And he's too far forward in the saddle. He should give the horse its head."

The hooves knocked on the third fence, but the bar didn't fall. Still, he had one down before the round was over.

"Four jumping faults," a calm voice announced from farther down in the announcing booth, and it was carried around the jumping enclosure on the public address system. The announcer then read off the elapsed time.

The crowd had given the first rider a round of applause, and another rider took the field as he withdrew.

Patches of high, white clouds were moving across the azure summer sky. There was a breeze, but only enough to dispel the heat.

McGarr touched the field glasses to the bridge of his nose and focused first on Menahan, who was sitting in the members' stand, and then on Murray, who was with his wife in a private box. The priest was smiling, looking around, another cigar in his hand, but Murray seemed glum, worried, staring more at the back of the seat in front of him than at the horse and rider in the ring.

And McGarr pondered Murray's involvement with horses, his need to be a part of the horse world on a scale so grand it had nearly ruined him. Murray— from the slums of Dublin, where the only horses he and McGarr had seen as children had been the drays that pulled the milk and bread and beer wagons and the thoroughbreds out at the race course in Phoenix Park, when the guard hadn't caught them wriggling under the fence, and those from afar.

The nation, he supposed, had succeeded in throwing off the yoke of direct British rule but would probably never rid itself of that alien culture. It had become too entrenched and horses were the totem. For those, like Murray, who were class-conscious, it was here at the Show that their aspirations could be realized in a way that was understandable to all. The new commercial and political ascendency—McGarr lowered the binoculars and looked down at the chestnut-colored boot Bechel-Gore had crossed over his knee—was merely replacing the old, or trying to. He supposed it was only natural, but it was not the Ireland of the Celtic Revival, the one that the poets, martyrs, and heroes of the revolution had envisioned.

But vision—who had it? Few, maybe none.

"Are you sure there's no way I can convince you to remove your wife and your horses from the Show?" he asked Bechel-Gore once again.

The man turned only his eyes to him. It would be tantamount to cowardice, and courage—in battle during the centuries of Britain's colonial and other wars —had been another hallmark of the old Ascendency.

They had come to Ireland as conquerors and had maintained a martial bearing throughout.

During the night white paint had been dashed across the black enamel of Bechel-Gore's Bentley that had been parked in the Shelbourne garage. "BRITS OUT." It was easy for unthinking and nationalistic Irishmen to understand the agony between Bechel-Gore and the Murrays of the new ruling class, but they didn't understand that such a gesture only made the man more certain of having to remain firm.

And McGarr himself, who believed in pluralism and tolerance, was in favor of that firmness, but it was Frayne who bothered him. Nearly thirty years of police experience told him that Frayne was a man who killed for the love of it. The British army, the I. R. A., murder for hire—it didn't matter, and the greater the risk, the greater the challenge. And if, say, Murray had hired him, he too would be wanting him to try something here at the Show where the first concern would have to be stopping the killer, quickly and finally.

"You're aware that in spite of the precautions I've taken—"

Slowly the long face turned to him. "Quite aware, Mister McGarr. Now—if you please, I'd like to concentrate on the competition."

McGarr only nodded and stepped down the narrow stairs of the announcing booth, admitting to himself that it was what he too wanted. If Frayne was present, two opportunities would arise: one for Frayne, but another for McGarr as well.

* * *

Keegan wasn't a religious man, but, if there was a God he had been praying to Him all morning long—that his back, which was galling him, would hold up until he could get himself in position; that he could shake the cop and that the others wouldn't see him or, if they did, they'd be looking for Frayne. And for simple justice—he was praying for that most of all—of the sort he could understand. For Maggie Kate and for the family.

"Down this way," he said to the cop, who had hold of his elbows as they walked down through the long rows of stables in Pembroke Hall, the upper halves of most of the large green doors open and the stalls empty, the horses either being shown or exercised.

"But I'm telling you, there're only horses here," McKeon replied, cautious now, sensing the urgency in the old man's voice and step.

"You'll be surprised, so. He brought her along for the hell of it, says he. But she's a beaut and she'll walk away with a sack of prizes. Up for auction too—he let it slip." He winked at McKeon.

"Here we are." He pushed open the door and stepped aside.

But McKeon turned and Keegan shoved him into the stall where the other man was waiting.

McKeon saw the punch coming down on him, but he was off-balance and had thrust a hand into his jacket for the gun. It caught him on the side of the head and drove him up against the boards that lined the wall, a glancing blow.

Keegan had closed the door behind them, and the other man—Boland himself—came on, wide and towering but old, like Keegan, his nose flattened off to a side of his face, his fists and arms raised, like somebody who knew what he was doing. And Keegan had pulled a gun, some sort of machine pistol that he held pointed at the floor.

McKeon kicked out with his foot, catching the big man on the side of the knee that was thrust forward. He staggered toward McKeon, who pushed off from the wall, lashing out with his right with everything he had. His fist landed squarely on the nose, but the man only flinched and his eyes bulged, his mouth opening in rage as he blundered forward.

Again and again McKeon struck solidly, his knuckles only seeming to ruffle the leather of the man's great, battered puss. The pug waited for the one punch that came up from the ground and drove McKeon's head back into the wall.

He felt only the snap of his teeth meshing together and the blow at the back of his head. Then everything was brilliant red, like a sunset.

Already Keegan had tossed the greatcoat into the straw, the hat alongside it.

He was wearing the blue coveralls of the R. T. E. tech-crew navvys, and he fitted on a blue cap. Against a wall was a mike wtih a long boom attached.

"You sure you don't need me?" the other man asked, dabbing at his bloody nose with a handkerchief.

"No, Dick, but—" he glanced up and their eyes met, "—thanks. I couldn't have taken him alone without—." He looked down at the gun and pulled the wire butt off the barrel. He wondered where Menahan had gotten it and what his hobnobbing with Murray meant.

But there was little time and he fitted the silencer on. It would affect the range and accuracy some, but if it wasn't heard over the roar of the crowd he could get off the entire clip and be sure.

And him up there in the announcing booth, in plain view through the large glass window, like a bloody effigy, he thought.

He hung the gun down inside a leg of the coveralls.

In the darkness of the trailer McGarr scanned the screens and the monitor that showed him where his staff was located—McKeon with Keegan in Pembroke Hall, having been there now (he checked the luminous dial of his watch) ten minutes; Ward with the mother and daughter who were in the exercise area of Ring 4, waiting to be called to jump; O'Shaughnessy with Bechel-Gore in the announcing booth; Delaney in a seat two rows in back of Murray; Greaves near Menahan; and the others whom he had positioned in various spots around the field.

He then scanned the TV screens, knowing he couldn't linger on any one of them long enough to study the faces but wanting more to know that everything was in place.

Bechel-Gore was the target, of course, but he could be hurt perhaps more grievously if either of the women were attacked. Would Frayne be thinking of that? No, certainly not. He had cause to hate Bechel-Gore, but McGarr judged that he was the sort who would go for the man himself and then again he'd have been given orders for pay.

If from Murray, would he have named the women?

McGarr thought for a moment. Perhaps the mother, who would be riding the Bechel-Gore mount, but certainly not the daughter. And if from Menahan? McGarr had been struck by the man's utter surety that he was clean and was likely to remain so, but if, say, he had hired Frayne—again, not the daughter. The mother, if the mother.

In any case, McGarr had had the jumping pocket, the laneway between, and the exercise ring virtually sealed off with uniformed and armed Gardai.

Without thinking, his hand went into his coat for his cigarettes. Empty. He crumpled the packet and threw it down, reaching for Flynn's on the table beside him.

Flynn only glanced at him. He was wearing earphones and a microphone on a wire that seemed to be pointed at his nose. He murmured another order to the cameramen who were following the action of the riders on the field.

Murray felt powerless, weaker than he had at any time in his life. Everything he owned or had touched —he turned to his wife, who was sitting beside him and who knew nothing of what had happened and was going on—had just seemed to crumble and pull away from him and not gradually but all of a sudden, overnight. What had it begun with? The horses, or was it the girl? Both really, but she had brought it all on.

She had caught him at a weak moment—there it was, the weakness again—when he'd forgotten about women and . . . and had even come to see him there in the library, flirtatious with those black, deep eyes, like other young girls who turned heads just for the thrill of it. But it was as though he had forgotten about that—he looked down at his wife's hand and picked it up, studying her palm—over the years.

And the things he'd suggested to her, the girl—every class of impossible . . . trips, holidays in Portugal, a flat in a posh section of London, when she really never intended anything with him and had just been playing him for a fool.

And then Sean was his son and she was his . . .

With that thought what he had succeeded in damping down all morning came blazing up now and made his temples hot. Guilt—that he'd ever gone so far as to try and wish a murder on his son, had convinced himself in his own mind that his son, his one and only child, was capable and indeed had . . . on top of the other thing.

Sean. Where was he? Murray looked around, but his eyes caught on the announcing booth at the other end of the enclosure.

Fool, he thought, what Bechel-Gore had made of him from the start, passing off animals to him that looked perfect in every regard and that veterinarians had said were sound but proved useless, slow as lead or barn rats or spoiled in training or some other class of thing. And how Bechel-Gore had gotten others to do the same and then snubbed him at hunts and at the ball.

Even now the nasaline drawl was a scald that rankled. "Mister Mick Murray, my dear. He's a politician, a big fellow—as you can see— in business and the newest and perhaps the grandest of Ireland's dealers in—" he had turned his eyes on Murray and the mustache had twitched, "—horse flesh." He had then turned his back, guiding the woman—some old cow and a member of his set—away.

But mostly Murray felt physically enervated, drained—he swirled his left shoulder—and as weak as a foal, and he wished he was someplace else.

"She's next," his wife said to him.

"Who?"

"The Bechel-Gore woman." Her tone was icy. She knew how he felt but not how much. And why, but not really why.

Two differences marked the entrance of Grainne Bechel-Gore onto the field of the jumping enclosure: scant applause, mostly from the members' boxes, and a harmony with the horse that McGarr had not noted in the other riders. She seemed not to have to control the large chestnut mare, and they moved together more easily than the other riders, even though flecks of spittle had gathered at the corners of the horse's mouth and the animal was lathered from the warm-up period in the exercise ring just prior to their being called.

And when the bell rang, the crowd quieted yet more, so that Flynn, who was sitting below where McGarr was standing in the dark R. T. E. trailer, had to say, "Volume, for chrissakes. What are we, at a funeral?"

Tracing the line of the hedgerow that bordered the field, she and the horse, cantering now, moved back toward the first gate, their movements contained and together, and McCarr found himself having to force his eyes to move to other screens—

the exhibition halls, the show rings outside the jumping enclosure, the farriery display that was closing down now, all the competitors trundling off their boxes of tools, their goggles set back on their foreheads and making their blackened faces seem to have two pair of eyes.

But he kept returning to her, from one camera angle or another, the best being those that showed horse and rider far below the fences, clearing them in one fluid motion and alighting gracefully, nothing out of place—not the hands too tight or her position in the saddle too far forward—and, unlike many of the other horses, Kestral seemed neither to be extending herself nor to be making an extra effort to keep her rear hooves from knocking on the rails. All was a flow, gentle and smooth and more like a dance—the high, curling arch—than an athletic endeavor, as they cleared each jump and moved toward the next.

Somebody touched McGarr's sleeve. "I don't know what to make of it, Chief, but we've got a navvy up on the roof of Anglesea Hall."

McGarr followed the guard over to the screens he'd been monitoring, and there on the green, corrugated metal roof of the general enclosure was the lone figure of a man dressed in blue R. T. E. coveralls and holding a long mike boom.

McGarr turned to Flynn. "Do you have a sound man up on the roof of the general enclosure, Dermot?"

"What?"

"This sound man. Here. The one with the boom and the mike—is he yours?"

Flynn whipped his head to the screen. "Yes. No. I don't know. I hope so, we need him."

"Well, can you focus in on him?"

"Why?"

"Just do it, goddammit."

"Jesus—what's the camera number? I've got a show to run."

"Eleven," said the guard.

"Eleven—in on that man on top of the jumping enclosure."

But McGarr didn't wait to see the picture. The man had dropped the boom and reached for the zipper of his coveralls and McGarr pivoted toward the door.

"Clean round," the voice over the public address system said, "and the best time of the day for Lady Bechel-Gore and Kestral.

"Miss Mairead Caughey is next, riding . . ."

They were passing each other right there beside the trailer and number board, and, glancing up at the figure on the roof, McGarr saw out of the corner of his eye the women reach out and touch hands.

The man stood and pointed something at the announcing booth, and McGarr drew his Walther but knew he had no chance of hitting him at that range. Still, he might distract—.

Bechel-Gore had stood to watch his two women passing below the booth, and just as O'Shaughnessy reached out to pull him back into the seat, the window seemed to explode, spewing a burst of brilliant, jagged glass around the interior of the booth. O'Shaughnessy and the others threw themselves to the floor. Bechel-Gore crumpled back on top of the superintendent, his hands to his shoulder and his jacket bloody.

The guard with the sniping rifles had been attracted by McGarr's shots and their fire knocked Keegan back and made his body jump in a wild and spastic dance before he fell and rolled slowly down the slope of the long, green corrugated roof.

But only McGarr and the guards seemed to be watching him.

The crowd in the general enclosure, as one, had risen up and begun fleeing, some back toward the pavilion and the exits, but most of the others onto the field, tumbling over the hedgerows, shrieking, dragging their children after them.

McGarr turned and looked for the women, but they had gone, following the direction that their horses had shied in, off through the jumping pocket toward the Simmonscourt Road.

When the shots began, the guards, who had been standing by Frayne and the other men from the farriery competition, had run into the jumping pocket, weapons drawn. With the confusion and the approaching horses and the others, who were panicking all around him, Frayne saw his chance.

But which of them. All that had been told him was that Bechel-Gore or his horse and a woman would be riding, but which one of them?

Frayne pulled up the leather apron and jerked the Skorpion from under his belt. He'd only got half the money, and without the kill—.

He caught the front one as she rode at him, and Ward saw her fall, cut back off the horse like a toy rider being knocked down by the swipe of a child's maddened hand.

But the other woman had bolted past Frayne and was gone behind the wall.

He hesitated a moment, crouching, pivoting, and saw the man making for him, tossing people aside with something black in his hand, and Frayne sprinted down the Simmonscourt Road toward the gate and the exit.

Only one other had seen and understood what had happened—Menahan. Throughout the confusion he had kept his field glasses focused on Mairead, and when she fell he shouted, "No! No, you bloody fool!"

Greaves, who was sitting behind him, watched him closely. The priest stepped out of the aisle and rushed down onto the walkway around the jumping enclosure. He took a few steps toward the field, hesitated, and then followed some of the crowd down the narrow lane between the members' stand and the grandstands, then through the green-and-white striped tents that enshrouded the tea gardens, pushing and shoving people roughly. He pulled open a flap of the tent and stepped through.

Greaves waited before going through himself, but he thought it better not to lose the man.

At the far side of the bandstand, the priest was having trouble getting through the shrubs and the low fence there, and turning his back to the benches, he saw Greaves.

He straightened up and seemed surprised, but he said, "Don't just stand there, man. Come help me. I'm a priest and I've got to get to the jumping pocket."

Frayne had lost the cop, the young one with the black hair and the gun in his hand, he was certain. But he waited behind the vans in the arrival and departure area to make sure nobody else had seen him

316

before he stepped toward the one he'd been told was his, the Skorpion back under the apron.

And Frayne was sure he'd gotten at least one of them and maybe the horse too, and he'd make the bastard pay even if—.

He tugged open the bay doors of the van and tried to see into the darkness and knew it was a mistake. There was somebody back there, and his gun was—.

The burst began at his crotch and ran up his chest, face, and forehead, and Frayne dropped back, dead before he hit the ground.

The other man tossed the Skorpion he had used into the straw and opened the side door, stepping out.

There he smoothed back his blond hair, fitted the chauffeur's cap on, and walked toward the Simmonscourt Road.

9

SNAPS, LITTERS,
SALVAGE AND TRUTH,
THE CONNECTION—FOGARTY
AND RUTH

McGarr was not the first to get to the girl. Fogarty and his cameraman were standing over her, the latter taking pictures. McGarr pushed through them and bent to her.

She was lying on her back, just as she had fallen, with one leg turned under her at an odd angle. The front of her blouse was covered with blood that also flowed from the corner of her mouth. McGarr opened the jacket and shirt. One wound in the upper chest, but she was having great difficulty breathing and her pulse was hardly there, the merest of threads.

"No—not that horse, goddammit!" McGarr heard a familiar and angry voice shout.

Several men were clustered around the horse, which was writhing on the ground only yards away.

It was Murray, and the men were intending to put the injured animal out of its misery.

Then Lady Bechel-Gore was there, kneeling on the ground by McGarr, stroking the girl's forehead and making low, keening sounds. Her eyes were wide but tearless, as though she could not believe what she was seeing.

Fogarty's man attempted to take her picture and McGarr rose up and shoved him away.

"Can't you see she's—" Fogarty began to say, but he was grasped by the collar and hauled off. It was O'Shaughnessy.

Chaos still obtained, and only when the doctors and ambulance attendants had arrived did McGarr move away from the girl. All the while he thought furiously of how it had happened and how his planning could have gone so wrong and how he could at least salvage some part of the situation.

"Is she alive?" somebody asked him. Bechel-Gore had a hand underneath his jacket and a uniformed guard was supporting him.

"Just barely, but I'm no doctor," McGarr stepped squarely in front of the larger man. "Now, you answer me this and answer me straight—those dossiers you were sent, that wasn't the first knowledge you had of your daughter's whereabouts, was it?"

Menahan was trying to push in close to the girl, but other guards were keeping him away. "But I'm a priest! She requires my office!"

Bechel-Gore's eyes moved to his daughter.

"Quick, quick!" a doctor was saying. "Out of the way! Get out of the way!" The ambulance was being backed toward them.

A shot sounded, people cringed and looked toward the horse, a leg of which twitched and then was still.

"No—I knew earlier."

"How much earlier?"

"Six months ago at least."

"But you didn't tell your wife."

"I was waiting until after, after the—"

Show, McGarr thought, the Show yet again.

"Because you had to pay for the information, and on top of all your other payments and having been injured you really aren't doing well financially, in spite of all the recent wins."

The ambulance doors slammed shut and the claxon sounded as it moved away rapidly.

Only then did Bechel-Gore turn his eyes to McGarr's. "I don't think I'll manage it, really. Not now. And frankly I don't know if I care."

McGarr did, however; he cared very much. "How much did you pay?"

Another doctor now moved toward them with two attendants carrying a litter.

"About twenty thousand pounds. I thought it would put the matter to rest."

McGarr wondered about the timing of Menahan's recent affluence and Bechel-Gore's payment. Between the two there was probably a great measure of—again the word—congruity.

"But still you continued the other payments—to Keegan and—"

"Of course, she's my . . . daughter." He turned to the attendants, who were trying to ease him onto the litter. "I can walk."

"Then this way," said the doctor.

McGarr swung around and found O'Shaughnessy, who had been observing the exchange. He nodded, and O'Shaughnessy moved toward Murray.

Ward pushed through the cordon of guards. "He's in a horse van that's parked in the departures area.

"Dead, dammit."

"How's—?"

The other police made way for McGarr. "Not very good."

Ward looked away.

Five hours later McGarr was pacing in front of a window in the dayroom at his offices in the Castle. Sitting in a chair was Murray, the father, the front of his shirt open and showing a large white bandage on his chest.

O'Shaughnessy was standing in the shadows, leaning against a wall.

McKeon was in a chair by the door, a hand to his mouth. All his lower teeth were now quite loose and they hurt.

Said Murray, "Listen, Peter, and it's the God's honest truth—I just thought I'd throw a scare into him."

"Is that an admission of guilt, Mister Murray?"

"Who's 'he?' " O'Shaughnessy asked.

"Christ," Murray looked away. "Can't we talk about this alone, McGarr?"

It depended upon what he had to tell him, but McGarr knew Murray was too crafty and experienced to admit to any crime and wise enough to know they had nothing on him.

"How did you get the bullet wound, Mister Murray?" O'Shaughnessy continued, but in a quiet, low voice. He'd keep at him for hours and days, if he had to.

"For Jesus' sake the last time, you culchie bastard—I shot myself while I was cleaning a handgun." Murray's face was the color of fresh liver, his eyes were bloodshot, and he was sweating; but without solid evidence they'd have to free him in forty-eight hours, that or impose the provisions of the Offenses Against the State Act and there too a judge would demand definite proof. And Murray had friends, journalist friends.

"And you were treated where and by whom?"

"Are you as thick as you look? I pulled it out with me teeth and spat it in the can."

"And did you . . ."

No—McGarr continued pacing—. Frayne was dead and with him had died the possibility of making the connection between him and whoever had hired him. And then the second Skorpion—rather the fifth—had been dropped into the straw on the floor of the horse van: that was the new connection.

There was a rap on the door and through the frosted glass McGarr could see the massive shape of Ban Gharda Bresnahan.

McKeon had stood, but McGarr moved toward her himself.

"Peter—for the love of God, don't leave me with these gobshites."

McGarr closed the door and took the sheaf of reports from Bresnahan.

She'd found a break-in report that had been added to the computer's memory unit only that morning. A pensioner in Ballsbridge had complained of a burglary that had occurred at the same time as the Caughey murder and three blocks away. The man had gone out for groceries and had returned to surprise the burglar. He described young Murray right down to the tan suit, the long, wavy hair, and the slightly bent nose. Fingerprints had been taken. All that remained was for the guards to lift Murray and lay the charges.

McGarr thought for a moment—he didn't know where young Murray had been during the Horse Show, but he didn't think that the boy was violent, and whoever was the connection had had contact with either Bechel-Gore or Menahan.

The next report cleared that up.

Paddy O'Meara, Bechel-Gore's chauffeur, had dropped out of sight. Bresnahan had called Coombe Memorial Hospital. Bechel-Gore had confirmed that O'Meara had taken the postal delivery of the returned tack from the Czech army horse purchase. It had been in those cartons that the six automatic weapons had been sent him.

McGarr signed the request of the detective who was investigating the Ballsbridge burglaries, and appended a note about young Murray's supposed drug addiction.

"All points on O'Meara. Tall, blond, in his late thirties."

"Already done, sir."

McGarr glanced up at Bresnahan. "Charge?"

"Murther."

"The English authorities?"

"Put in that request first. Armed and dangerous."

McGarr nodded once.

Armed. The Skorpions. Five of six recovered and McGarr was willing to bet the last was the one Murray and whoever had been with him had used at Keegan's place in Drogheda. They'd never find it, of course, but he again thought of the connection between Murray and Frayne, whose boot prints had been found there in Drogheda; and between Paddy O'Meara and Menahan, who had as much as admitted having told others about Bechel-Gore's child, some of the locals out in Leenane. Menahan would know O'Meara and well, their being roughly the same age.

—The third report said Menahan, after having left the hospital, had returned to the Caughey apartment where Monsignor Kelly had been waiting for him on the doorstep. They had had a loud argument and Kelly had left. Later piano playing could be heard above.

Menahan. The piano. McGarr remembered Friday night and the way the twilight sun had made the gold letters seem as though they were lit from within and the photographs and the two women who'd been talking below in the back gardens. Missus Brady and —what was the other one's name? Harmon. No. Herman. No.

McGarr reached for his smokes. Some sort of a bird. Walking toward his cubicle, he remembered. Herron.

She was at home, and after he'd identified himself, he asked her if she might know where Missus Brady's husband drank, which she did, of course.

Back in his offices at the Castle, McGarr removed Murray from O'Shaughnessy's clutches and saw to it his shirt was buttoned and his tie in place.

On their way down the stairs they met Fergus Farrell, the Commissioner.

"Back so soon. Short holiday, what?" said McGarr, moving past him.

"Where're you going?"

In the doorway McGarr could see several guards who were keeping the reporters back. The voices of many rose to them and curses and shouts.

"Mick and I thought we'd pop out for a sup. Hot up there."

Farrell, who knew Murray, nodded to him. "But don't you think—"

"Not me. Had enough of that for the day. I think we'll unstring the bow and that class of thing, eh, Mick?"

Murray didn't know how to reply and he was watching McGarr closely. He didn't care for his tone and the playful cast to his eye.

Farrell liked it much less.

McGarr paused on the top step. When the reporters had quieted, he said. "You know what happened today, but not why. Fogarty can tell you that. I'll have the rest for you tomorrow, and that's a promise."

"Will there be an arrest, Chief?"

"Yes."

"Is Murray the man?"

McGarr glanced at him. "I don't know."

When McGarr slid into the Cooper, the others turned on Fogarty, who said, "He's lying. I don't know a goddamned thing."

"'Truer words . . .'" thought McGarr.

10

FITTING A GREEN ISLE,
WHERE IT ALL COMES DOWN—
THIN AND BRASH—
TO A SMILE

A heavy, summer downpour had wet the city streets, and the tires hissed on the macadam.

"Isn't it curious," said Murray, "that after being kids together and all it should come down to this."

McGarr reached for his flask and then, offering it, glanced at Murray's puffy face. "Are you trying to tell me something?"

"No—indeed not, but it's as good as dashed, my—" he gestured with the flask, "—life, you see." His smile was thin. "But it's curious too, you know. At least now there seems to be some . . . adventure in my future, if you know what I mean."

It was a nice observation but odd, coming from Murray, and McGarr drove on.

He found Brady, and while Murray waited in the car he explained what he wanted.

Menahan was still at the piano when they arrived. He objected but put on the only suit that McGarr could find in the Caughey woman's former— now Menahan's—closet. It was made of some fine, light gray material and fit him well. And a derby. McGarr found that there too. Vanity, he thought, and pride.

The light at the bottom of the Caughey staircase wasn't strong, the setting, obscured by the rooftops of the houses across the street, cast only a pale mauve glow. But McGarr suspected the little lad's eyes were sharp, and he had his father there with him in the closet for support.

McGarr handed the derby to Murray. "You first, Mick."

"I don't understand."

"Just put it on, open the door, and walk up the stairs."

Murray looked down at the derby, turning it in his hands. "You wouldn't happen to have—"

McGarr again reached for the flask, then opened the door and said into the empty hall, "Ready?"

He heard a muffled reply. Tony Brady, the boy, was standing in the dark with his eye to the crack between the stairs, his father behind him.

His mother was watching with Missus Herron, the two of them out on the front lawn with their arms crossed over their chests, cardigans hanging loose by their sides.

Murray handed the flask back to McGarr and fitted on the hat, his jowls rippling as he adjusted it. He seemed to gird himself, then reached for the handle, pulled open the door, and stood there a moment, diffident, before he moved forward.

When Murray returned, McGarr took the derby from him and moved toward the priest, who was smiling.

"You to play, Father."

"I don't know what you're trying to prove here,

Inspector. The word of a child, you know, isn't admissible in any court of law."

"Only the truth, Father." McGarr glanced up the street. House lights had been extinguished, and people were standing in the darkened doorways. At least several press people had learned of McGarr's whereabouts and were out on the sidewalk. "And I'm sure in all his innocence little Tony Brady can tell it us."

Fergus Farrell opened the gate and approached them.

Still with the smile on his face—forced, it was, making him look more like a commercial traveler than a priest—Menahan raised the derby and fitted it on his brow.

But before he could move forward, Missus Brady stepped up to the hedges. "If all you're after wanting to know is if Father John Francis came back on Friday afternoon, Inspector—he did. And didn't I see him with my own two eyes, dressed as he is. Had his back to the door so I couldn't see his face at first, and I heard Missus Caughey ask who was it and he gave no reply. It took her sometime to get down the stairs, you see, so I had a . . . peek.

"The father said he forgot his key. Isn't that so, Father?"

Menahan turned but not to her, only McGarr. What little of his smile remained made him seem ill. "That's not enough, and you know it."

"Ah, but I don't, Father. The truth is sometimes—" he appropriated Menahan's own words, relishing the opportunity, "—difficult, is it not? Just like the situation you tried to generate.

"Let me piece it out for you.

"You didn't find it sufficient to shop the truth to Bechel-Gore two months ago. He paid you a full twenty thousand pounds, but he did nothing with it, so you turned to Murray here and made it work for you twice. You told him everything, about how Bechel-Gore had gotten Grainne Keegan pregnant and that the child had been taken by Grainne's older sister and brother because they thought she wouldn't be a competent mother and, later, they saw a way of getting back at Bechel-Gore.

"For Murray here, who was way out of his element in the horse business, the situation was ready-made. He'd committed himself to his operation, and if he could just get it going, make a showing, he'd be able to float another loan or unload it. At least he'd be able to keep his head above water.

"But in spite of the Skorpion you supplied Murray with—through Paddy O'Meara, your boyhood chum who was working for Bechel-Gore—he blew it. He hired Frayne and some others with I. R. A. connections to raid Keegan's place in Drogheda where he'd established an identity as Doctor Malachy Matthews. But instead of throwing a scare into Keegan and making him want to go for Bechel-Gore, they almost killed him. Murray himself took a slug and it made him wary. He'd had enough.

"It was then, Father," McGarr said derisively, "that you saw your opportunity to—" he turned and faced Menahan directly, "—rid yourself of many of the people—Margaret Kathleen Caughey, in particular—who would keep Mairead from you.

"You murdered her, Father . . ."

Menahan went to object, but McGarr held up a

hand. ". . . coldbloodedly, right upstairs in front of that chair. And you then commissioned Jack B. Frayne, who was a psychotic and whose record was public knowledge, to initiate, along with several of the others who had worked for Murray, an attack on Bechel-Gore, to feed Kestral the apples, to shoot at him and miss. The whole attempt was to make it seem like a feud between Bechel-Gore and the people on whose former land he lived. They had wronged each other for years and it would appear that things were just working themselves out. And if the police could get beyond that, there was always Murray. He'd committed himself personally, even had a bullet wound that would tie him in.

"But Frayne—now, he's the *interesting* case," Mc-Garr's voice was icy. "He turned out better than your wildest dreams, didn't he? At least for a while." Mc-Garr studied Menahan's facial features closely, the fleshy cheeks and the bright, dark eyes that held his gaze. "He just liked to kill and it didn't matter much who—Bechel-Gore, if he could have gotten a clear shot at him, his accomplices in the kip, the Netherlander we found in the back of the car, and, alas, he even tried to kill your Mairead."

Menahan's slight smile was set, stonelight and implacable.

"Frayne was a—" McGarr remember Descartes and tried to think of a term that was mathematical, "—variable. Wild and unpredictable and a liability because he knew enough to incriminate you. So you sent him to the Horse Show, thinking he'd create some sort of havoc, perhaps slay the mother or Bechel-Gore, if Keegan himself didn't get them first. Only

Paddy O'Meara could put a bend on you, and you knew him too well. He'd keep his mouth shut if you could just get him away. It was he who was waiting for Frayne in the back of the van at the Show Ground and with the final, the sixth Skorpion.

"Now, *why* is the curious point, is it not, Father?" McGarr spoke through his bottom teeth, remembering the way that Menahan had spread himself across the front seat of the Cooper that morning, godlike, his tone patronizing, his gestures didactic. "You saw your chance here," McGarr swirled his left hand and the man flinched, "to play at god, didn't you? The mother said she was going to take Mairead away from Dublin, and you, you decided it would be easy and perhaps a bit of fun to manipulate all—" what was it Menahan had said during the first interview?—"all God's pap, the coarse and talentless, just to keep her with you.

"Bechel-Gore's knowing of her would open up another direction. She'd probably want to stay with her parents out there in Galway and you'd remain as her teacher at least a while longer. But the money you extorted from him showed your true 'nobility,' Father—you being one of the 'big' persons yourself. And it titillated you too, didn't it? With enough of it—why, you wouldn't need Bechel-Gore or Murray or any of them. And if you played things right you could find yourself suddenly with quite a bit of it and in control of a big talent, like hers, and she a handsome young woman who stood to inherit a smart sum herself.

"Just like—" again McGarr remembered Menahan's dossier, "—a mathematical equation, you could re-

331

duce things down to zero or at least one, Mairead, or perhaps two, *you* and Mairead, when in fact the equation solved out to no more than avarice and lust and a particularly repulsive piece of a corporeality, physical and otherwise, Father, namely yourself.

"We'll see how 'god's pap' judges seven deaths and perhaps an eighth, and she—" McGarr with his hands, "—your big talent."

Menahan only closed his eyes and folded his hands across the top of his belly in a manner that was definitely priestlike.

"Don't you feel anything, even for her?" McGarr demanded.

Slowly Menahan opened his eyes. "Oh, surely, Mister McGarr. Most definitely. But you see—" he turned his head to him, his smile soft, almost beatific, "—Mairead will survive. That's assured."

"By whom?"

Menahan only closed his eyes and shook his head slightly. "And I must warn you here and now," his voice still carried the soft, pleasant tone, "if you arrest me, I'll slap a lawsuit on you and, mind, I've got the will and the money to make it stick. And after triple damages I'll have to consider you a benefactor."

McGarr's body tensed, but he held himself back. "Hughie!" he called to Ward. He was willing to take the chance.

Sinclaire again enjoyed the flight, which had begun early in the evening that seemed to fall rapidly as they headed out over the Atlantic. They had a few drinks, a snack, played cards, and he even managed to get a little sleep. But waking every now and again, he kept half an eye on the tall, blond man who said he was a groom.

He had arrived at the airport only minutes before they took off, but the pilot said one of the Murray partners, from whom he, as Holohan, had bought two horses, had arranged for the service, and Sinclaire was genuinely pleased.

An hour after they were up, Sinclaire knocked on the cockpit door, pretending to want a look at the controls. He made small talk as he showed the pilot his Garda Soichana badge and the note he had written in the toilet.

Now, as the new day was dawning, the plane banked gently toward an island that appeared small and very green from afar, its beaches buff against the silver-gray sea.

"What's that?" the young man asked, standing to look out the windows that were canted toward the earth.

"The Azores," said Sinclaire. "We'll refuel and get to stretch our legs."

"Janie, but don't it look—" His eyes fell on Sinclaire, who removed the newspaper on his lap.

The barrel of the Walther was pointing at O'Meara's belly.

"I've been instructed to take you alive, Paddy, but it's all one to me."

McGarr, O'Shaughnessy, and McKeon were waiting at the Dublin Airport for the plane to put down.

Ward was at the Coombe Hospital where the girl had been moved from the intensive care section to a private room.

AN OCCULT NOVEL OF UNSURPASSED TERROR

EFFIGIES

BY William K. Wells

Holland County was an oasis of peace and beauty . . .
until beautiful Nicole Bannister got a horrible package that triggered a nightmare,
until little Leslie Bannister's invisible playmate vanished and Elvida took her place,
until Estelle Dixon's Ouija board spelled out the message: I AM COMING—SOON.

A menacing pall settled over the gracious houses and rank decay took hold of the lush woodlands. Hell had come to Holland County —to stay.

A Dell Book $2.95 (12245-7)

Dell Bestsellers

- [ ] **RANDOM WINDS** by Belva Plain $3.50 (17158-X)
- [ ] **MEN IN LOVE** by Nancy Friday $3.50 (15404-9)
- [ ] **JAILBIRD** by Kurt Vonnegut $3.25 (15447-2)
- [ ] **LOVE: Poems** by Danielle Steel $2.50 (15377-8)
- [ ] **SHOGUN** by James Clavell $3.50 (17800-2)
- [ ] **WILL** by G. Gordon Liddy $3.50 (09666-9)
- [ ] **THE ESTABLISHMENT** by Howard Fast....... $3.25 (12296-1)
- [ ] **LIGHT OF LOVE** by Barbara Cartland $2.50 (15402-2)
- [ ] **SERPENTINE** by Thomas Thompson $3.50 (17611-5)
- [ ] **MY MOTHER/MY SELF** by Nancy Friday $3.25 (15663-7)
- [ ] **EVERGREEN** by Belva Plain $3.50 (13278-9)
- [ ] **THE WINDSOR STORY**
  by J. Bryan III & Charles J.V. Murphy $3.75 (19346-X)
- [ ] **THE PROUD HUNTER** by Marianne Harvey .. $3.25 (17098-2)
- [ ] **HIT ME WITH A RAINBOW**
  by James Kirkwood $3.25 (13622-9)
- [ ] **MIDNIGHT MOVIES** by David Kaufelt $2.75 (15728-5)
- [ ] **THE DEBRIEFING** by Robert Litell $2.75 (01873-5)
- [ ] **SHAMAN'S DAUGHTER** by Nan Salerno
  & Rosamond Vanderburgh $3.25 (17863-0)
- [ ] **WOMAN OF TEXAS** by R.T. Stevens $2.95 (19555-1)
- [ ] **DEVIL'S LOVE** by Lane Harris $2.95 (11915-4)
